*THE **TERMINATORS***

DONALD HAMILTON

A *MATT HELM* NOVEL

THE *TERMINATORS*

TITAN BOOKS

The Terminators
Print edition ISBN: 9781783293025
E-book edition ISBN: 9781783293032

Published by Titan Books
A division of Titan Publishing Group Ltd
144 Southwark Street, London SE1 0UP

First edition: June 2015
1 2 3 4 5 6 7 8 9 10

A CIP catalogue record for this title is available from the British Library.

Printed and bound in the United States.

Did you enjoy this book? We love to hear from our readers.
Please email us at readerfeedback@titanemail.com or write to us at
Reader Feedback at the above address.

To receive advance information, news, competitions, and exclusive
offers online, please sign up for the Titan newsletter on our website:
www.titanbooks.com

THE TERMINATORS

1

The weather in Bergen was just about what you'd expect at that time of year. Nobody visits Norway in the autumn for fun.

In summer, you go to see the fjords and the midnight sun. In winter, I guess you can go for snow and skiing if you're bored with more fashionable locations like, say, Switzerland. But in the fall, Scandinavia is usually a gray and miserable place; and when I reached Bergen it was raining hard and the streets were full of citizens in boots and slickers, indistinguishable as to sex. Apparently no Norwegian female under the age of fifty would be caught dead, nowadays, in a neat swingy skirt and sheer, sexy stockings. The current Nordic vogue seemed to involve enormous drab, baggy slacks kind of bunched up over yellow rubber boots, cowboy-fashion.

In Bergen, it didn't really matter. The place itself was pretty enough, or would be when they finished building it, or rebuilding it—at the moment, its most conspicuous feature was the giant construction cranes that stuck up all over the city like towering mechanical weeds in an otherwise pleasant garden. Nevertheless, it was a picturesque seaport surrounded by spectacular mountains; but the women didn't live up to the scenery. Even when I did manage to identify a member of the opposite sex of suitable age, she wasn't worth the trouble. I'd never seen such a bunch of plain Scandinavian females in my life.

I felt kind of cheated. Generally, if you're a man, you can count on a little interesting, blond, visual entertainment in that part of the world. Well, I hadn't come there for entertainment, visual or otherwise.

"Sorry, Eric," Mac had said over the phone, using my code name as always. "The climate probably won't appeal to you after Florida, but we owe these people a favor."

"And I'm it, sir?"

"I'm afraid so," he said. "They need an agent with a fairly lethal reputation, for some reason; and apparently they have none of their own. Unfortunately, you have made yourself rather well known, in some circles, as an expert in violence. Such publicity—any kind of publicity, for that matter—is generally a handicap in our kind of work, but it should operate in your favor here, since that kind of an image is just what these people seem to require."

"Not to criticize, sir," I said, "but it looks to me as if your friends are just shopping around for a human lightning rod. What do you want to bet I'll be left out in the open with my lethal reputation, as you so flatteringly put it, while the electricity fizzes all around me and they hide in the storm cellar watching the show?" I sighed. "Oh, well, I guess that's how we earn our government pay, taking the heat off characters with more scruples and less survival potential."

Waiting for his response, I looked towards the lovely, tanned, bikini-clad lady—named Loretta, if it matters—waiting under a palm tree near the phone booth. I shook my head ruefully to let her know that the news was just as bad as we'd expected it to be when I got the signal, never mind how, to call Washington at once. Nothing lasts forever, and we'd both known it wasn't a permanent arrangement, but saying goodbye wasn't going to be much fun. Heading towards the bleak and frozen north under orders, I was even, as Mac had suggested, going to regret saying goodbye to sunny Florida, although it's got too many people in it these days to qualify as my favorite state.

"As you say, Eric, that is the purpose of this organization," his voice said in my ear.

"Who are these refined operators who can't dredge up anybody scary enough from their own ranks?"

"That, I am told, is something you do not really need to know."

I made a face at the beautiful lady I'd be leaving soon. "The old need-to-know gag," I said grimly into the phone. "Jolly good, as our British colleagues would say. I'm supposed to die for these gentle jerks without even knowing who they are?"

"We hope it won't come to that, Eric. To make reasonably sure it doesn't, I'm arranging for you to have a little reliable support available along the way. This is strictly between the two of us, you understand. There are certain things the people with whom you'll be working do not need to know, either. In a minute, the girl downstairs will come on the line and tell you how to make contact…"

I should have guessed. After all, I'd been involved in Mac's brand of interdepartmental cooperation before. As a matter of cold fact, I've never known him to do a friendly favor for another government outfit that didn't turn out, in the end, to have served some devious purpose of his own.

Years ago, I might have kidded myself that the fact that my superior was arranging for me to have expert help available on a mere loan job showed how much he treasured my services—maybe even my friendship— and how much he'd hate to lose them. Knowing him somewhat better now, I didn't figure it was very likely that he'd set up an elaborate support organization in distant Scandinavia just to protect the life of a single agent, no matter how valued and experienced. Obviously, we were sharpening two axes on a single grindstone, me; and as usual when I got involved in one of Mac's trickier operations, I was going to have lots and lots of fun keeping the two edged tools apart.

The transatlantic crossing had been the standard airborne ratrace, Pan Am division. It used to be that a first-class plane ticket entitled you to a special waiting room, a special plane entrance, and special consideration. Now all you get for your—or the government's—several hundred extra bucks is a few inches more seat and a couple of free martinis. I also got the privilege of viewing a movie I didn't want to see. There were only five of us elite passengers up forward. Four wanted to sleep and the other wanted the movie, so we all saw the movie. That's called democracy.

After a brief stop in Glasgow, in the rain, we landed in Bergen, in the rain. The airport bus transported me to the Hotel Norge in the rain. I checked in and read a letter that had been awaiting me; and now, after a day's rest that had let me get slightly hardened to the change in climate and time zones, I was out in the cold northern rain again, looking for a restaurant called Tracteurstedet, a name I won't try to translate because I don't know how. I used to speak a little Swedish, enough to make Norwegian, a closely related language, mildly comprehensible; but I hadn't been in Scandinavia for a good many years and my Nordic vocabulary seemed to have gathered considerable rust in the interval. On an important mission, I'd probably have been run through a refresher language-course as part of the routine preparation, but on an impromptu friendship deal like this it seemed that I'd just have to struggle along on what little I could remember.

The restaurant was down near the docks, in the area that, the guide book informed me, had housed the Hanseatic—that is, German—merchants who, in the old days, had played an important role in Bergen's commerce with the warmer, softer world to the south. They had specialized, I gathered, in dried fish. I found the colorful blocks of ancient wooden houses facing the harbor, all right; but the eating place eluded me. Apparently it wasn't visible from the street.

At last, spotting a cruising Bergen police car—a Volkswagen bus marked POLITI—I flagged it down and got some directions in halting English, enjoying every minute of it. I mean, when your profession is on the edge of the law, and sometimes even on the wrong side of it, you can generally get a childish charge out of boldly approaching the cops for help, like an ordinary, innocent citizen.

Following police instructions, I entered a narrow walkway between the old buildings and found myself in a maze of courts and lanes paved with elderly, splintery, wooden planks. There didn't seem to be anybody around. At last, far back in this dim rabbit-warren, I found a two-story building with illuminated windows and the right sign by the door. Inside, a few people were sitting on benches at heavy, rustic, wooden tables. I managed to convey to the gent behind the Bergen version of a snack bar that I desired a full dinner, and he directed me to a larger room upstairs where a disapproving waitress with no English whatever gradually made it clear to me that hard liquor wasn't legal here and it was naughty of me even to ask.

Well, I should have remembered that European martinis are not only unreliable, but difficult to come by.

I should also have remembered that Scandinavia rivals Britain in the mad complexity of its liquor laws. I should have grabbed a couple of the duty-free bottles available at the Glasgow airport and, if I really required stimulation, I should have had a reviving snort at the hotel before embarking on this expedition. Now I was stuck with beer or wine. Choosing the former, I reread the communication I'd been handed when I arrived.

It was addressed to Mr. Matthew Helm, c/o Norge Hotel, Ole Bull's Plass, Bergen, Norway, please hold. Well, that figured. You wouldn't employ a character for his dangerous reputation and hide him under an alias. Writing to him, you'd put his real name conspicuously on the envelope so that, if the people you wanted to impress were on the ball, they'd read it and be suitably terrified. The fact that, after being informed of his fearsome identity, they might then take a few shots at him just for luck, wouldn't concern you greatly. After all, that's what dangerous characters are for, to be shot at, isn't it?

The letter was written in a feminine handwriting, in blue ink. Okay, so far. At least I wasn't going to have to cope with one of the green-ink girls—it's been my experience that when they feel compelled to dip their pens in outlandish colors, they tend to be kind of impossible in other ways as well. The letter read:

> *Darling:*
> *I'm so happy you can get away from Washington at last.*
> *After all the delays, it's got a little late in the year for our*

cruise up the Norwegian coast, but that's all right. Now we'll probably have the ship to ourselves; and what's a little weather between friends? (We are friends, aren't we, whatever else we may be?)

I've made all the arrangements, as you asked, and your ticket is enclosed. We have separate cabins, but right next door. I hope you don't mind. They're very small cabins, I understand; and anyway, while I really don't care what people think, I don't see much point in either offending them or going through the motions of pretending to be man and wife. Do you?

Before the boat leaves, you might have dinner at a quaint little Bergen restaurant called Tracteurstedet near the docks. A friend tells me they have a beef dish that's out of this world. I thought the Norwegians couldn't cook anything but fish. If you get a chance, check and let me know.

As you can see by the enclosed schedule, we shove off at eleven p.m., but you can board any time after nine. It will be simpler if I just take a taxi direct from the airport and meet you on board, as I'm catching a late plane from Paris.

Please, please, don't let anything stop you this time.
Madeleine

I frowned at the thin, elegant sheets of paper, and the thin, elegant handwriting. Sometimes this kind of careful doubletalk is concocted, after endless conferences, by committees of experts: but I had a feeling this letter had been composed as well as written by a real, flesh-and-blood woman; a woman I was soon to meet, who wasn't really looking forward to meeting me.

It was right there in front of me. She'd put in all the essential, official stuff: the warning that something or somebody might try to stop me, the order to pay a visit to this restaurant before sailing time, and the necessary travel information. She'd also, however, managed to include a little unofficial message of her own. No Washington committee dealing with undercover operations would give much of a damn, as long as it wasn't conspicuously out of character, whether a couple of agents working together on a job traveled in two cabins or one. If anything, one cabin would be preferred, since it would provide better protection for both agents, and would cost the government less.

But our girl Madeleine—whatever her real name might be—did give a damn. She cared very much, in fact; so much that even before meeting me she was telling me to keep my cotton-picking hands to myself. She'd obviously been told enough about me to get a strong negative reaction. Maybe she disapproved of dangerous characters with lethal reputations; or maybe they simply scared hell out of her. In any case, the message from my future lady colleague was clear: two cabins and no funny-business. The man-and-wife routine was definitely out. But definitely. We were going to be friends, just friends, and I'd damn well better not forget it.

I grinned, and stopped grinning. Professionals, whether

male or female, don't generally worry all that much about who sleeps where. Her concern for her virtue labeled the lady as a stuffy and probably rather stupid amateur. This was no surprise, of course. Any outfit that had to borrow a nasty man from another department to frighten people with couldn't be very professional. Nevertheless, the prissy attitude of my associate-to-be was another warning, if I needed one, that whatever happened I'd better not count on much useful assistance from her.

I sighed, folding the letter and putting it away, remembering another female operative with whom I'd once worked; a real little trouper who, the minute we hit a hotel, had unblushingly invited me to pick out the nightie in her suitcase that did most for my virility. She'd calmly put it on and climbed into bed, saying that we had a long way to travel together as married folks, and we might as well start getting acquainted. Yet she'd been no nympho, just a practical girl solving a practical problem the simplest and most direct way; a brave kid who'd died a few months later in southern France...

I looked up to see the waitress standing over me expectantly. I made an apologetic noise, put the letter away, picked up the menu, frowned at it, and shook my head.

"Sorry, I don't dig that *Norska* stuff," I said. "Haven't you got one in English? *Engelska?* No? Well, just bring me something with meat in it, okay? Meat. Beef. *Boeuf?* No, that's French, dammit..."

"Can I be of help, sir?"

It was the male half of the couple at the next table,

a husky, weathered character in his sixties with cropped gray hair, wearing tweeds and a strong British accent. His companion was younger, a slim, pale girl in gray slacks and sweater. I'd noticed them when they came in, a few minutes after me—as a matter of fact, I'd recognized the man and been surprised to see him, since he wasn't the kind of errand-boy I'd expected to meet—but I had not, of course, paid any attention to them since.

I said, "Well, if you don't mind... I'd kind of like a steak or something. I've been eating fish ever since I got here. What's Norwegian for beef?"

The man said, "The word is *ox køtt*—ox meat. They don't have steaks here, but the first meat dish on the menu is rather good, don't you know? Would you like me to tell her?"

"I'd sure appreciate it," I said. "Ox meat, for God's sake! Thanks a lot."

"It's perfectly all right, old chap. Happy to be of service."

His British was a little overdone, perhaps; but then, so was my American. He spoke to the waitress in reasonably fluent Norwegian. After being thanked once more, he turned back to his companion, who gave me a brief, polite, restrained little smile before picking up the conversation that had been interrupted by my gastronomic and linguistic emergency. An hour later, well fed and beered, I emerged on the street that ran along the misty harbor. There had been a man lounging in the shadows near the corner of the restaurant, but nobody'd jumped me or shot at me as I made my way out of the Hansa merchants' ancient dark lanes, although it was an ideal place for an ambush.

I was a little disappointed. I'd kind of hoped for some kind of action to give me a hint of what I was going to be up against. Well, whoever we were dealing with, they'd missed their boat. I'd been walking around practically naked for a couple of days. All these current anti-hijacking procedures make it tough for an honest agent to earn an honest buck, or even stay alive; but now I had my gun and knife back, slipped to me under the table, after being transported across the Atlantic by a different route, by the tweedy pseudo-British chappie who was actually a very solid American citizen, an ex-congressman in fact, named Captain Henry Priest, USN, Ret. Obviously, he was having himself a lot of fun playing secret agent, phony accent and all.

His presence changed the picture rather drastically. I'd been thinking of this friendship deal in rather vague and general terms; but Hank Priest was a real friend of Mac's, with a real claim on the organization for services rendered not long ago, when we'd needed his help badly. If, after losing his bid for reelection, and later losing his wife in a boating accident—I'd read about it in the newspapers—Captain Priest had consoled himself by becoming involved in some kind of hush-hush government project that required a little assistance of the kind that only we could give, he'd know where to go; and if his request was at all reasonable and legitimate Mac would undoubtedly grant it, maybe even straining the rules a bit, since we did owe the guy a favor. The only question was: why hadn't Mac simply told me I'd be working with Hank Priest once more, instead of handing me the old need-to-know routine?

Well, my superior does like to be mysterious, sometimes unnecessarily so; but in our business it doesn't pay to take anything for granted. I had to go back to the hotel anyway, to check out and pick up my suitcase—it hadn't seemed advisable to explore the wilds of Bergen burdened with forty pounds of luggage. Back in my room, I placed a call to a number in Oslo, the national capital, a couple of hundred miles to the east across a lot of rugged mountains. After half a dozen rings, a male voice answered.

I said, "Okay Priest."

The voice said, "Priest okay."

I hung up, making a sour face at the phone. Hank Priest might be okay as far as security was concerned; he had been reliable the last time we met and apparently he still was. He might be a pretty good congressman, when the voters allowed him to work at it. He might even, before retirement, have been a fine seaman and naval officer. I had no reason to think otherwise. But just what the hell was the picturesque old seadog doing here with his lousy old tweeds and his pale young brunette?

Well, whatever it was, it was bound to be a high school production and I wanted no part of it—which didn't alter the fact that I obviously had a large part of it whether I wanted it or not.

I picked up my suitcase and went downstairs to check out and take a taxi back to the harbor, past the Hansa section where I'd had dinner, to Festnungskaien, which I managed to translate loosely as the Fortress Dock, presumably named for an ancient stone structure on one of the hills nearby.

2

The ship looked black and enormous, lying at the dock in the misty darkness. I guess I was judging her by the pleasure boats I'd been playing around with recently in more tropical waters—a ton-and-a-half outboard is quite a husky runabout, and a ten-ton sport fisherman isn't something you want to start dreaming about unless you can shell out half a hundred grand without hurting. This was actually a fairly small steamer; but she'd still weigh in at well over two thousand tons.

Although far from new, she was clean and freshly painted; but I quickly learned that she was no luxury cruise-ship with service to match. The uniformed gent at the gangplank just took my ticket, told me that my cabin was one deck down on the starboard side, and let me find it for myself, carrying my own damned bag.

The Norwegians call it their National Highway Number One: the regular daily ship service up the coast. It's also known as Hurtigruten, which translates loosely as "the speedy route." I guess it does beat walking, at that, and maybe even driving, since the roads along that rugged, mountainous, fjord-slashed shoreline mostly have to go the long way around, where they exist at all.

If you've got an active imagination, you can visualize the main Scandinavian peninsula as a large dog standing on its forepaws (don't ask me why) near a fire hydrant called Denmark. The belly, washed by the Baltic and the Gulf of Bothnia, is Sweden, which also includes the forelegs. The back, exposed to the North Atlantic, is Norway, which also includes the head. Oslo is tucked away well up under the chin. Bergen is out on the face, halfway between the nose and the ears. The ship route runs from there up the mutt's back, clear around the rump—the North Cape, well above the Arctic Circle—and down to Kirkenes on the Russian border; the ice-cold ass-hole, if you insist on completing the picture. A round trip takes some eleven days and is popular in midsummer with sun-worshippers, who get a thrill out of experiencing twenty-four continuous hours of daylight on the roof of the world. In midwinter, it works the other way, of course; but I'm told that few people seem to be interested in seeing that much darkness.

The ticket I'd received wouldn't take me that far. It was a one-way job entitling me only to a four-day voyage as far as Svolvaer, in the Lofoten Islands just off the coast, opposite Narvik on the mainland. Having been there once, I knew that Narvik is the ice-free Norwegian port that handles the ore from the great Swedish iron mines across the mountains in Kiruna—at least the ore comes out that way in winter when the Gulf of Bothnia freezes over. It's the sort of detail you notice when you don't know what the hell's going on. Whether it was actually significant as far as the present operation was concerned, I had no idea. What would happen after Svolvaer, if we got that far—destinations marked on tickets mean very little in this racket—was up to the gods, or a girl called Madeleine.

I'd checked both cabins, as well as I could, for electronics; and I was examining my stateroom when she arrived. I was standing there wondering how a race of reasonably husky people like the Norwegians manage to do their sleeping in the narrowest, shortest beds on earth. My fairly expensive Bergen hotel room had boasted, if that is the correct term, a pair of diminutive cots I wouldn't have wished off on a couple of stunted kids. This tiny cabin was equipped with sleeping-shelves—you couldn't conscientiously call them berths—one on each side, that were not only ridiculously inadequate in the transverse direction, but weren't significantly over six feet long, leaving me with several extra inches to dispose of somehow. It occurred to me that my prospective partner's elaborate efforts to preserve her virtue had been quite unnecessary. We might as well have saved public money by sharing one cabin. Only a pair of oversexed midgets could have managed successful passion in the cramped space provided...

"Matt, darling!"

She was standing in the doorway. It was no time for

taking inventory. After all, we were supposed to be, at least, very good friends. She was stepping forward, arms outstretched; and I took the cue and embraced her heartily and kissed her on the lips—cool and damp from the rainy night outside—without having had much of a chance to determine what I was greeting so affectionately. I only knew that it smelled nice and felt feminine in spite of being snugly wrapped in a tailored pantsuit of brownish tweed rough enough to earn the approval of Hank Priest in his British incarnation.

I felt her stiffen in my arms when I carried the exploration a little too far. Apparently I'd read her written message correctly: no funny business. I withdrew my scouts from the forbidden territory; and we clung together a moment longer and parted with reasonably convincing reluctance—all this, presumably, for the benefit of a husky, red-faced, fairhaired sailor in dungarees and a navy-blue turtle-neck, who was standing out in the passage with a white suitcase in each hand. It seemed that there were ways of getting porter service on board, after all, if you knew how and were properly constructed.

"Darling!" said my colleague-to-be. "Oh, darling!"

Her eyes were angry. Even play-acting, apparently, before an interested audience, I was supposed to keep my cotton-picking hands from wandering.

"It's been a long time, Madeleine," I said soulfully.

"Too long, dear. Much too long!"

She was properly constructed. She was, as a matter of fact, much better than I'd expected. As a rule, the ones who are afraid of it are the ones to whom it will never happen; but this one wasn't going to wither on the vine unpicked unless she worked at it hard. She was a fairly fragile-looking girl in spite of her tweedy, trousered outfit; a slight figure with dark, carefully arranged hair, and delicate, accurate features in a small, heart-shaped face. She was carrying a purse, a raincoat, and what I at first took to be a cased camera, and then realized was a pair of small binoculars. I wondered if it was part of her tourist camouflage, or if she was actually expecting to have to spot a distant object invisible to the naked eye, and if so, what.

"Give me a moment to clean up, darling," she said. "I just stepped off the plane and into a cab. It's wonderful to see you, Matt, it really is!"

Our greeting dialogue wasn't the greatest, I reflected; but then we weren't really trying to fool anybody, just to make them think we were trying to fool them, if I had the game figured correctly. Even that, as far as I could see, wasn't absolutely essential. After all, judging by what Mac had said, I'd been hired as a menace, not as an actor. That meant the people I was supposed to be menacing were supposed to know it, or what was the point? And if the folks who were supposed to be scared knew enough about me to know what a scary fellow I was, they'd also know, most likely, that I'd never seen this very attractive, very proper lady before in my life.

"I won't be a minute," she said.

I made a burlesque thing of checking the time. "I'll

hold you to that, doll," I said. "One minute. Sixty seconds. No more."

She laughed; but her eyes had narrowed slightly. I'd gone and done it again; the crude gent with the wandering hands and the big mouth. Calling her "doll" was, apparently, not showing proper respect, or something. I watched her turn away and I sighed, reflecting grimly that it was going to be a great four-day boat ride, relaxed and informal and friendly, just fun, fun, fun all the way. Well, hell. Maybe I should look upon it as a challenge to my *machismo,* as the Mexicans call it and make a real project of finding out what kind of a girl or woman was hiding behind the frigid, protective shell. But my experience has been that kissing Sleeping Beauties awake isn't all it's cracked up to be. It's more fun when they already know where the noses go.

I shook my head ruefully, and busied myself unpacking my suitcase while I waited. I'd laid out my pajamas and toilet kit; and I was tucking the bag into the wardrobe, out of the way, when it occurred to me to glance at my watch again, a bit uneasily. Six minutes.

Of course, the lady probably hadn't taken the time limit I'd set her very seriously. She could even be putting me in my place deliberately. Nevertheless, the old hunter-hunted instinct was stirring in its primitive way. It had been a hell of a quiet evening so far. It didn't feel right. Somebody'd had me brought a long way because I was supposed to be familiar with violence; yet no violence had occurred. Or had it?

I stepped quickly out into the passage and knocked on the door of the next stateroom. There was no answer. I checked the door cautiously. It wasn't locked. Well, it wouldn't be. The general passenger instructions issued with my ticket had informed me that for safety reasons—I suppose so you could get out in a hurry if the ship started to burn or sink—the staterooms were not supplied with keys. If you wanted to protect your belongings while you stepped ashore at a port along the way, you were supposed to see the purser, and he'd do the honors.

I worked the handle, gave a little push, and watched the door swing back into the cabin. There was nobody to be seen inside and there was only one place for anybody to hide. With my hand on the gun in my jacket pocket, I sidled into the stateroom, kicked the door shut, and yanked open the wardrobe. It was empty.

Standing there, I drew a long breath. It was no time to get mad. It was no time to stand around telling myself selfrighteously that nobody'd informed me I was supposed to be guarding any body besides my own. It was time to think very clearly and work very fast. I made a hasty survey of the cabin. Her two white suitcases lay on one berth, unopened. Her large brown leather purse, her little binoculars, and her tan raincoat, lay on the other. There were no signs of violence, except that what should have been there wasn't: the lady herself. It was hardly likely that she'd departed voluntarily, leaving passport, money, ticket, optical equipment, everything, lying in an unlocked cabin for anybody to grab.

Well, there was one possibility. I stepped back out into the passageway, closing the door behind me. I told myself firmly that I was a courageous and patriotic undercover agent accustomed to facing danger and death for my country. I made certain there was nobody in sight in either direction, and yanked open the door of the ladies' room across the hall, prepared to flee in confusion, muttering that, as an ignorant Yankee, I hadn't known that DAMER meant dames. The place was empty, with no feminine feet showing in either of the stalls.

I withdrew hastily, reached into my own stateroom for my hat and coat, and headed for the deck above, knowing, of course, that I was too late, I had to be. I knew what I'd have done, if I'd been in the place of the red-faced blond sailor; and the biggest mistake you can make in the business is to figure that other people are any less decisive and ruthless than you are.

The proof was that he was right there, lounging near the gangway, with a smaller, younger man beside him. They were watching the boarding and loading process idly, as if they had nothing better to do, and maybe they hadn't, now. My man no longer looked like any kind of a sailor. A quick shaking up had made the light hair look longer, under the battered, old, felt hat he was now wearing. The jeans and sweater were the same but now there was a necklace of big beads around his neck. A pair of well-stuffed packs, the gaudy nylon kind with aluminum frames, were parked on the deck beside the two men. They were, at a glance, just a couple of the semi-hippie types you encounter everywhere these days, seeing the world with their belongings on their backs.

There was only the one gangway. Forward, a crane was hoisting some big crates aboard; but unless the whole ship was in on the gag, he could hardly have got her ashore that way. Anyway, if they'd gone to the trouble of smuggling her ashore, they'd probably keep her alive, at least for a little while. I could work on that later, if necessary. Right now I had to act on the worst assumption I could dream up, remembering that when a ship is at a dock, everybody seems to congregate on the shoreward side watching the action. A man can practically count on having the seaward decks to himself for any nefarious purpose he may have in mind.

I drew a long breath and, without looking at the pair by the rail, walked forward to the officer who'd taken my ticket earlier, and indicated that I'd like to step ashore for a moment.

"Yes, you have an hour and ten minutes, sir," he said in good English. "But please do not forget, we sail promptly at eleven."

"I won't forget, thanks."

I walked down the sloping, cleated gangway to the dock, marched straight ahead until I was out of sight in a narrow space between two large, windowless buildings on the shore—warehouses, perhaps—and began to run. Coming out on the street beyond the buildings, I turned left, pounding along at a good clip. Reaching the far end of the structures, I turned left again, back towards the water, and hit the edge of the dock far enough ahead of the ship that I couldn't be seen by anyone on the passenger decks aft. A seaman on the towering bow might spot me, but if he was just an honest seaman he wouldn't care.

I stood for a moment catching my breath as I studied the black water of the harbor, speckled with steady rain. There were swirls and miniature whirlpools of current out there, glistening in the docklights and the lights of the far shore, moving sluggishly seaward with the ebbing tide. I glanced at my watch: eleven minutes had passed since she'd left my cabin. Say it had taken him five to get the job done, that left six: one tenth of an hour. At two knots, a current would carry a floating object two tenths of a nautical mile in that length of time, or four hundred yards.

I started running again, loping to the end of the long wharf…

Not quite to the end. I was just taking a last look out there before turning inland, wondering if it would be worthwhile to go on along the street, or road, that followed the rocky shoreline ahead, when I saw something out in the dark water thirty yards from shore. Staring, I saw it make a kind of crippled movement, and another, as if trying weakly to kick its way towards land. Okay. With time short, aware that I'd start checking soon, our husky blond friend had been hasty and careless. He'd counted on the cold water and the current to finish the job. He hadn't made sure before he put her over the ship's rail; not quite sure.

I raced around the end of the dock, ducked under a

fence cable, and slid down the rocks to the water, getting rid of hat, raincoat, jacket, and shoes. I put my wallet on top of the pile, and tucked my gun underneath, wondering why the hell people couldn't ever seem to get themselves drowned—or half-drowned—in summer. She came drifting past the end of the pier as I launched myself. The water was just as cold as I'd anticipated; and I'm no great swimmer even when I'm not freezing to death. I just kind of hacked my way out there awkwardly, grabbed a fistful of wet tweed, chopped my way back, and dragged her onto a shelving rock. As I eased her down gently, so I wouldn't bruise her any more than she was already bruised, my fingers encountered an ugly, unnatural depression in the skull under the soaked hair…

"Helm?"

I almost missed the faint whisper, as a car roared by on the road above. "Here," I said.

"My head… He had a gun. He made me go on deck, and then he hit… It was the sailor, the one carrying the bags. Watch out… watch out…"

"Sure," I said.

"Cold," she breathed. "It's so cold and dark… Helm?"

"Still right here," I said.

Suddenly her voice was quite calm and clear, although still very weak: "Ivory… I'm sure that man was working for Ivory, the one who hit me. He wants the Siphon—"

"The what?"

"The Siphon, the Sigmund Siphon!" She was impatient with my stupidity. "And the information; the data to

make it work. Ekofisk, Frigg, Torbotten. The drops are
Trondheim, Svolvaer. Deliver to… Don't remember. Oh,
damn! Denison, the man Denison works for. Deliver to
him. No, I forgot, the Skipper will deliver. Contact in
Narvik. Narvik? The ferry? Somewhere up in there. Can't
remember. My head. They'll tell you what you need to
know. Get in touch with them."

"Who'll tell me?"

"The Skipper will tell you."

"The Skipper?"

"Hank. Captain Henry Priest," she whispered, "and his
pale, doting little shadow… Madly in love with a man old
enough to… Stupid little girl, really. Oh, never mind. I'm
wandering. But ask them. The money's in my suitcase,
two envelopes. The thick one's for Svolvaer, of course,
to pay for the plans of the Siphon. The other's for the
contact in Trondheim. Trondheim? I think that's right. The
binoculars, you'll need the binoculars… No, darn it, it
won't work. Not for you; not for a man. They're expecting
a woman. Can't change; they'll know something's gone
wrong, and panic. Very timid people…"

"Do they know you?" I asked.

The painful, determined whisper continued as if I
hadn't spoken: "Ivory's after it, too, hired by somebody;
and that smug little hypocrite his daughter pretending she
doesn't really approve—"

I interrupted sharply: "The timid people in Trondheim
and Svolvaer from whom we'll be buying all this stuff.
Do they *know* you, doll?"

It brought her back from wherever she'd gone for a moment. "Don't call me that!" she snapped. "It sounds so cheap… No, they don't know me… And you really should do something about your habit of pawing girls in public, Mr. Helm. It's not very nice, you know. I must insist that in the future…" Her voice stopped abruptly.

"Sure," I said, after waiting out a long moment of utter silence. Headlight beams swung over my head suddenly, and the sound of the car washed over me. When it had died away, I rose slowly. I said, "Sure, kid. In the future."

Then I was sorry I'd said it, because she wouldn't have liked being called "kid." Not that it mattered now.

3

Tracteurstedet, the restaurant with the untranslatable name—untranslatable by me, at least—was still open for business. The watcher I'd spotted in the shadows, earlier, was still where I'd left him, right on the job; a small, rather shabby man, from what I could make out. Then I saw another, larger, male shape back up one of the alleys. It's nice in the movies. You can tell the white hats from the black hats; and sometimes even the Union Blue from the Confederate Gray. Well, as long as they minded their business, whatever it might be, I'd mind mine.

Standing among the old wooden buildings in the steady, cold, Norwegian rain, I studied the lighted windows for a moment. I was feeling a bit shy after my evening dip in the harbor. I saw that there was an outside staircase leading directly to the upstairs diningroom, bypassing the snack bar below. I took that, and looked through the glass of the door. They were still where I'd left them over an hour ago: Hank Priest and his rather colorless young lady-friend.

There are two kinds of operations. There's the precision mission in which Agent A stays at point B for C number of minutes after which he proceeds at D miles per hour to point E. This hardly ever works as planned. Somewhere along the line somebody slips by thirty seconds and the whole schedule goes to hell. Opposed to this is the seat-of-the-pants operation where you're told to hang around a likely area as long as you feel you may be needed there, and then go to some other spot of your choice, where your talents may come in handy, as fast as your instinct tells you. With luck, and the right people, this sometimes clicks. Apparently, I had some right people on my side tonight. At least, something had kept them dawdling over their coffee so I could find them when I needed them.

I opened the door and, overcoming my shyness, marched right over to the table hoping that, in this dismal weather, my coat and hat would do a reasonable job of covering the fact that underneath I was actually wetter than any normal rain would account for.

"Excuse me," I said when the two of them looked up at me. "Excuse me, I was here before, sitting right over there, remember? You were kind enough to help me with the menu."

"Yes?" It was the girl who spoke.

"I seem to have misplaced a book," I said carefully. "I was wondering if I'd left it here."

"A book? What kind of a book?"

"A guidebook," I said. "A rather special guidebook. I'll be lost without it."

"Oh. Well, I'm afraid it's not here, at least I didn't see... Why don't you ask the waitress, Hank?"

"Of course." Priest called the woman over and spoke to her in Norwegian. He turned back to me, shaking his head. "No, she says you left nothing behind, old chap."

"Oh, hell," I said. "Well, thanks anyway. Sorry to bother you."

"No bother at all."

I walked out. At the bottom of the stairs I retrieved a bundle I'd tucked out of sight; then I stepped around the corner of the building to wait, shivering uncontrollably from time to time, but the cold was irrelevant. We dedicated professionals, sustained by our fierce sense of duty, protected by our rigorous training and conditioning, are immune to hardship, or supposed to be.

The relevant fact was that it was conveniently dark back here in the Hansa boys' historic old compound—I hadn't come across any references to Hansa girls in my hurried research; maybe they'd all stayed home in Germany where it was warm. Anyway, it was dark and it was raining harder than ever. Both facts were in our favor if our retired naval hero—the Skipper, for God's sake!—would just get his damned seagoing butt off the bench and out here before I froze to death.

Then they were coming down the stairs. Priest was helping the girl with her coat, gray like her sweater and slacks, one of the long, tailored, cover-up jobs reaching almost to the ankles. The two of them stopped at the foot of the wooden stairs, looking around.

"Over here," I said.

Priest was struggling into a shapeless, colorless, British-type raincoat. He had on a tweed cap that matched his suit. He must have had lots of fun getting the props together for his I-say-old-chap act but, I reminded myself, the guy had stuck around where I could find him. After all, he wasn't a total greenhorn. He'd been through some wars. He might not be much of an undercover operative, but apparently he did have a useful feel for a combat situation, if you want to call it that.

He had something else. Just before stepping off the bottom of the stairs, he made a small signal with his left hand. The man at the corner of the building nodded, and strolled across the little courtyard, and signaled to the man up the alley, who joined him. Both headed towards the street, and vanished. I wondered briefly how our tame nautical expert had managed to recruit local help— at least they had that look—but after all, he did seem to speak the language; and an ex-Norwegian named Priest wasn't any more unlikely than an ex-Swede named Helm. Maybe he had family in these parts. I watched him approach with the girl.

It was hardly a time for social amenities, with a crisis on our hands and the rain pouring down. Still, aside from our brief encounter earlier in the evening, we hadn't seen each other for a couple of years, and some kind of relationship had to be established, or reestablished.

"A long way from Florida, Captain," I said. "I was very sorry to hear about Mrs. Priest, sir."

I mean, the dead girl might have got by with calling him Skipper, and I'd known him well enough once to call him Hank for a week or two, but you've got to be careful with these gold-braid guys, particularly the retired ones. Some of them can't seem to forget the rank they once held and it breaks out on them like a rash any time they find themselves with a little authority. I was going to have to work with the man. I didn't want to antagonize him right at the start. I didn't want to make the same mistake twice in the same night. After all, if I'd taken the trouble to show the proper gentlemanly deference to the girl called Madeleine, maybe she wouldn't have felt it necessary to go off and powder her nose and get herself killed.

"Never mind the condolences," Priest said curtly and for a moment I was glad that I'd sirred him properly. Then he grinned, displaying the little squinty, seadog wrinkles around his eyes. "And never mind buttering up the old retread with all that phony respect, son. I know what you think of amateurs in a situation like this—just about what I used to think of landlubbers on shipboard." He held out his hand and I shook it. "As we say in the Navy, it's good to have you on board, Mr. Helm."

"Maybe," I said. "And maybe it's not as good as somebody hoped it would be. As they say in NASA: 'Houston, we have a problem.' A serious problem."

There was a little silence. I was aware of the girl turning her coat collar high against the rain, but she said nothing.

"Evelyn?" Priest asked at last.

"Evelyn?" I said, frowning.

"Evelyn Benson, alias Mrs. Madeleine Barth. Has something happened to her?"

I said deliberately, "Barth. Well, it's about time somebody told me my lady-love's last name—my late lady-love's last name."

Priest drew a long breath. "She's dead? Who—"

"Does it matter right now?" I asked. "I know the guy, and I'll deal with him if it becomes necessary, but first we'd better decide on some kind of alternate plan, if possible."

The pale girl stirred beside Hank Priest. "You're supposed to be a tough, experienced, competent agent, Mr. Helm. That's why you were picked to help us. You were supposed to keep Evelyn safe—"

Priest said, "Never mind, Diana."

"But—"

"I said, never mind!" Captain Priest hadn't spent all those years in command for nothing. His voice had a nice military snap to it. He went on: "As Matt has already hinted, very delicately, the briefing was inadequate. We were so afraid of betraying her to the others that we apparently didn't give sufficient information to the man who was supposed to protect her. My fault. I didn't expect... I assumed his mere presence would be enough to discourage any attempts... He stopped, and glanced my way. "Where is she?"

"Among the rocks at the end of Festnungskaien with a nasty, fatal dent in her cranium."

He winced, but didn't protest the graphic description. The girl, however, seemed about to resent it vigorously;

but he cut her off before she could speak.

"You have more experience with this sort of thing, Matt," he said. "What can we do now?"

"About her?" I said. "I'll give you a number. Call it, and she'll be taken care of discreetly, saving the Bergen police a lot of trouble. Such accidents happen in this business; and we keep people around who know how to deal with them, even in this cold corner of the world."

Mac had indicated that there were things, like how much expert help was being provided me, that I didn't need to tell a lot of people about, presumably not even Hank Priest. Let the old salt think that it was all just routine and that we normally kept burial details standing by to gather up the stiffs as they fell, all around the world from the frozen north to the frozen south.

He didn't seem particularly interested, however. He was more concerned with the dead girl.

"Tell us what happened."

"I went to my cabin," I said. "She came, kissed me dutifully and we went through the long-time-no-see routine. There was a sailor-type waiting in the hall with her bags. I'd seen him before, lounging by the gangplank when I came aboard. He hadn't offered to carry anything for me, but what the hell, she was prettier than I was, it figured okay. But obviously the guy had been hanging around waiting for her."

"You mean, you think he knew her by sight?" Priest frowned. "I really thought our security was better than that."

I shook my head. "If they'd known her by sight, they wouldn't have cut it so close. I mean, why wait and risk taking her out from under the nose of a trained bodyguard, if I may flatter myself a bit, if they could have hit her anywhere? I think they knew the ship and the cabin but not the girl—not until she showed her ticket to the purser and he told her where to find her stateroom. That gave them the identification they'd been waiting for, and they moved in, or he did. The ship's people knew he was a passenger, but if he wanted to help a good-looking girl with her luggage, it was nothing to them. She, on the other hand, thought he was just one of the crew doing his job. As did I, more or less. When she went to her cabin to tidy up a bit, he went with her, of course, with the bags."

"You should have stayed close to her!" the girl in gray said quickly.

"Yes, ma'am," I said. "I should have stayed close to her; and I surely do thank you for pointing it out. When I decided she'd been gone long enough, and went looking, she wasn't there. Her purse was open on the bed. I figure she'd been fumbling for something to tip him with when he put a gun in her back and marched her up to the deserted deck above, on the side away from the dock. He clubbed her over the head and dumped her over the rail. Then he joined a friend who'd probably been acting as a lookout; and the two of them went back to watching the passing show. Well, I managed to second-guess him well enough to make the intercept and fish her out, but she died on me. Scratch one Barth."

The girl said sharply, "Evelyn was a rather nice person, Mr. Helm! You might at least show a little—"

"Cut it out," I said. "We haven't got time for showing remorse for our errors, or respect for our dead, sweetheart. The ship sails in twenty minutes. Somebody up the coast is expecting—"

"Well, they're just going to be disappointed, aren't they?" the pale girl said. I remembered that Priest had called her Diana. She didn't look much like a Diana to me. She went on sharply: "I mean—since we're being so brutal—if Evelyn's dead, she's dead. There's nothing we can do about it now, and standing here in the rain isn't going to help—"

"That's where you're wrong," I said. "Standing in the rain may help a lot. It will help even more if you go over and stick your head under that leaky rainspout."

Her eyes widened. "Why in the world should I—"

"Because your hair's too light, Diana X, or whatever your name is. Getting it good and wet will darken it just enough, I figure, until we can get the right chemicals to do the job. Anyway, your hairdo's different, pulled back schoolteacherishly like that, but if you loosen it up and let it kind of wash down your face, maybe nobody'll notice, particularly if you're wearing my coat over your head like a tent to keep the rain off, the way girls do, hopefully, even after they've got themselves thoroughly soaked in a storm. The only catch is, we've got to get going before it double-crosses us and stops raining hard enough to make your act look plausible."

The girl was staring at me, aghast. "You're mad!" she breathed, and turned to Priest, and said, more uncertainly:

"He's crazy. Isn't he, Skipper?"

I said, also speaking to Priest: "Evelyn Benson told me several things before she died, among them the fact that the people with whom she expected to make contact up north knew that a woman was being sent—*but they didn't know what woman.* They didn't know Madeleine Barth. That means, since they seem to be kind of shy folks who'll panic if the signals are switched on them, that I can't make the deal with them, whatever it is. But Miss X, here, can."

The girl spoke in a soft, preoccupied way. "My name is Lawrence, Mr. Helm. Diana Lawrence."

"Hi, Diana Lawrence," I said. "Well, what about it?"

The funny thing was that, now that the initial shock of my suggestion had worn off, she was interested. She was giving it serious consideration; and it wasn't merely a question of her duty, or of her loyalty to, or love for, the older man beside her, who was responsible for this project, now threatened. I remembered the dying girl referring to her scornfully as his pale, doting shadow.

But it wasn't dutiful compulsion I saw in her eyes. What I saw was a kind of fascination; a low-down, reckless, to-hell-with-it-let's-flip-it look. Apparently this pale kid in gray had always, shy and withdrawn, dreamed secret dreams of suddenly becoming a sexy, fearless, wicked Mata Hari. Her hands went up and started withdrawing the pins from her sedate, now rather damp, hairdo…

"No, Diana." That was Priest. "It's too risky. You've had no training, no preparation…"

"You warned me there'd be risks when you offered me the job," the girl said. "Robbie ran risks. Evelyn ran risks. Why shouldn't I run risks, Skipper? What's so special about me?"

I asked, "Who's Robbie? I've got names coming at me faster than I can field them tonight."

"Robbie's dead," said Diana Lawrence. "Never mind about Robbie, Mr. Helm. You said we were in a hurry. Well, hurry up and talk him into it."

I shrugged, and turned to Priest. "Give it some thought," I said. "At the moment, we're short one Barth, female. Either we put a substitute into play or we concede the game." I shoved the soggy bundle I was holding into his hand. "There you are. That's what Mrs. Madeleine Barth was wearing when she went over the ship's side. That's what she'll be expected to come aboard in, if she comes back aboard. I don't suppose they'll be much fun to put on, but it wasn't much fun getting them off her, either. I'd hate to think I'd done it for nothing, but it won't kill me. Just say the word, Captain Priest, either way, so we'll all know where we stand, sir."

Sometimes even the best of them have to be reminded who's supposed to be running the show; particularly when it's a kind of show they're not really used to running. Priest glanced down at the rolled-up garments he was holding, sodden with rain and harbor water. He looked at me, frowning a little.

"It's an ingenious idea, son," he said. "But why go to all that trouble? If we do decide to put her aboard, why can't she just go aboard as Diana Lawrence?"

I said, "Aside from the fact that I don't particularly want to arouse curiosity and suspicion by trying to explain to the ship's company why I've traded one girlfriend for another, I'd rather not hand the opposition any victories I don't have to, Skipper. If they're allowed to think murdering young ladies under my nose is easy, they'll be right back on the job tomorrow, plugging for victim number two. However, if I can shake them up a bit, with an apparent failure, and a few other shocks I have in mind, depending on how it develops, Miss Lawrence's future becomes considerably brighter." I glanced at the girl. "Are any of the people with whom we'll be dealing likely to recognize you?"

"Probably not," she said. "The contacts up north certainly won't. As for the gang that's trying to muscle in, if that's the right underworld phrase, it depends on how thoroughly they've checked us all out. My feeling is that I'm... well, too unimportant and inconspicuous for them to have noticed me particularly."

I studied her a little more closely. Any girl who'll admit that she's unimportant and inconspicuous has got to have something going for her, if only honesty. I turned to Hank Priest.

"My point is, if we're going to use her, we might as well use her as Madeleine Barth, if she's willing to tackle the impersonation, and she seems to be. The big decision is whether to use her or not. If not, have you got an alternative, sir? Besides getting a bottle and getting drunk,

I mean; and even that isn't really practical, considering the crazy liquor laws they have around here."

Except for a slight frown, he ignored my frivolity. He said, "You seem to forget that at least one man saw Evelyn board the ship as Madeleine Barth: the man who murdered her. According to you, he had an accomplice who may also have got a good look at her. Even if you manage to get Diana aboard undetected, her impersonation isn't going to fool them for very long."

I said, "Captain Priest, sir, may I remind you of your own words? This is the sort of thing I have experience with, remember? I wouldn't be asking Miss Lawrence to climb into a dead girl's clothes if I didn't think she could get away with it. Leave Ivory and his cohorts to me."

"What do you know about Ivory?" Priest asked quickly.

"Just what a dying girl told me," I said. "She indicated he was probably responsible for the attack on her; an interloper trying to horn in on our game, I gathered. She also said we'd be dealing with a mystery man whose name she couldn't recall—the crack on the head had made her memory a bit spotty—but whoever he was, he had in his employ a guy named Denison. What do we know about a Denison, Skipper?"

"Nobody knows much about Denison. He's just a kind of bodyguard and dirty-works man for Kotko. You may have heard of *him*." Priest grimaced. "I don't like having to cooperate with a robber-baron type like that; but he does have the know-how we need for this job, so we've come to an agreement with him. The details don't really concern you."

Nothing is harder on the digestion of a man in my line of work than details that don't concern him. "Kotko," I said grimly "That would be Lincoln Alexander Kotko, the notorious invisible millionaire who shaves his head in imitation of a Prussian Junker or a couple of Hollywood actors; the guy who owns all the oil wells Faisal can't be bothered with."

"That's a slight exaggeration but you've obviously got the right man in mind."

Well, I hadn't really thought it was going to be Arctic iron ore this time around. I groaned. "Then this whole crazy business is just another petroleum caper? With Mister Kotko involved—I hear he insists on the Mister; and he's rich enough to make it stick—it's got to be petroleum."

"Yes, of course," Priest said. "What did you think we were all doing up here, son? You must have heard of the recent big North Sea oil discoveries: Ekofisk, Frigg, Torbotten. The information we're trying to obtain—we've promised it to Kotko, who'll put it to use to our benefit, and of course his own—is being delivered in two installments, one dealing with Ekofisk and Frigg, and the second with Torbotten and some other subjects."

I said carefully, "Those other subjects you touch on so delicately, Skipper. Could one of them, by any chance, be something going by the odd name of the Sigmund Siphon?"

There was a little silence. Priest sighed. "Evelyn really

laid it all out for you, didn't she?"

"Not really. She just gave me a lot of funny names to play with. When I get them all sorted out, maybe I'll know something. Or maybe you'd like to break down, sir, and tell me all about it and save my brain all that wear and tear."

He hesitated. "It's a fairly long story, and we haven't got time for it right now. Later, if you don't mind, Matt."

"Righto, Skipper," I said. "But you had better give me a little information about this Ivory character right now, since I may stumble over him or his boys again before we can hold a formal conference."

Priest nodded. "Very well. Ivory is our private code name for a certain Dr. Adolf Elfenbein, a scientific genius who retired from university research some years ago to put his geological knowledge to profitable use in very non-academic ways."

"Elfenbein," I said. "German, or Norwegian, for elephant-bone: ivory. Cute. Evelyn mentioned a daughter."

"Yes. There was a wife, Irene, who was very much involved in her husband's schemes, but she died of cancer last year. The daughter, Greta, had been studying music in Switzerland, but she came home to stay with her father in Hamburg maybe to take over her mother's part in the family business, so to speak. Judging by her snapshots, she's fairly small and rather attractive. Elfenbein himself is a rather mild-looking, little, white-haired man, but don't be deceived. He's intelligent and he's dangerous and he's built up the nucleus of an efficient international organization that hires muscle as required. Keep it in mind, since you're probably going to have to deal with him somehow. He works on commission; and apparently he's being employed by somebody—we haven't identified the employer, but we're working on it—who wants the same thing we do."

"Which is?"

Priest hesitated once more, which seemed a little odd, since he wasn't what I'd call a hesitant man. "Can't you figure it out for yourself, son?" he asked. He sounded almost embarrassed.

I studied his weathered face in the light from the restaurant windows. "Let's see just what we have here," I said slowly. "There's a respectable, retired naval person with a fine service record and a good credit rating but he's got some real funny company. A geological genius with larcenous impulses. A mysterious and unscrupulous financial type specializing in oil. And added to this interesting mixture are a nice, big, newly discovered petroleum puddle under the North Sea and a worldwide energy shortage that's got everybody in a continuing panic." I frowned. "The only catch is, if I've read my newspapers correctly, that all this North Sea petroleum has been neatly divided up among the bordering nations. The U.S. doesn't border on any part of the North Sea, as far as I can recall; and neither does Mr. Kotko, not to mention Dr. Elfenbein. So I don't quite see…" I stopped, and looked, and saw the answer in his face, and whistled softly. "Captain Priest, sir, I'm ashamed of you. Going into partnership with the infamous, piratical Mister Kotko to… Why, that's downright dishonest, sir! What would George Washington say?"

Priest cleared his throat. "Officially," he said, "officially, Mister Kotko is a successful and highly regarded businessman against whom nothing illegal has ever been proved. His company, Petrolene, Incorporated—I should say, his most conspicuous company—has a filling station on every U.S. street corner. You've probably got a Petrox credit card in your wallet; I know I have. Hell, son, we should all be proud to be associated with such a sterling character in a patriotic enterprise like this." His voice was dry. "Anyway, there are very few Georges in Washington today, Mr. Helm."

"Well, there never were many."

"What there are in Washington," Priest went on deliberately, "are a great many small and scared men who shit their pants full during the last fuel crisis and are willing to go to great lengths—*very* great lengths—to keep their trousers clean in the future. If you know what I mean, Mr. Helm."

I said, "I'm catching on fast."

I looked at him for a moment longer, with considerable respect. I wouldn't have thought the conventional-looking old sailor had it in him. The U.S. Navy is a great institution, no doubt, but imagination is not one of the traits for which its graduates are usually noted. This was an interesting and ambitious project, kind of like robbing the U.S. Mint or swiping the British crown jewels.

Actually, I guess, it was more like planning to walk off with a Grand Canyon that didn't belong to you, or stealing yourself a Matterhorn and a few associated Alps.

My own line of work didn't leave me in a very good position to criticize the caper on moral grounds but I did wonder a bit about its feasibility. Of course, unlike Mister Kotko, I had no special knowhow in this area. If he was involved, it meant the thing could probably be pulled off somehow.

"The Sigmund Siphon," I said softly.

"I'd rather you forgot you ever heard about that, son."

"Sure."

Priest hesitated, and glanced at Diana Lawrence, standing there silent, and back to me. "Do you really think this impersonation scheme of yours will work? It seems to me there are too many loose ends—"

"I'll do my best to tie them up," I said.

He hesitated, weakening. "Well, just don't forget for a moment that they've already killed once on that ship, even if they don't know it."

"Mr. Helm will protect me, I'm sure."

That was the girl. She'd finished loosening her hair while we talked and it was still raining hard enough that the darkened tendrils were now streaming wetly down her face just as I'd suggested. Most girls don't take well to water except on the beach but it seemed to improve this one—or maybe it was the anticipation of becoming an honest-to-God, real-life Wonder Woman that had put a hint of pink into her normally colorless cheeks.

She spoke to Priest: "We've got to do *something* if we're going to salvage anything from this mess. What Mr. Helm suggests seems to be, as they say, the only game in town. Please stop being paternal, Skipper, and give me those clothes. And turn your backs, both of you...

4

The only spot on the ship from which I could watch the boarding ramp unseen was the deck directly above: the upper passenger-deck outside the first-class lounge and dining room. If was one stage up from the level to which Evelyn Benson had been taken for her final dive, two from that of the cabin where her substitute now awaited me, protected, I hoped, by the gun I had lent her, with hasty instructions in its use.

Leaning against the rail up there in a manner I hoped looked relaxed and casual, I wondered if the shipping line kept a doctor handy with a sure cure for galloping pneumonia—I hadn't taken time to change into dry clothes. I controlled the shakes with a heroic effort, and watched the last crates of cargo being swung aboard, forward. Beyond this scene of activity was the long, empty, lighted dock in the rain. At least it was empty when I first looked...

I suppose I'd been expecting him. At least, I wasn't

really surprised when Denison stepped out into the light some fifty yards away. He did it very deliberately, coming into sight around the corner of one of the warehouses and stopping in the cone of illumination of one of the lamps over there, looking directly at me.

He was a big man, bigger than I remembered, wearing a belted trenchcoat, dark across the shoulders with rain, and a hat with a brim wide enough to look slightly Wild West, at least in these effete European surroundings. Even at that distance, there was no doubt at all that he'd seen me on the ship's upper deck, and that he wanted me to see him. Now he raised his hand in a kind of salute, or maybe it was a kind of challenge. I made an answering gesture and watched him turn without haste and go out of sight.

Of course, I hadn't seen his face well enough under the wide hatbrim to identify him in a court of law but I didn't need to see it. I'd worked with him often enough and long enough, after first breaking him in—on-the-job training, so to speak—to know him anywhere: Paul Denison, code name Luke, once a friend of mine, and the man who'd repaid me for the education I'd given him by teaching me a valuable lesson in return. He'd taught me it didn't pay to make friends in this business.

He'd put his lesson across the hard way, by almost getting me killed. Two others had died. It had not been a very nice affair and the fact that he'd sold out for money hadn't helped. Fear, yes. You can forgive fear. You'd damned well better forgive it, unless you're brave enough to be sure it will never happen to you, and who is? But *money*?

I reflected grimly that it was beginning to make sense, Mac's arranging for me to have all kinds of secret, expensive support on what had seemed on the surface to be just a simple matter of repaying a favor we owed his old fishing buddy, Hank Priest. It had made sense ever since I'd heard Denison's name on a dying girl's lips. Mac was not a forgiving person. He'd put out the word on Paul Denison, priority one, immediately after I'd made it home and reported what had happened—Denison, presumably, had hoped there would be no survivors, but he wasn't that good a Benedict Arnold then. I reminded myself he might be better now. He'd had a good many years to practice in, seven to be exact.

As soon as I'd been more or less fit for duty once more, I'd been given the job of making the touch. I'd been the logical choice, of course, knowing more about our agent Luke—now our ex-agent Luke—than anyone else in the organization. But it had been a kind of left-handed reprimand, anyway. It had been Mac's way of making sure I remembered never again to trust my life, or anybody else's, to simple, stupid friendship. The hints of betrayal had been there, but I'd disregarded them because they'd involved my good *amigo* and protégé, Paul Denison. The message I was supposed to get, and got, was that the mistake had been mine and it was up to me to correct it, permanently.

However, while I was preparing to carry out the assignment, and waiting for some hint of the location of my quarry, the whole thing had been called off.

The word on Denison had been canceled, without explanation. Around that office, you don't ask questions, particularly about a critical and embarrassing subject like an agent gone bad. As the man responsible for a very recent disaster mission, I'd been in a particularly poor position to play detective. I'd kept my mouth shut, and the name Denison had simply disappeared from our vocabularies as if forgotten; but I should have known Mac hadn't forgotten.

Neither, for that matter, had I. To hell with Frigg, Torbotten, and Ekofisk. To hell with a guy named Robbie, barely mentioned, whoever he might be or have been. To hell with the pirate petroleum-tycoon who liked to hear himself called Mister Kotko. To hell with an ex-university scientist called Elephantbone, now lucratively self-employed, and his daughter Greta, and his wife Irene, defunct. I'd had a bushel of names served up to me tonight, but there was only one that really counted: Denison. And the fact that Mac had sent me here, with help, meant that maybe, just maybe, some situation had changed enough, somewhere—or could be changed enough—so that I'd be allowed to do something about it…

Forward, the crew was securing the cargo boom. On the dock, a couple of men approached the gangplank in a purposeful way, obviously about to remove it. There was a shout from the deck just below me, and they stood back briefly to let a youthful male figure with a backpack hurry ashore. I stepped away from the rail above in case he should throw a last glance over his shoulder, but he didn't.

A moment later the ship was swinging free of the dock. Normally, I'd have stayed to watch how the gold-braided gent on the bridge managed the job of getting the big vessel away—in this business, you never know. Once, I found myself several thousand feet up in the air in a small plane with a dead pilot. I won't say I got that flying machine down undamaged because it wouldn't be true but what counted was that, having paid some attention to the landings I'd witnessed over the years, I managed to keep myself without damage while I was cracking it up. One day, somebody may hand me a freighter or an ocean liner without a book of instructions, and a few minutes spent watching a good shiphandler at work will pay off. But there'd presumably be other opportunities for observation up the coast; at the moment I was too cold to wait around.

Two decks below, I knocked a certain way on the door of the cabin assigned to Mrs. Madeleine Barth. The voice of the new incumbent answered promptly. I stepped inside and looked at the hole in the end of the short barrel of my own .38 revolver.

"Good girl," I said, closing the door behind me. "But just point it elsewhere now, please."

Diana Lawrence laid the gun on the berth and rose, pulling uncomfortably at the jacket of her borrowed outfit. She was a deceptive girl in more ways than one, I reflected. Physically, she'd seemed about the same size as Evelyn Benson, if anything a little smaller; but apparently her colorless personality had fooled me. There was more girl there than I'd thought. The now damp and shapeless brown tweed pantsuit was short and tight on her. If she hadn't been designed along very narrow lines, she'd never have got into it. She pushed some stringy hair out of her face, and regarded me warily. I had the impression that, waiting, she'd had some uneasy second thoughts about this far-out impersonation drama dreamed up by me, in which she had the starring role. Maybe she'd even had some second thoughts about me.

"Well?" she said.

"I think they fell for it," I said. "Your gangway performance was great. I think you convinced them that Madeleine Barth has returned from the grave, a little shaky and very self-conscious about her disheveled appearance, but very much alive. Anyway, the blond thug sent his kid helper ashore at the last moment; or maybe the orders came from someone else on this ship. We can hope he went to summon reinforcements, now that getting rid of Mrs. Barth has turned out to be more difficult than expected."

Diana frowned. "That's a hope?"

"Well, if it's true, it means they bought your act," I said. "It also means they're shorthanded here on board, until the reserves report for duty. And it means that one of the only two people we're fairly sure can identify you— well, unidentify you—isn't around for the moment."

She hesitated, and said a little uncertainly, "Of course you know best, but should we… should we be talking like this, Mr. Helm?"

"Talking?" I said. "What do you mean?"

"Well, if we were overheard… There are things like microphones and such, aren't there?"

I grinned. "Swell. We're going to make a first-class operative of you, Diana Lawrence. However, I checked both cabins when I first came aboard, as well as I could. I think they're clean."

"Oh."

We stood there for a moment, silent. It had been a rushed acquaintanceship all the way. This was the first time we'd really had an opportunity to stop and see each other clearly. I don't know how I looked, but if it was anything like I felt, it was terrible. She looked even worse, if possible, if only because girls are kind of supposed to be neater and prettier than boys. Now, after being dressed up in another woman's sodden, slightly too small clothes and run several blocks through heavy rain she looked hopelessly bedraggled and at the same time a little ridiculous, like the old movie in which the comic gets caught in a thunder-shower in his cheap new suit and it shrinks on him.

The thought seemed to occur to her at the same time and she glanced down at herself wryly. A funny little smile twitched the corners of her pale lips as she looked up once more.

"We're a pair of clowns, aren't we?" she said. "You'd better get into something dry before you freeze to death. Helm?"

"Yes."

"Why?"

"Why what?"

"Why are you doing it?" she asked. "On this mission, you're contract labor, if you don't mind my saying so. It's nothing to you. Why did you go to the trouble of working out this elaborate scheme to retrieve the disaster, *our* disaster, and practically cram it down our throats."

I hesitated. I couldn't tell her, of course, that I was doing it largely because of Denison; but there were other reasons. "Nobody dies for nothing," I said.

"What?"

"It's an old saying we have," I said. "People die, sure. It can't always be helped. But we can see to it that everyone who dies, dies for something. Well, Evelyn Benson died. Maybe I could have saved her. Maybe I should have. So I didn't have things carefully explained to me. So I wasn't warned. So what? Guys like me aren't supposed to have to be warned. If you must know, I was just too goddamned cocksure that I had it all figured out, that if anybody came to kill, he'd come for me. Okay. She's dead. It's too late for me to do anything about that. But I can try to see that whatever she wanted done gets done, even without her."

Diana Lawrence was watching me oddly. "You're a… a funny man," she said. "I mean—"

"Hilarious," I said. "I'll keep you in stitches clear up the coast. Stay here. I mean that. Don't even stick your head out of this cabin—particularly not your head. Somebody might recognize it, or what would be worse, not recognize it, if you follow me. You're Madeleine Barth sleeping off the effects of a mild concussion and a

THE TERMINATORS   61

cold midnight swim. As long as nobody sees you, nobody can say otherwise. The ladies' john is just across the way. If you need it, say so now, and I'll watch the hall while you… No?"

She smiled faintly. "No, thank you very much," she said. She hesitated. "Am I… am I supposed to know what you're doing?"

I looked at her for a moment. "You're a bright girl. I'm sure you can figure out what's got to be done next," I said. "Keep that gun handy, and shoot hell out of anybody who opens that door, as long as it isn't me."

5

The ship's first-class lounge looked out upon the bow deck with its mast and cargo booms, only dimly visible in the darkness outside the rain-wet windows. I hoped the guy up on the bridge could see more out there than I could and that he had an efficient radar to help him. We seemed to be proceeding at a good clip, judging by the sound of the machinery below, and the map of Norway I'd studied had indicated that it was a hell of a rocky, reef-strewn coast to go blasting along blindly on a stormy night. I consoled myself with the thought that this ship, and presumably this captain, had been making it for years, clear up beyond the Arctic Circle and back. Maybe it was easy when you knew how.

A TV set was going in the lounge, tuned to a Norwegian quiz show that had the studio audience roaring with appreciative laughter. Only a few of the people scattered around the room were paying any attention. The rest were manfully, or womanfully, trying to ignore the noisy box as they chatted, read, or napped, bracing themselves against the motion of the ship in their comfortable, clamped-down chairs. Again, as on the plane, I found myself wondering about a society that permits one person with a coin, or the strength to manipulate a switch or just make a request, to inflict his entertainment preferences on everybody around; but it was hardly a time for solving odd social problems...

I saw the red backpack, mate to the one I'd watched being carried ashore, parked by the lounge door. Then I spotted the owner, in the corner to my right where he could see who entered while ostensibly enjoying the funny, funny show on the black-and-white screen. I say ostensibly, because when I first saw him he was being seriously distracted by a pair of nylon-clad legs belonging to an attractive, nicely dressed young lady passenger sitting on a nearby sofa. I didn't blame him for his preoccupation, considering the scarcity of that kind of entertainment in Scandinavia, these trousered days—but the older man seated beside the girl was rather small and inconspicuous, with fine, white, carefully combed hair that let the pink scalp show through on top.

A rather mild-looking little whitehaired man, Hank Priest had said, describing Dr. Adolf Elfenbein. *Fairly small and rather attractive,* he'd said, referring to Greta Elfenbein. Well, that was fine, the enemy high command was in sight, but it could wait. At the moment I had business with the lower echelons.

My man glanced around, nudged by some primitive

instinct, and saw me standing there. For a moment, he couldn't decide how to treat the discovery; but I was looking straight at him, and there was really nothing to be cute about, so he looked back with a direct challenge in his eyes. We both knew what he'd done tonight, he said to me silently across the room and what was I going to do about it, hey? Of course, I knew he was a successful murderer and he thought he'd failed; but that was my little joke, and I wasn't going to share it with him or anybody else, if I could help it.

His eyes were very blue, I saw, and his ruddy, ragged, thirty-year-old face might have been considered handsome by some. I had a hunch he was rather impressed with it himself; and not only with his looks, but with his strength, his courage, his skill, and his ruthlessness. So much the better. The vanity boys are almost always pushovers, if you handle them right. I jerked my head slightly, requesting his presence outside. He gave no answering sign. I grinned mockingly, reached down, and picked up the gaudy red nylon pack and walked off with it, aware of his eyes widening abruptly in an outraged way…

It was too bad, really. It was a reflection on the personnel policies of the Elfenbein outfit. They should have hired somebody less concerned with his own brave image; less ready to challenge and be challenged. Of course, I had everything going for me. The man had undoubtedly been briefed. He'd been shown the dossier and told I was supposed to be dangerous.

He'd even, apparently, been ordered to steer clear of

me and take the girl instead; the easy pickings. He was, by his looks, the virile kind who'd feel that was an insult; a hint that somebody thought he wasn't good enough to run in truly fast company. He'd be hoping for an excuse to forget his instructions and cut me down to size: the local fast-draw kid eager to make a name for himself by tackling the stranger in black with the tied-down guns and the big reputation... Okay, so it was corny, but punks are punks the world over, and have been since history began. In the primeval cave, on the streets of Abilene, or along the coast of Norway, they're all the same. At least I hoped so.

I pushed open the door to the deck outside, and was greeted by a fierce blast of wind with some rain and spray in it and by the rhythmic, surging hiss of the ship driving hard through the black, stormy night. There was nobody out on deck. I moved aft, bracing myself against the ship's roll and the thrust of the wind, half-dragging the heavy pack. Slinging it over a shoulder would have been easier, but I didn't want to be tangled up in it if he should come with a rush.

He didn't. I guess he was puzzled. Maybe he couldn't believe I was being as obvious as I seemed, deliberately spitting in his eye, so to speak. There had to be a trick, a trap, somewhere. I guess he had a little caution in his system after all, but it wasn't enough to keep him from following. He called after me once from the door, and came after me, and shouted again, angrily. I turned, and gave him that mean grin again, and threw his pack over the rail into the sea.

That shocked him. It tripped the trigger inside him, as I'd hoped it would. Caution forgotten, insulted and furious, he moved forward deliberately, stalking me; a big man with lots of light hair whipping past his face. I was aware that the Vikings, no sissies, had worn it long but I still wasn't quite hardened to the sight of a man with flowing golden tresses. It still seemed feminine and unnatural to me in a combat situation, along with the fancy necklace he was wearing over his dark turtleneck. There was a gun in his hand now, but with the jolting wind, and the erratic motion of the ship, he wanted to get close enough to make quite sure. Maybe he was remembering a girl who'd come back to life because he hadn't been quite thorough enough, or thought he hadn't.

I guess he also wanted to frighten me a bit before he killed me. They generally do if you make them mad enough. You can practically count on it.

I knew the instant he made up his mind to shoot— well, to shoot the next time the deck was halfway steady. It showed in his eyes and in his stance. As the gun started to line up, I threw myself low and to one side, swinging my arm in an arc parallel to the deck. The belt I'd held coiled in my hand whipped out, weighted by its heavy buckle. It wrapped itself around the ankle of his advanced leg before he could pull back. He really wasn't very good. He should have fired, of course, and to hell with dodging. What harm could a belt do in the hand of a dead man?

But, trying to avoid the flashing buckle, too late, he missed his opportunity to nail me. Then I'd yanked the foot out from under him. He came down awkwardly on his tailbone, legs apart; and the gun flew out of his hand and skidded away along the deck. He tried to scramble after it, another mistake. He should have let it go and come for me barehanded. Big and strong as he was, he'd still have had a good chance.

But he went for the weapon instinctively and I hauled back and managed to stretch him out before the belt unwound itself and came loose in my hand. Dropping it, I rose, and stepped forward and kicked the side of his head, hard, as he tried to get to his knees. Dazed, he covered up, expecting another kick. I turned and grabbed his ankles instead, and dragged him to the rail with a rush, and heaved up and out. For a moment he was draped there ridiculously, head down, with his feet kicking over the side and his fingers trying for a grip on the metal mesh of the rail. A chop at one clutching hand, a kick at the other where it clung to the grillwork and I grabbed a couple of fistfuls of the long hair, finding a good use for it at last, and levered him the rest of the way over, hoping there was no one on the deck below to hear the wailing cry he let out as he fell.

I stood there a moment, breathing hard. Instinct, and perhaps a glimpse of movement, brought me around fast. A small figure was making for the fallen gun. Concentrating on the man, I hadn't been aware of another presence. The girl almost made it, but I got there first and put my foot on the weapon before she could reach down and grab it.

She straightened up to face me; the young lady I assumed to be Greta Elfenbein; the attractive passenger from the lounge sofa; the little dark-haired, dark-eyed one with the nice nylons; but it was not a good night for pretty ladies and their pretty clothes. The howling wind along the deck was dismantling and demolishing her as she stood there, destroying her careful hairdo, getting under the pleated skirt of her neat, gray suit and streaming it from her waist like a storm flag, yanking her tailored jacket into wild, unbuttoned disorder, dragging her thin blouse, flapping, out of her waistband.

"You… you *killed* him!" she shouted accusingly. Her English was good but accented. "You threw him in the sea to drown!"

"He had it coming, Miss Elfenbein," I yelled. "Don't send any more of your friends after Madeleine Barth. Not unless you've got friends to spare."

Her eyes told me I had the right girl, not that I'd had any serious doubts. I waited for her to speak. I could see that she wanted to say something that was fierce and threatening, and at the same time full of disdain and dignity; but with one hand busy keeping her whipping, snapping hair out of her eyes, and the other engaged in getting her crazily blowing skirt down where it would conceal at least a little of her panty-hose, she didn't have much dignity to work with. She turned and ran forward and disappeared into the cabin.

It would take a little time for her to put herself back together, both physically and mentally. Not wanting to get involved in another major confrontation tonight, I made a slow business of putting my belt back on and picking up the pistol and examining it by one of the weak deck-lights. It was a small Spanish job stamped: *LLAMA, Gabilondo y Cia Vitoria (Espana) Cal. .380.* Strangely, it was a miniature replica of the Colt .45 Auto, complete with exposed hammer and grip safety. There's nothing wrong with the big Colt, of course, except that it kicks too hard for some people. It's a great old cannon but I couldn't see much point in faithfully copying a relatively clumsy and awkward military sidearm in three-quarter size for use as a pocket pistol. It was kind of like building a small working model of an antitank gun to use for a deer rifle.

Having stalled long enough, or what I hoped was long enough, I pocketed the weapon and went inside. The girl was nowhere to be seen. In the lounge, the sofa on which she'd been sitting earlier was empty. The white-haired man, presumably her father, was missing also. Perhaps they'd retired to their quarters to hold a council of war: subject, retribution. I hoped they'd come to a sensible decision. I thought they probably would. Judging by what I'd been told, Dr. Adolf Elfenbein had been working at his particular racket long enough not to blow his stack at the loss of a little low-grade manpower.

When I knocked on the cabin door two decks down, Diana's voice told me to come in. Inside, the light was still on and she was sitting on the berth as before, armed, alert, and ready to repel boarders. I'd kind of expected to find that she'd retired, or at least got out of her ill-fitting, borrowed costume but she'd only discarded the jacket and combed her hair. Obviously, not quite knowing what to expect, she hadn't wanted a sudden crisis to catch her with her clothes off.

It showed a commendable attention to duty and the revolver was steady in her hand. It occurred to me that, for a member of an outfit so ineffectual that it had to use imported muscle, she showed a surprising tolerance for firearms. Generally, an inexperienced young lady—I'd had to tell her the difference between hammer and trigger—grasps a loaded gun as if it were a live and angry rattlesnake.

"Is everything all right?" she asked. "You were gone a long time."

"Everything's fine," I said. "Any trouble here?"

"There hasn't been a soul around to bother me." After a moment, she said, "I figured it out. What you had to do."

"Good for you," I said. "Point that thing somewhere else, will you? The theory is, you don't aim it at anything you don't want to shoot."

"I'm sorry."

She lowered the weapon. She'd had time to warm up and dry off and the white turtleneck she was wearing—Evelyn Benson's white turtleneck—while not quite immaculate after its dip in the harbor, was a lot more becoming without the too-tight jacket buttoned over it. With her hair nicely combed, she looked reasonably human once more. She had a symmetrical, oval face, I noted, and odd, greenish eyes. Once you got used to it, the pale skin was kind of striking, setting her apart in a world of conventionally tanned or rosy beauties. She really wasn't a bad-looking girl.

"The man who murdered Evelyn," she said. "He'd seen her up close. I fooled him on the gangplank, at night, hurrying past him in her clothes with my hair all down my face and your coat over my head; but if he saw me in daylight, he'd know. So... so he had to be killed."

"Yes," I said.

"Did you?"

"Yes," I said. "Of course. That's what you people got me here for, wasn't it, my goddamned lethal reputation? I said I had a few shocks in mind for the opposition, remember?"

She hesitated. "What about the other one?" she asked. "The one who went ashore. He probably saw Evelyn too, you said."

I studied her for a moment, puzzled. It wasn't going at all the way I'd expected. Working with a shy, sheltered maiden brought up on tender principles of humanitarianism and nonviolence, I'd been braced for the old hand-wringing, breast-beating, bleeding-heart act, or at least a few conventional expressions of shock and dismay, but I wasn't getting them.

"The kid?" I said. "Not to worry. He's just juvenile help."

"But you'll have to deal with him, too, sooner or later, won't you?"

Her voice was quite calm and matter-of-fact. I realized that I'd got hold of something kind of special here, maybe even unique, but it was too early for me to tell whether it was good or bad.

"He's on shore," I said. "We're afloat. We don't have to worry about him tonight."

"You're really taking this masquerade seriously," she said. "I mean, killing a man to protect it."

"Well," I said, "let's just say it made a hell of a good excuse."

She was silent for a little. "Vengeance, Mr. Helm?" she murmured at last.

"I don't go out of my way for it, usually," I said. "I certainly won't jeopardize a mission for it. But if it's right in front of me for the taking, sure, I'll take it. People shouldn't go tossing people into the drink if they're not prepared to do a little swimming themselves."

She licked her lips, watching me. There was a funny gleam in the greenish eyes. "Was that what you did, threw him overboard?"

"That's right," I said. "I got him separated from his gun, kicked him in the head, and dumped him over the side." I glanced at her. "Why?"

She said steadily, "Because, since I'm here, I don't want to miss anything, Mr. Helm, not even murder. I want to learn all about it. Everything." She drew a long breath and when she spoke again, her voice wasn't quite so steady: "I... I've always been a very nice girl. I don't mean I'm a virgin, or anything silly like that but I've worked hard at being a truly *civilized* person. You know. Peaceful. Considerate. Kind. Intellectual. Sympathetic to all the good, worthy, conventional causes. Nonviolent, of course, because that's the only way to be, isn't it? I mean, we've all got to be that way, or get that way, if the world is going to survive, don't we? People like you, people with guns, are ugly, dangerous anachronisms threatening our peaceful modern society... *What* peaceful modern society, Mr. Helm?"

I didn't answer. She didn't expect me to answer. I just listened to the steady rumble of the ship's machinery, that turned the tiny cabin into a very private place, insulated by the noise from the rest of the universe.

"I'm tired," she said softly. "I wish I could make you understand how tired I am of pretending to be something I'm not—I don't mean just an imaginary Madeleine Barth; I've been an imaginary person all my life—and pretending the world is something it isn't, like everybody else of my generation. Who's kidding whom, Mr. Helm?"

If there's a screwball with an identity crisis around, we'll get him every time. Or her.

I said, "Sweetheart, I think you got the wrong door. The psychiatric department is down the hall to the right."

"You don't understand," she said, unruffled. "I've found what I was looking for right here, waiting in this cramped little stateroom in a dead person's soggy clothes. I've died of fear ten times while you were gone, don't you know that, Matthew Helm? And I've loved every terrified minute of it!" She'd got to her feet as she talked. Now she glanced at the blunt revolver she was still holding, and tucked it into her waistband. "And I've happily killed two dozen people with that, one every time the door rattled, don't you know that?"

"Quite a trick, with a five-shot gun," I said.

"Five? I thought they all shot six times."

"Don't count on it," I said.

"What are we talking about?" she asked.

I said, "You know damned well what we're talking about, and the answer is no."

"No?"

"No, I won't go to bed with you, just to make your thrilling evening complete, Miss Lawrence."

There was a little silence, then she laughed quite cheerfully. "Oh, dear," she said. "Is that what I was leading up to? I guess it was." She grinned at me impishly. "And of course, you're perfectly right not to humor the shameless whims of an unbalanced female who really ought to be in a clinic with bars on the windows. I mean, if you took ungentlemanly advantage of her aberration, you'd never forgive yourself, would you?"

Something had changed in the room, the way the atmosphere changes noticeably after a weather front moves through. She was looking up at me, laughing at me with those odd, greenish eyes in that strangely pale face. I found myself thinking uncertainly that, well, hell, there was really no good reason for me to fight for my virtue, or hers. The girl might be a kook, but she was a grown-up kook. We had a long boat-ride ahead of us. If it made her feel thrillingly wanton and wicked to precipitate tonight what would probably happen between us later, anyway, under the intimate circumstances of our mission, why should I hold back like a timid bride?

Just to keep up appearances, I said defensively, "Look, you're supposed to be Mrs. Madeleine Barth, a very proper lady who carefully arranged for us to have separate cabins on this trip." When Diana said nothing, I went on feebly: "Anyway, none of these damned Norska bunks are big enough for two."

"Do you want to bet, Mr. Helm?"

I didn't bet. It was just as well. I'd have lost.

6

Breakfast was a self-service meal, with a fine display of anchovies and herrings on the big table at the end of the first-class dining room. With silent apologies to my Scandinavian forebears, I passed up this fishy feast and tracked down a couple of boiled eggs and some bacon, a glass of orange juice, and a cup of coffee. In the meantime, my current partner in business, and other endeavors, was heaping stuff on her plate in the manner of a lady who doesn't have to worry about her waistline.

It disturbed me to note that this morning she looked very good, slim and willowy in her own nicely fitting gray slacks and the neat little short-sleeved gray sweater she'd been wearing when I'd first seen her in Tracteurstedet—I'd smuggled the garments aboard under my jacket. Her long coat had been too bulky and had been left with Hank Priest. She had a kerchief over her hair to hide the fact that it wasn't quite as dark as Mrs. Madeleine Barth's hair was supposed to be. She looked quite bright and attractive, and I didn't like it, remembering how drab and colorless I'd thought her the evening before. While I'd have liked to think that a night in my company could cause a perfectly plain female to blossom info quiet beauty, honesty forced me to admit it wasn't likely. The change must therefore be in the way I was looking at her. Changes like that you've got to watch.

There was, of course, also the fact that she looked as serene and untouched as if she'd spent the night chastely alone in her narrow Nordic berth. Professional caution made me wonder uneasily, for a moment, if maybe she wasn't a truly clever little actress putting me on for some sinister purpose. Well, if she was, I had to hand it to her: it was a great act.

"No," she said, sitting down at a table by a window.

"No what?" I asked, seating myself to face her.

"No, it's not an act, darling. That's what you were just thinking, isn't it, looking at me so suspiciously. You were wondering if maybe… maybe I hadn't lured you into bed for wicked conspiratorial reasons of some kind."

I sighed. "Kooks I can stand, but clairvoyants give me the creeps."

"Then you're in fine shape," she said, "because that's all I am, just a simple country kook. And the funny thing is, I never realized it until a few months ago. I thought… I thought everybody had those crazy, uncivilized impulses from time to time. And I never dreamed I'd really have the nerve to…" She stopped, and laughed abruptly. "You were wrong, Matt."

"How wrong?"

"Those beds. You said they weren't big enough, remember?" She blushed, and busied herself with some pickled fish on her plate. "Matt."

"Yes?"

"I feel all funny inside. Reckless-funny. Does it show?"

"Not one little bit," I said. "You look very genteel and proper, as a matter of fact." After a moment, I went on, "You did say the Elfenbeins probably don't know you by sight? I hope you're right, because if I've got the right people spotted, here they come."

"Don't hoard the salt, darling," she said. "Other people eat eggs, too, you know… It's really magnificent scenery, isn't it? I understand it gets even more spectacular up north."

She'd turned to watch the rocky coast passing off to starboard, illuminated by shafts of bright sunshine as the clouds of last night's rain broke up. It was nicely done, giving them no more than the back of her head and a thin profile to compare with any description the blond man might have given them. Then they were coming past us. Greta Elfenbein had changed to brightly checked red-and-white slacks, which was a pity, considering her legs. A white ski-sweater made her look like a sporty elf. Adolf was wearing a dark blue business suit and a conservative blue tie. In daylight, close up, he was just an ordinary-looking, mild-looking little blue-eyed gent in his fifties. All he needed was a backwards collar and a prayer book to appear like a gentle village parson, instead of the very clever scientific character he was supposed to be, with a gang of unscrupulous thugs under his command. They went on to the serving table without glancing our way.

"Yes, that's Adolf Elfenbein all right," Diana said softly. "At least he fits our description; and so does she."

"How the hell did you get involved in all this, anyway, Diana?"

"It's a long story. Don't ask if you don't want to know." I said, "Somewhere up the line, my life may very well depend on your reactions. Naturally I want to know what kind of a female nut I've got for a partner on this screwball operation."

She laughed again. "Well," she said, "it was the gas shortage that did it, believe it or not."

"Since you give me the option, I don't believe it," I said. "I mean, it was a damned inconvenience and still is from time to time; but I can't see you getting so upset about it that you volunteer for a crazy, crooked, international mission to swipe fuel for all the thirsty Cadillacs of America. Hank Priest, sure. Those old Navy boys come all over patriotic from time to time: my country right or wrong, and all that jazz—"

"Actually, the Skipper is avenging, or atoning for, his wife's death, didn't you know?"

I frowned. "I thought Mrs. Priest drowned in a boating accident. That's the way I read it in the Florida papers."

"Frances Priest drowned because their thirty-foot sport-fishing boat—the Skipper's pride and joy, called the *Frances II*—had just ran out of fuel when she fell overboard, so he couldn't go after her. The current carried her away, or something. You'll have to get the nautical details from the nautical expert, but it was a traumatic experience for him, as you can imagine: a man who'd spent his life at sea losing his wife like that! I guess he decided that no more nice U.S. ladies were going to die for lack of diesel oil, if he had to go and steal it. Anyway, he worked out this scheme and sold it in Washington. He used to be a congressman, you know, so he knew his way around and they were all in a panic at the time. This was back when things were really tight and they were scared to death of an honest-to-God revolution at the gas pumps. They were ready to grab at any idea, no matter how far out. As for the illegality of it, well, that city isn't noted for its respect for the law these days, or hadn't you noticed? So here we all are. The Great Petroleum Caper."

"Involving The Wonderful Sigmund Siphon," I said. "That's a terrific name, but what does it mean?"

"I don't really know what it means," she said. "Security is very tight on the subject, Mr. Helm, and you shouldn't even breathe the name aloud."

"Sure, sure," I said. "But does it tap the oil well itself or the pipeline where it runs under the sea or what? Either way, it's got to be quite a trick, doing it undetected several hundred feet down. Of course, the North Sea is a good place for it, with the weather as lousy as it generally is. You can lose yourself out there in a hurry, most of the time. Even, I suppose, in a goodsized tanker with a big hose running over the side."

She said, rather stiffly, "Really, I'm under orders not to

talk about it to anyone, Matt. I won't help you speculate about it. As a matter of fact, I don't really know. Well, I do know what a siphon is, roughly. And I guess it's all right to tell you that this thing was invented by a kind of defrocked technician with an affinity for the bottle, now working around the fringes of the oil industry at any job he can get. Meanwhile he cooks up wild inventions, each one of which is going to make his fortune. Well, this one may just do the job, if the Skipper is right about it."

"Jeez," I said. "It's a goddamned circus, that's what it is. A couple of mad scientists, a mysterious oil tycoon with a passion for privacy, and some traumatized victims of the energy crisis."

"You forget that man called Denison."

I said, I hoped casually: "Oh, sure, Mr. Kotko's dangerous Mr. Denison. Add him to the list. You didn't tell me how the gas shortage got you here."

She said, "Actually, I don't know that I'd call myself a victim of the crisis, darling. I may actually be a better girl for it, or at least a less hypocritical one. It made me think for the first time in my life, really think. I mean, there I was pedaling my ecological ten-speed bicycle on my way to save the world and make it beautiful, and shaking my fist dutifully at all those obscene, polluting Chrysler Imperials whizzing past—and suddenly, no more gas. You know, darling, bicycling when you feel like bicycling or want to prove something is one thing. Looking forward to a lifetime of sitting on that hard little seat and pushing those crazy pedals and getting your hairdo ruined and your

pants or stockings greasy is something totally different."
She shook her head ruefully. "It was… a real shock, Matt.
Suddenly I realized that all my life I'd been taking my
opinions from other people. I'd been thinking just what
all my concerned, idealistic friends had been telling me
to think. At least I'd been thinking I was thinking it, if you
know what I mean."

"Give me time," I said. "I'm a few thinks behind, but
I'll catch up eventually."

"Suddenly," she said, "I realized that I—me, Diana
Lawrence—-didn't feel like that at all. I made the
dreadful discovery that I really *liked* big, comfortable,
air-conditioned cars, and I was going to miss them
terribly if they disappeared. And once I started looking,
I kept finding more disillusioning things about myself,
for instance that I really *liked* warm, soft, lovely fur
coats and I wasn't really all that disturbed about the poor
little animals who'd lost their lives to make them. Well,
leopards and such, okay. They're endangered; and I don't
want to be the one to push them over the edge to extinction
but I never heard that the mink situation was even mildly
critical. I even discovered—this is a terrible confession,
and I probably shouldn't tell you—that I was pretty tired
of hearing about those darling little seals brutally clubbed
to death by those dreadful men on the goddamned Pribilof
Islands, wherever they are. Hell, maybe the poor guys
were just trying to earn a living, and that was the safe and
efficient way to do it, and maybe the herd could spare a
few seals now and then. Aren't you shocked?"

"I'm tough," I said. "I'll recover."

It's part of the required duties of a secret agent. He's supposed to sit there showing wide-eyed interest, hoping for some useful nuggets of information, but it isn't always easy. I mean, ten-speed bikes and fur seals, for God's sake! I reminded myself that she was a nice kid, or at least an interesting one, and I had, after all, asked for it. I changed position slightly so I could watch the Elfenbeins hitting the herring hard. I decided that tomorrow I'd better try it. I'd done it before, long ago, and survived; and why fly a third of the way around the world just to eat the same old bacon and eggs?

"But the thing that really got to me," Diana was saying, "when I started *thinking*, was the busybodies who, not satisfied with saving the environment and the animals, kept trying to save *me*. Without even asking my permission! Here I'd been applauding uncritically every time somebody hung a new safety gadget on my car and now I realized suddenly that I was sick of it. I was sick of people who were forever saving everything from everybody, and everybody from everything. I was fed to the teeth with all the screaming seatbelts and wailing ignition locks—now you can't even start the stupid machine without getting yourself all safetied up! What's that junk doing in a car? A car's for *driving*, isn't it? If you want to be so damned safe you can stay *home*, can't you? And anyway, if I want to go through a windshield headfirst, that's my own goddamn business. Isn't it?"

"So you decided to go through a windshield headfirst

just to show them, and here you are?"

Diana laughed. "Something like that. What I really
decided was that I was fed up with being so damned
concerned, so damned idealistic, yes, and so damned safe.
I didn't really know what I was going to do about it; but
then one afternoon at a Washington cocktail party I got
into an argument with a well-heeled society female with
whom I'd served on some worthy committees. She tried
to tell me how we should look at the bright side of the
crisis. What she considered bright was that all the people
who'd loved fast cars, or snowmobiles, or dune buggies,
or speed boats, or travel trailers, would all be grounded,
and wasn't it wonderful, my dear? I mean, think of all
those broken-hearted folks with their beautiful, expensive,
useless toys—well, like the Skipper and his fancy fishing
boat—and this bitch was *gloating* about it, damn her! If
that was high-minded idealism, I thought, to hell with it!"

Diana paused to look out at the mountainous coastline
sliding by. I asked, "What happened?"

She grinned. "Well, I practically shocked that buxom
biddy out of her expensive foundation garment by saying
that I thought the internal combustion engine had been a
good and faithful servant to mankind and if we did have
to bury it, the least we could do was show some grief
and appreciation, instead of spitting on the grave. She
isn't a lady with a great sense of humor, so the argument
got pretty hot. I mean, she actually accused me of being
a Traitor to the Cause. I noticed this rather striking,
weathered, grayhaired character standing by, looking kind

of amused. The next morning he called me up and said he was Captain Henry Priest, USN, Retired, and would I care to have lunch with him? His intentions were strictly honorable, he said; he was forming a certain organization with government blessing, and he had employment he thought might suit me, judging by the way I'd talked the night before..." She paused and shrugged. "Well, that's about it, Matt. It was just the kind of crazy, crummy, dangerous, antisocial thing I'd been looking for to get the taste of all those goddamned crusades out of my mouth. The blackfooted ferret was just going to have to do without me for a while. I was going out and steal a lot of smelly oil and I wasn't going to buckle a single seatbelt while I was doing it!"

I said, "*The Liberation of Diana Lawrence*, we'll call it when we put it on the screen."

She looked at me for a moment; then she reached out and put a hand on top of mine, a small gesture of protest. "Don't," she said quietly. "Don't make fun of me, darling. Don't make fun of us. Don't spoil it."

"Sorry," I said.

"It's really a terrible thing," she said. "None of those people were real; and the world they lived in wasn't real. They'll never find, or make, that dreamland of theirs where the streams run nothing but distilled water, and the breezes blow nothing but pure oxygen and nitrogen mixed one to five, and no animals or people ever die. This is real. You're real."

"Thanks," I said dryly. "If that's a compliment."

"Death is real," she said. "I learned that last night, waiting in that cabin for somebody to come in and murder me like they'd murdered Evelyn—if I didn't shoot them first. It was wonderful. Why didn't anybody ever tell me that the only way to be alive, truly alive, is to risk being dead? It had never happened to me before. I'd always been protected before. It was horrible and marvelous and I wouldn't have missed it for the world."

"You're a screwball," I said.

She gave me a sudden, boyish grin and squeezed my hand lightly before taking hers away. "Well, as they say, it takes one to know one," she said.

Of course, she was perfectly right.

7

Around noon, we pulled into a picturesque little harbor called Ålesund and I stood on deck watching the docking procedure with interest. It looked very easy. The ship just made its approach well out, somebody forward heaved a light line ashore, and a man grabbed it and hauled across a husky wire cable with a big loop on the end, which he fitted over a giant cleat on the dock. The ship, still gliding ahead slowly, came to the end of the cable and was drawn right alongside by her own momentum, after which the other docklines were put ashore. Simple. I wondered how many years of practice it had taken the guy on the bridge to make it look that way. There was a familiar, youthful, figure in jeans and wind-breaker among the people clustered on the pier. I went below. Diana was reclining on the unmade berth when I knocked and entered her cabin.

"I told you to keep that gun handy, always," I said.

"It's handy, darling. I just didn't want it in plain sight in case you were the stewardess coming to make the bed."

She sat up and pulled her hand out of a fold of the blanket and showed me the ugly little snubnosed weapon. "Is he there?" she asked. "The other one, the one who went ashore last night?"

I nodded. "He's there. The lad seems to take his duties seriously, whatever they are. Judging by my map he must have made a hell of a drive overland to rejoin us, with all kinds of ferries to catch across the fjords. Or maybe he had a friend with a fast yacht or handy helicopter."

"Is he alone?"

"As far as I can see but that means nothing. If he brought reinforcements, they'd be keeping out of sight."

"What do we do now?"

I looked around for something I needed, or thought I might need: a towel. A rather damp one hung over the edge of the washbowl in the corner. I rolled it up and stuffed it into my overcoat pocket.

"You," I said, "do nothing. Don't leave this cabin. If he sees you, and makes the connection, the only way I can keep him from telling the Elfenbeins this isn't the dame he helped dump over the side in Bergen, is to kill him. So keep out of sight while I figure out how to get rid of him without distressing the local constabulary. They're nice Norwegian boys, and we don't want to bother them with any unnecessary dead bodies."

Diana hesitated. "That's… kind of risky, isn't it, Matt? Leaving him alive, I mean."

I looked at her sharply. The funny green glow was in her eyes again. They're the most dangerous people on earth: the ones who've been brought up on the cruel fairytale that peace is the natural state of mankind, and that violence is a rare and disgusting aberration. Once they realize how badly they've been conned, if the discovery doesn't shatter them completely, they tend to go so far in the other direction that no self-respecting Mako shark will associate with them.

I said, "You're a bloodthirsty bitch."

"No," she said, "just a practical one."

"Well, maybe," I conceded. "But it depends. On whether homicide is feasible at this point, in broad daylight, without time to set it up properly or get help lined up."

She shrugged. "You may be right, darling. I haven't had a great deal of experience at this sort of thing—less than twenty-four hours, actually. But—" She stopped.

"What?" I asked.

"Be fair, please," she said quietly. "If I were a professional agent, you wouldn't look at me as if I were some kind of a mad vampire lady, merely because I point out that a certain person is a serious threat that might better be removed."

I regarded her for a moment. Again she was perfectly right. I sighed. "My apologies. You are not a bloodthirsty bitch, Miss Lawrence. Okay? Now keep that gun handy, and don't let anybody in you're not sure of. This may take time, so don't get impatient and start roaming around. I'll be back as soon as I can."

They were just shoving the gangway into place when I

got back upstairs—excuse me, topside. Parson Elfenbein and his pretty daughter were not in evidence. The youth whose friend I'd been so mean to last night was still waiting among the greeters and prospective northbound voyagers down on the dock, with his gaudy nylon pack at his feet. He picked it up when the gangplank was opened to traffic, but he had to wait to let the shoregoing passengers get off the ship first, and I was among them.

Ålesund was a colorful little community clinging to the side of a mountain valley half-filled with water. Beyond the town limits, the hillsides above the fjord were covered with small evergreens that looked as if they led hard, precarious lives. The dock was fairly long and had a lot of big crates piled on it awaiting shipment to somewhere. I scanned it hastily as I moved downwards with the rest of the landing party, looking for a spot quiet enough for what I had to do.

Then he was right in front of me and it was time for me to go into my act. After all, the groundwork had been laid. My lethal reputation, as Mac had termed it, was supposed to have preceded me. Now, if ever, was the time to cash in on it. He pretended not to recognize me, of course; just glancing at me casually and returning his attention to the ship, looking for someone else. He'd performed his mission, whatever it was, and now he wanted to find his immediate superior and make his report.

"*Han kommer inte,*" I said deliberately, standing there. "He won't be coming. Ever. *Han kommer alldrig.*"

It was Swedish, not Norwegian, and I didn't know how

good Swedish it was after all the years, but it got through. The kid looked at me sharply, lowering his pack. He was blond, like his late partner, but he didn't have the same red-faced, rawboned, rugged look. He was rather a pretty-looking young fellow, as a matter of fact, moderately tall but without much flesh on his substantial Scandinavian bones. He'd have looked swell as a lean young ski instructor in stretch pants, with a charming accent, telling the matrons politely to keep their feet together and their weight forward. People kept pushing past us as we stood there, but they didn't count.

The boy licked his lips and glanced towards the ship once more. "Bjørn?"

"Was that his name?" I asked. "Bjørn means bear, doesn't it? Well, your big, blond bear went swimming. Out there somewhere. *Han simmar därute någonstans.* Only I think he's probably stopped by now. Do you understand what I'm saying, sonny?"

"I understand," he said. "I speak Swedish, and also English, a little."

"Good for you," I said in my sneering, overbearing way. "Bjørn made a serious mistake, you understand. He was very rude to a friend of mine. A lady friend. That wasn't very nice of him. He really shouldn't have done that, should he, sonny?"

"Please do not call me sonny, Mr. Helm. Yes, I know your name, of course. My name is Erlan Torstensen. And I do not believe what you say about Bjørn. He was very strong, very experienced—"

"Look down, Erlan Torstensen," I said.

He looked, and I heard his breath catch a little. There was a moment of silence. Up on the ship they were preparing to swing out one of the big cargo booms for unloading.

"Do you recognize the pistol, Erlan?" I asked softly, concealing the little Llama once more. "Do you think your friend Bjørn liked me well enough to give it to me as a present? If so, you are more stupid than I think. I took his silly little gun away from him and I threw him overboard in the storm. What do you think I am going to do to you?"

He licked his lips once more. "I am not afraid, Mr. Helm."

I stared at him for a moment, unbelieving. Then—I couldn't help it—I burst out laughing. A couple of young girls moving past looked our way curiously. I noticed that their glances lingered a bit on Erlan Torstensen. He was a real handsome boy, and a real joker, telling me he wasn't afraid, as if it mattered. Well, of course it mattered, it was the whole point of the exercise, making him afraid; but I can never really understand anybody who thinks his goddamned courage is important enough to discuss in public, as if the world wasn't lousy with heroes already.

"Come with me," I said. Torstensen hesitated. I said impatiently, "*Komm med mej!* Snap into it! Pick up that pack again and march along like a good boy. Over there to the right behind those crates…"

I wanted to breathe a sigh of relief when I got him there, but of course it would have been out of character for the super-tough and super-confident character I was playing. But anybody dumb enough to talk about his fears or lack of them was dumb enough to do just about anything, even with a gun covering him.

"All right, Erlan, you can put it down again," I said, and he lowered the heavy backpack to the dock. We had the little alley between the rows of packing cases all to ourselves and they were stacked high enough that we couldn't be seen from the decks of the ship. I said, "Let's talk sensibly now. First, will you take my word that your friend is dead, or should we find Miss Elfenbein and have her confirm it? She saw it; she'll tell you what happened. Bjørn was a little rash, Erlan, a little overeager, a little too anxious to prove what a brave, strong fellow he was. I think he must have spent too much time lately blackjacking helpless, unsuspecting women. He forgot that there are people who do fight back. Do you believe me now?"

He nodded slowly. "You have Bjørn's gun. I believe you."

I said, "Well, I don't know how you feel about your friend—"

"He was not my friend," young Torstensen said stiffly. "He was a man with whom I was ordered to work, a rather vulgar and unpleasant man, but a competent operative, I was told, from whom I could learn many things."

"Good, then there are no personal feelings involved," I said. "You will learn nothing more from Bjørn, but you may learn something from me. Like how to stay alive. Or how to die. It's up to you, Erlan Torstensen. The next time I see you, I'll kill you. So you had better not let me see you again, had you?"

The boy watched me intently but didn't speak. I listened for the big crane, but they didn't have it working yet. There was nothing for it but to keep making with the menacing verbiage.

I went on: "If you want to live, Erlan, I suggest you rapidly take yourself far away where there's not the remotest chance of our ever meeting again. Because if we meet, I will go for you instantly, wherever it is. Don't think I'm bluffing, sonny. I never bluff. On the street, in a crowded theater, on a bus or train or streetcar, wherever. If I ever see your face again, I'll shoot; and I'm a damned good shot. Maybe they'll catch me and put me in jail for it, but you'll be dead. I guarantee it."

The boy said, "Either you are mad or—"

"Don't say it," I said. "Don't even think it. I told you, I don't bluff. We had a long talk about you, Mrs. Barth and I. She doesn't like you very much. She doesn't like being hit over the head and thrown into the cold water to swim for her life; and you were there, too, right along with Bjørn. She told me I ought to kill you before you got orders to try it on your own. Last night she said to me, 'That's fine, Helm, you've taken care of the big dog, now finish the job and go wring the pup's neck for me so I can relax. She's a rather vindictive lady, Erlan, in spite of her prissy looks. I spoke up for you. Well, not for you, really, but I pointed out that while I didn't much object to disposing of you at a suitable place and time, right here and now there was too much risk of trouble with the authorities, and we can't afford that. So we're giving you a chance, *one* chance. But only one. If you show up again, here in this town or anywhere along the route, that's it, Erlan. Scratch one Torstensen." I looked at him for a moment; then I gestured. "Okay. That's all. Pick it up and get going. And keep going."

He hesitated. Then he reached down for the backpack and turned and walked away. They'd got the ship's crane working at last—about time—and there was a lot of whining of gears and motors, and thumping of crates, and rumbling of steel-tired dollies. I grimaced, knowing that most of my fancy menace had been totally wasted. Frightening people is for the birds, anyway; or for the syndicate and its professional bullies and terrorizers. They seem to have a more impressionable class of customers. The folks with whom we deal generally don't terrify much. You've got to shoot them to really impress them.

I pulled out the pistol once more, and quickly wound around it the damp towel I'd appropriated from Diana's stateroom.

"Erlan!" I called.

He heard me over the dockside noise. Three fast steps would have taken him to safety, but unafraid young Norse heroes don't run. He stopped and turned to face me courageously. I fired. The report was a muffled crash that seemed very loud in the narrow space between the crates.

The bullet passed him closely and buried itself in a big carton behind him, with a slapping sound. He jumped, controlled himself, and stood very still. I walked up to him deliberately.

"Remember," I said. "Any place. Any time. Just like that, only a foot and a half to the right. If I see you again, you're dead. *Om jag ser dej igen så är du död*." I grinned at him wolfishly. "Okay. Just a little demonstration, sonny. On your way now."

They take guns more seriously over there. I saw that I'd made my point at last. The boy's blue eyes were wide and shocked; I saw real fear, at last, in his face. I'd actually discharged a firearm in a public place in broad daylight and nothing was happening to me, not a thing. The big noisy crane was swinging its load ashore as if nothing had occurred. Cars were driving by on the nearby street. People were talking beyond the stacks of cargo, their voices reaching us in snatches through the other din; and a deadly, jacketed, caliber .380 bullet, locally known as a 9mm *Kurz*, or Short, had passed within a few inches of him...

He came out of his trance, slung the pack over one shoulder, and turned and hurried away. I heard his footsteps quicken to a run after he'd gone out of sight.

Busy getting shreds of toweling out of the automatic's works, I turned sharply as something moved at the end of the row of crates behind me. I cleared the mechanism, and dropped the weapon into my pocket, but kept my hand on it.

"You ought to be ashamed of yourself, Matt, going around frightening little children," Denison said, coming forward.

"Hi, Luke," I said.

8

He didn't like it. He hadn't been called that for a long time. His eyes narrowed briefly; then he grinned.

"You know," he said, "I've been trying to remember that old code name of mine ever since I saw you on the ship last night, and I just couldn't bring it back. Do you think that might be what the shrinks call Freudian forgetfulness?"

"Hell, you're the one who called us the Four Apostles, which shows how much you know about the Bible," I said. "On that crummy little fishing boat that put us ashore on that dismal coast, remember? Matthew, Mark, Luke, and John. Only, Mark and John got caught in an unexpected revolution, remember? At least it broke in a way three of us hadn't expected. And down there is where they invented the *ley de fuga*—you know, give the guy a running start and shoot him in the back, and say he was trying to escape. I understand a certain Lincoln Alexander Kotko did real well with the help of the new regime after things settled down; he's been pumping oil out of there ever since. They tell me it's made him big enough that he's now dealing with major powers instead of crummy little military *juntas*."

"He was big enough then," Denison said. "Plenty big enough to have you called off my trail, afterwards. That was part of the deal: protection. And it still goes, so don't finger that gun so hungrily. Your chief—what did we use to call him, Mac?—knows that if any of his people lay a finger on me, his whole outfit will be reorganized out of existence, now. L.A. owns enough elected and appointed politicians in Washington to see to that."

"L.A.?" I said. "Does he often get mixed up with the city of Los Angeles? Or does he figure that he's so much more important that no confusion is possible? Anyway, I thought the gentleman in question insisted on being called *Mister*."

"It depends on who's doing the calling," said Denison, a little smugly.

There are three kinds of organization men. The armed forces have theirs, all sucking up to the local general or admiral, but there's a difference. Way down deep they know they're not totally dependent on the Old Man's whims. They've got the Uniform Code of Military Justice to fall back on. And in civilian government service we also know that, while it's nice to get along with the department or bureau chief, there are limits to what he can do to us if we don't. But in the private sector you'd damn well butter up the old boy behind the big desk or you'll be out on your ear. It makes for a real harem mentality and Denison was proudly flaunting his status as senior concubine, one of the few people granted the privilege of referring to Mister Kotko by his initials.

"I gather you've actually seen the great, elusive, bald man, then," I said. "He does exist?"

"He exists, all right. Don't kid yourself for a moment that he doesn't. All you have to do is fire that little Spanish automatic and you'll learn all about Lincoln Alexander Kotko, *pronto*."

I said, "Hell, you make it sound almost worth shooting you for."

Denison grinned and shook his head. "You can't be all that mad at me after seven years, *amigo*. You never were that good a hater."

"Maybe I've been working on it. Maybe I've improved."

He shook his head again, smiling. "If you really hated me, Matt—I mean, *hated* me, personally—you'd kill me now and to hell with orders. Tell me something, how did you get away that night? Was it the girl, Elena or Margareta, or whatever her name was? She turned up missing next morning; did she tip you off at the last moment and go with you? Hell, I thought she was my girl."

"She was," I said. The girl's name had actually been Luisa, and I didn't for a moment believe he'd forgotten it, any more than he'd forgotten Mac's name, or his own. However, if that was the game he wanted to play, I was happy to oblige. I went on: "She loved you, and she didn't want you to have a friend's life on your conscience. They think a lot of friendship down there. Unfortunately, she caught a bullet as she was showing me the back way out—well, we both caught bullets, but I survived mine."

"Yes, your survival quotient was always pretty damned high," Denison said. There was a little pause. He said, "You're looking good, Matt."

"You, too," I said.

He was. He looked as if he had been eating well and sleeping between silk sheets in very attractive company. He had the well-tailored, well-manicured, well-barbered appearance that all the big boys, legitimate or otherwise, seem to insist on for their henchmen. Under the wide, rakish hat, he was wearing his wavy brown hair a little longer than I remembered, in deference to modern male, fashion. He had a nice, smooth, expensive tan that made his big teeth look very white when he grinned again, with a glance in the direction Erlan Torstensen had taken.

"You really leaned on that kid," he said. "*High Noon* stuff: *Get out of town or get dead.* Did you mean what you told him?"

I made a face. "How the hell do I know? If he shows again, we'll see whether I meant it or not."

"Where does he fit?"

"One of Elfenbein's boys," I said. "What's the matter, haven't you done your homework, Paul? Getting sloppy in your old age?"

"We don't give a damn about Elfenbein," he said. "He's just a small-time operator; clever, sure, but strictly minor

league. All that interests us about Adolf Elfenbein is that
he's interested, if you know what I mean. He's sharp, and
he's got a hell of a lot of good geological experience and
training: if he wants something up here—or thinks it's
worth his while to take on a client who does—it's worth
wanting, and can be had. But otherwise, unless he really
threatens to louse up the deal, to hell with him. He's too
small for L.A. to bother with."

"Thanks a lot," I said. "In other words, you're leaving
Adolf to me. I appreciate that."

"You can handle him," Denison said. "What we're
worrying about is you—you, and this retired naval hero
you seem to have taken under your wing, or vice versa.
An old friend of Mac's who helped you all out of a hole
a while back, isn't that right? We were glad to hear that,
and check it out; otherwise we might have thought you
had some other ideas when you offered to give him a hand
with this operation. But your chief's old friend had better
produce, Matt. He's made a lot of promises, now he'd
better come through. Pass it along. L.A. will do his part,
he's interested in getting part of the local action on the
terms agreed on, but you'd all damn well better do yours."
He gave me his quick grin once more. "But on second
thought, if you need any help dealing with Elfenbein,
don't hesitate to call on me, *amigo*. I'm here to protect
L.A.'s interests; and if the little white-haired doctor is too
tough for you, I'll be happy to give you a hand, for old
times' sake."

"Sure," I said. "For old times' sake."

There was a brief silence. Paul Denison started to turn away, and looked back. "It's a funny thing," he said, "when I heard you'd got away, I was glad, believe it or not."

I didn't say anything. After a moment he turned and walked away. I gave him a few seconds' start, and moved after him, coming around the piles of crates in time to see him climb into a fancy, silvery Mercedes, between ten and twenty grands' worth of car—it's hard to keep track of all the current prices. I watched him drive out of sight. It was too bad, I reflected. I'd brought that guy up right. I'd taught him the ropes; but after all the years as Kotko's errand boy he seemed to have forgotten his basic indoctrination, talking like a movie character with a bad script—about whether or not I hated him, for God's sake, as if my personal feelings would make any difference to what happened between us now!

I glanced back at the ship, and hoped Diana was sticking to her cabin and not getting too bored or scared in there—well, she was the kid who thought being scared was wonderful, I reminded myself, so that part didn't matter too much. I walked into the town—another pretty, coastal community under heavy attack by tall building cranes—and found a character who could talk some English, and got directions to the telephone office. Most towns of any size have them over there and you can make a call anywhere without worrying about being overheard by anybody who gives a damn. I found the place and pretty soon I was in a booth along the office wall talking with the gent in Oslo I'd never seen, who shortly had me connected with Washington by some kind of electronic magic I wouldn't have understood even if somebody'd bothered to try to explain it to me.

"Eric here, sir," I said. "I've just been chatting with an old friend of ours. He says I don't hate him."

"Indeed?" Mac said, sounding weak and distant. The magic connection wasn't very good. "Is he correct?"

"Does it matter?"

"It shouldn't."

"Nevertheless," I said, "maybe I should have the current word on Paul Denison, sir."

"There is no current word on Paul Denison, Eric. Mr. Denison is a respectable citizen employed in a responsible secretarial capacity by a certain Mr. Kotko, also very respectable—at least no one has ever proved otherwise. Since Mr. Kotko is a wealthy and influential man, on an international scale, his employees enjoy a certain immunity. Seven years ago, he made it clear that violent political reprisals would follow any action against, or harassment of, Mr. Denison. Just what he had in mind was never specified, but there was no doubt that he had influence enough to make things, shall we say, awkward? For an important national objective, the risk might have been considered acceptable but not for an internal disciplinary problem. In other words, Eric, I did not feel then, and do not feel now, that dealing with one defector is worth jeopardizing the effectiveness of the organization as a whole. Therefore, until the situation changes, or can be changed, Mr. Denison is untouchable.

I hope I make myself clear."

"Yes, sir," I said. "Very clear."

"Anything else?"

"Frances Priest. How did she die?"

There was a little pause. "I'd be interested in your reason for asking, Eric, if you'd care to state it."

I said, carefully, "I know the guy is a friend of yours, sir. However, I kind of like to know if a man I'm working with, or for, has all his marbles. Has Hank Priest shown any signs of senility lately?"

"None of which I'm aware."

"Then we can't have heard the same story about Frances Priest," I said. "Because the information I got, kind of shorthand and secondhand, says that Captain Henry Priest, USN, Retired, a professional naval officer who once commanded enormous vessels in complicated battle maneuvers and on lengthy voyages, took his simple little thirty-foot sport-fisherman, the *Frances II*, out for a simple day's spin. During the course of this brief outing, this trained and experienced seaman managed to (a) let his boat run out of fuel, and (b) have his wife tumble overboard and drown. On the face of it, that's pretty lousy boating, sir. I couldn't do much worse myself, and I don't pretend to be a sailor. So what I want to know is, is the guy competent or isn't he? I mean, if he wants to drown his wife, okay, that's between him and her; but I'd kind of object to his doing it to me, or running me into some kind of stupid deadfall up the line just because he wasn't quite focusing at the time."

"I don't think we need to worry about Hank's competence," Mac said. "He encountered an unfortunate combination of circumstances that could hardly have been anticipated, or avoided." I didn't say anything. I just waited. I mean, it was a tricky business, questioning him about his long-time fishing partner—he wasn't a man with a lot of friends. As a matter of fact, Hank Priest was the only one I'd met in all the time I'd worked for him. Still, it was about time for him to dish up a little background information on this job he'd sent me on practically blindfolded, and to hell with his finer feelings. After a moment, Mac went on: "You only met Hank once before, didn't you?"

"Yes, sir, that time we were kind of operating out of his home on Robalo Island a couple of years back," I said. "That is, until last night in Bergen."

"I think you should keep in mind," Mac said, "that he's spent practically all his life on ships, from choice. He actually loves the water. He'd planned to spend his retirement mostly afloat, fishing and cruising. He'd used a large part of his life savings to buy the *Frances II*. When he lost his bid for reelection he told me that in a way it was a great relief. He'd made his final gesture towards public service. Now he could relax and really retire and get out in his boat the way he'd planned. And just about that time the Arabs shut off the oil. You remember how it was, Eric, with long lines at the filling stations. Well, the marinas were often even worse; and as it happened, diesel fuel was particularly short in his part of Florida. Most of the time he couldn't take the *Frances* out at all that winter. When he did, he had to stay close to harbor—after spending fifty thousand dollars he couldn't really afford on a boat he'd expected would take him anywhere he felt like going!"

I felt a little uncomfortable. Mac didn't often go in for this kind of eloquence. Well, friendship was a funny thing, as my encounter with Paul Denison had just reminded me.

Mac said, "Hank is used to authority, and he has some fairly positive ideas. After serving his country all his life, he felt he'd earned the right to spend his retirement as he pleased—the right, and the fuel. After all, he said, they'd been happy to sell him a fifty-grand yacht; now they could damn well supply the stuff to run if. Anything else was simple fraud; like selling you a building lot that was under water so you couldn't build on it. People were arrested for pulling crooked deals like that and he wasn't swallowing any flimsy excuses about Arabs…

I watched a pretty girl typing behind the counter across the room. It seemed to me I was collecting a lot of life histories these days, complete with psychological analyses. Well, maybe they'd add up to something in the long run.

"As you can imagine," Mac said, "Hank's attitude didn't endear him to the people at the local gas dock. It was a time when they were feeling very independent, as you may recall. That morning, he'd been informed that there was finally some diesel oil available. He arrived in the *Frances* to see another boat about the same size pulling away. He read the figures on the pump and asked for a similar amount, but the attendant wouldn't give it to him, on some unconvincing excuse or other. There was a scene. Frances calmed Hank down and he settled for a smaller quantity. They went fishing down the coast, the first time in several weeks. Hank had planned to return in time to catch the last of the favorable tide through the pass—you remember that narrow inlet between the islands, with its strong currents—and he'd allowed himself fuel enough to get home on, with a small reserve. However, as they were heading home, they saw smoke astern, and had to turn back to rescue a couple of boys whose boat had caught fire. One was badly burned. By the time they had the youngsters on board and patched up temporarily, they'd used up their reserve and the tide had turned against them in the pass."

"Tough," I said, since it was time for me to say something to show I was still on the line.

"Yes," Mac said, "it was a difficult decision. Normally, Hank told me later, he'd simply have anchored and waited for the next good tide rather than run the tanks dry fighting the current and have to radio for a tow. However, the burned boy needed medical attention, so he called the Coast Guard, told them the situation, and cruised slowly to meet the vessel they promised to send out. At the entrance, with no Coast Guard yet in sight, he sent Frances up to handle the boat from the tuna tower, from which she could see better to pick the favorable eddies, while he stood by up forward to drop the anchor if the power should fail. When they were halfway through the inlet, it did. Hank let go the hook and just about that time the burned boy in the cockpit started screaming. Frances started down the steep ladder to attend to him, maybe hurrying a little too fast—she wasn't exactly a young girl, remember—and right then the anchor dug in and brought the boat up short. She lost her grip and went over the side. Hank tried to reach her with a life preserver and a line but an eddy had already swept her too far away. He cut the anchor loose so the boat would drift after her, but it grounded on a sandbar. By the time the Coast Guard boat finally arrived, she was gone. They didn't find her until several days later, dead." There was a little pause. "As I said, an unfortunate combination of circumstances."

"Yes, sir," I said. "Unfortunate. What happened to the attendant? The man at the gas dock?"

There was a little pause. "How did you know something happened to him?"

I said, "Five gallons more would have seen them through that tide race, and Frances Priest would still be alive," I said. "Hank couldn't help but realize it. Hell, two more gallons would probably have done it, and the guy had held back just to be nasty, right? If it had been my wife, I'd have gone back there and beat him till he rang like a gong. It wouldn't have done my dead wife a damned bit of good, but it would have made me feel a hell of a lot better—and anyway, people who play petty little ego games like that might as well learn to take the consequences, when there are consequences. I'd have considered I was performing a public service."

I heard a dry laugh several thousand miles away. "I didn't realize you and Hank Priest had so much in common, Eric. He did exactly what you suggest, to the extent of putting the man into the hospital. It caused considerable trouble and of course he had to pay the medical expenses and some compensation; but the authorities decided not to prosecute the assault charge, under the circumstances. Later, he admitted to me that it had been a childish, damnfool thing to do. That was after he'd evolved his present idea. He said that Bismarck or Clemenceau or somebody—I meant to check his source; but I haven't had an opportunity—once said that war was too important to be left to the generals; well, obviously petroleum was too important to be left to the oil men. If the stupid bastards, his words, couldn't produce enough to keep us running over here after they'd got us totally dependent on the stuff, it was time, he said, for sensible people to take a hand."

"Sensible," I said. "Yes, sir. Well, I'll let you know how this sensible larceny turns out—but just how far do I go to help him carry out this wild-eyed scheme of his?"

Mac was silent for a second or two. When he spoke, his voice had changed slightly. "I think you may be making a serious mistake, Eric," he said. "Do not for a moment underestimate Hank Priest. Do not for a moment dismiss him as a picturesque old seadog dabbling clumsily and inexpertly in violent terrestrial matters with which he has no experience. This may be the image he is trying to project for you at the moment—we all play these little games—but I advise you, for his sake as well as your own, to take no stock in it whatever."

I sat there for a moment, remembering certain things, like the men lurking in the shadows in Bergen in the rain. I drew a long breath.

"Yes, sir," I said. "I am very glad you said that, sir. Because that is exactly the way I had him pegged."

"In the early days of World War II," Mac said, "before I was instructed to set up the organization of which you later became a member, I worked with an intelligence group assigned to maintain contact with the Norwegian underground movement. This was the Quisling era, you may recall, when large numbers of Norwegians were resisting the German occupation, and the dictatorial efforts of the puppet regime in Oslo, by any means available. We were giving them all the help we could. Our best man up north—our best along the entire coast, for that matter—was a certain U.S. Navy lieutenant of Norwegian extraction, selected, I suppose, for his knowledge of the language and the country. He was more than a courier and contact man; he planned and led a number of guerrilla operations so ingenious and effective, and I might add so totally ruthless, that the Germans put a very high price on his head. Of course, that was a good many years ago, but no man ever really forgets that kind of experience."

"Hank Priest?" I said.

"Yes, that is where I first met Hank," Mac said. "We've kept in touch ever since."

Something stirred in my mind, and I said, "Those boys all had code names, didn't they?"

"He operated under the name Sigmund. Why? Does it mean something to you?"

I frowned through the glass of the booth at the pretty blond typist across the room. Fortunately, engrossed in her work, she didn't notice, so her feelings weren't hurt.

"It means something," I said. "I'd hate to try to say what, right now."

"It meant something to the Norwegians at the time," Mac said. "If Sigmund should ever return to Norway, he would not have to look far for help in whatever he wanted to do. He was a hero to those people; he still is. And don't forget, men who have once tasted of that kind of secret and violent life often don't need much of an excuse to revert to it, no matter how peaceful and profitable—and dull—their current existence may be."

I said slowly, "If he's got that kind of Resistance assistance ready to pop out of the *fjords* and *fjells*, what does Sigmund want with me?"

"Most of his former Norwegian associates are rough farmers and fishermen, local people. He said he needed someone who could play the part of an American tourist; someone trained in current techniques, with enough of a reputation in modern undercover circles to discourage interference."

"Well, despite his vast wartime experience, Mr.

Sigmund seems to have overestimated what a reputation can do," I said wryly. "We've got interference coming out our ears over here. But never mind that, sir. Tell me, how many people know this about Priest? Would Denison know it, for instance?"

"Paul Denison is just a little too young to have taken an active part in World War II. He could therefore hardly have picked up the story in the line of duty and it was never written up afterwards. If he checks the files—well, as far as the Navy was concerned, Hank was simply on detached duty connected with intelligence, details unspecified. All other records were destroyed to protect the people involved. I would say there's hardly any chance of Denison, or any other investigator, stumbling across the information at the American or British end. As far as Norway is concerned, if Hank wasn't betrayed back when there was a large price on his head, it's unlikely that anybody would reveal his identity now. Those who loved him wouldn't betray him and those who didn't— there were a few; one makes enemies in a job like that— wouldn't dare risk the wrath of his friends, even now. I would say Hank has nothing to fear from the Norwegians."

"Yes, sir," I said. "The big question is, what have they to fear from him?"

After a brief pause, Mac said, "Perhaps you had better explain what you have in mind."

"You know damned well what I have in mind, sir," I said. "If I add up all the information I've received so far, I come to the logical conclusion that the Skipper, as he likes to be called around here, is deliberately making use of his tough old Norwegian comrades—patriots all, or they wouldn't have risked their lives against the Nazis— to steal Norwegian oil."

Mac said carefully, "When you put it like that, it does sound a bit implausible, doesn't it, Eric?"

"Implausible," I said. "Yes, sir. Logical it may be, but it never was a very convincing story. With what you've told me, it becomes damned near incredible. I have a strange hunch there are things I'm not being told. Any comments, sir?"

He didn't speak at once. I sat there and listened to the hum of the electrons, bridging the several thousand miles between us. When his voice came again, it sounded formal and remote: "Actually, the true nature of Captain Priest's enterprise, and its success or failure, is no concern of this department, Eric."

I whistled soundlessly through my teeth, recognizing the symptoms. Washington is the city of doubletalk and my chief is its unrecognized champion. I mean, when he doesn't want to say something, he can find more different ways of not saying it than any man I ever met. I was beginning to think that he was setting some real records in this case.

"That sounds real great, sir," I said sourly. "Just what the hell does it mean?"

"It means that we are obliged to contribute only what we were asked to contribute: your presence and your reputation, Eric. No further assistance was requested, so we have no obligation beyond this. At least you have none, as far as Henry Priest is concerned. There is, of course, another desirable objective you should keep in mind, but we've already discussed that."

"Yes, sir," I said, reflecting that it would have been nice if he'd drawn these fine lines for me a couple of days ago. I didn't say that, however. "Spell it out, sir," I said. "I seem to be a little slow today."

His voice was deliberate and emotionless: "As I said, your *official* duties in connection with Hank Priest are limited to those described. Unofficially, I am making a request that you are at liberty to disregard if you so choose, or if circumstances so dictate. I have known Hank Priest for a long time. He has been a good friend. It is possible that he does not realize that this is not wartime—at least not the war he knew—and that Sigmund is out of date. Regardless of what help he may find elsewhere, I would like you to take care of him to the best of your ability."

9

After paying the nice Norwegian lady at the counter for my lengthy call to Oslo, and winking at the pretty blond girl at the typewriter who'd restored my faith in lovely Scandinavian womanhood, I left the telephone office. Outside, the sun was shining brightly for a change—well, as brightly as it ever shines that far north at that time of the year. The little town looked clean and pretty but while the houses were colorful and picturesque by American standards, they didn't seem very old by the standards of Europe, where a dwelling erected in the days of Columbus is considered barely broken in. Of course, this could be a new section of town but I remembered that the Nazis were supposed to have systematically destroyed a large number of communities along the Norwegian coast when they pulled out in 1945, necessitating complete rebuilding...

"This way, please."

The man had fallen into step with me as I moved along the busy sidewalk. He was a red-faced, white-haired, wiry little gent with a rolling, seaman's gait. I had a hunch I'd seen him before outside a Bergen restaurant. His dark suit was shabby and his dark work-shirt was frayed but he was wearing a tie. They all wear neckties over there when they come to town, at least the older ones do. It's a mark of respectability. His gnarled hands were in plain sight.

"Sure," I said. "Lead on."

We walked side by side down the main street, made a turn, and stopped in front of a restaurant in the middle of the block. It looked like a reasonably high-class place for the size of the town.

"He waits inside," said my guide.

"Thanks."

Entering, I could tell at once I wasn't in a U.S. eatery, because there was an old man drinking his after-lunch beer near the door, slipping leftovers from his plate to his black-and-white spotted dog curled up under the table. I thought it looked kind of cozy and homelike. I hesitated. An elderly waitress looked around and jerked her head towards a door at the end of the room. I marched to it, and through it, closing it behind me. I found myself in a small meeting or banquet room. Hank Priest, alone at the end of the big table, looked up from a plate containing a couple of large sausages and some other stuff, and waved me to a chair beside him.

"Hungry?" he asked as I sat down.

I hesitated. "Well, I'm going to have to feed Diana when I get back on board ship," I said. "The poor girl's sitting in that cabin with a .38 Special in her hand, slowly starving to death."

"She'll keep; she's a patient young lady. I have some things for you to take to her: hair dye and clothes. Meanwhile, have a little *pølse*—sausage to you."

"Yes, sir," I said.

He grinned. "Oh, that's right, you're a goddamned transplanted Swede, aren't you, son, just like I'm a transplanted Norwegian. I don't have to tell you about *pølse*."

"Actually, the Swedes call it *korv*," I said.

"What did Denison have to say when you talked with him on the dock?"

His voice was casual, but his eyes had narrowed slightly, watching me. I didn't know whether he expected me to act guilty about chatting with Denison, or just startled that he knew about it.

"He said he was here to protect L.A.'s interests," I said. "We peasants call him Mr. Kotko, but Denison is a privileged employee of long standing, and has permission to use the great man's initials. It makes him happy all over, like a great big, bouncing puppy."

"You know Denison? My man said you greeted each other like old friends. Or old enemies?"

"I know Denison. His code name used to be Luke, when he worked for us."

"Arthur didn't tell me that."

Arthur was Arthur Borden, the man I generally refer to as Mac. His true identity is known only to a few. Priest, as a long-time friend, was one of the few.

"There are some things you probably didn't tell him, Skipper," I said. "There are a lot of things nobody told me."

"Well, if you've got business with Denison, don't let it interfere with your work for me, son."

"No, sir."

The aging waitress I'd encountered outside came in with a plate of sausages and a mug of beer, although I'd seen no signal passed. Maybe everybody got sausages and beer today. After she'd departed, I took a bite. They were very superior sausages, way out of the hot dog class.

"You'll be happy to know the boy you put the fear of God into got into his little sports car and drove straight out of town," Priest said. "You won't have any more trouble with him. From what you were overheard to say to him, I gather you had some trouble with his partner last night."

I regarded him grimly—Sigmund, the legendary underground hero brought back to life for reasons yet to be determined. I should have known, of course. If I'd been sharp, I'd have spotted him a couple of years ago when we'd first met, but I'd had other things on my mind at the time. I'd overlooked it then, and having got into the habit, I'd overlooked it last night. If I'd sensed anything at all, I'd attributed it to the Navy background. At a casual glance he was still the pleasant, stocky, crisply gray-haired, retired military gent whose liquor I'd drunk in Florida, with his deeply tanned face and the humorous, squinty little wrinkles around his faded blue eyes; but looking more closely I saw what I'd missed before.

A lot of those uniformed, career characters are mere pushbutton, remote-control killers. They keep their hands clean and don't really know what death is all about. To them, it's a technical, scientific exercise in velocities and trajectories. That is, of course, particularly true of the Navy, where the big guns do the dirty work beyond the horizon and the spotter planes radio back the score—come to think of it, I guess the big guns are pretty much obsolete, but the operating principles remain the same. Naval warfare is seldom if ever a gunwale-to-gunwale, pistol-and-cutlass business nowadays. I wouldn't be surprised if there are naval officers around responsible for hundreds of deaths in action, in one war or another, who have never come within a mile of a live enemy, or a dead one.

But this wasn't one of them. This was a man, I was realizing belatedly, who'd seen death at close range, who'd administered it with his own hands, coldly and efficiently, maybe even smiling a little with those pale Norse eyes. I remembered Mac's description of his wartime way of working: ingenious, effective, and totally ruthless. I drew a long breath, and reminded myself not to be so damned hasty about sizing up situations, and people, in the future. I'd already made a couple of bad mistakes here.

"Oh, that big, blond guy?" I said to Priest. "He had trouble. I had no trouble."

It was a little gaudy. Hell, let's be honest, it was Tarzan pounding his chest, and making with the victory cry of the Great Apes. I guess I was trying to make some kind of an impression on the older man facing me, who'd once rated pretty high in something approximating my own line of endeavor. Or maybe I was just trying to correct an impression already made.

I couldn't help realizing, of course, that he must have had a good laugh watching me doing my best, like a dutiful seeing-eye dog, to show the blind and bumbling old seafaring gent through the dark, unfamiliar mazes of shoreside intrigue. Unfamiliar, hell! He'd been there before me; he knew the way as well as I did—at least he'd known it once, and once is all it takes. Well, I'd asked for it. I'd been a little too eager to play the cynical pro dealing with naïve amateurs, without bothering to check just how naïve they really were. I saw an amused gleam in the sea-faded blue eyes.

"Very well, Matt," Priest said. "By now you must have been told I once spent quite a bit of time along this coast. I still have contacts here—well, you've seen some of my old associates hanging around. If you should need help, local help, don't hesitate to ask."

It was a good thing, I reflected sourly, that I had no designs on the throne of Norway. With the amount of assistance I'd had offered me on this job, I could have taken Oslo without firing a shot.

"Yes, sir," I said. "But the only help I really need at the moment, sir, is whatever is required to let me understand how you can get all these nice Norwegian citizens to help you rob their country of its precious natural resources." He watched me, still smiling a little, but his eyes had narrowed again. He didn't speak and I went on: "Or could it be, sir, that you're telling your Norska troops one thing, and your Amerikanska forces something else?"

He grinned abruptly. "It's the old underground razzle-dazzle, son," he said cheerfully. "You tell your eager young resistance fighters, full of piss and patriotism, what they want to hear. You certainly don't ever tell them the truth. Hell, they might panic if they knew the truth. Or get sick to their delicate little guts. Or they might even spill it to somebody who shouldn't know. You never can trust an idealist with the truth, Mr. Helm, you ought to know that. Truth is the one thing he just can't stand."

"Or she?" I said, watching him.

"Precisely," Priest said. "Just because a young girl's beautiful idealism has got temporarily reversed, like the polarity of a circuit, doesn't make her any less of an idealist, does it?"

"I think you're underestimating the kid, if we're talking about the same thing," I said. "Of course, there was Evelyn Benson, too. And a guy called Robbie nobody's bothered to tell me much about. The mortality seems to be high among reversed idealists, if that's what they were." Priest said nothing. I went on: "And then there's a guy called Helm. No idealist he, backwards or forwards. Does he get to hear the truth, sir?"

Priest laughed shortly. "If I'm not confiding in men like old Lars, who just brought you here, who once fought beside me and saved my life, what makes you think I'll confide in you, son? This is a fairly important project, and security is absolutely imperative."

"Yes, sir," I said. "Excuse me while I puke, sir. That word always does something funny to my insides."

He stared at me bleakly. "You're going to have to

take me on faith, Mr. Helm. When you come across contradictory bits of information you don't like, just remind yourself that this mission was not initiated to make you happy. What you don't like may confuse somebody else, somebody we've got to keep confused in order to succeed. When your faith wavers, son, remind yourself that this operation has been cleared in Washington; it has even been cleared with your own superior. Tell yourself firmly that Captain Henry Famham Priest, USN, is a man who's served his country all his life and is pretty much in the habit; he's not likely to go Benedict Arnold all of a sudden in his old age." The pale eyes watched me unblinkingly. "Either that, son, or you're going to have to haul your ass the hell out of here. I can use you but I can do without you. Make up your goddamned mind."

I let a little time go by in silence; then I said, "That's quite a speech, but may I make a suggestion, sir?"

"What?"

"Don't use the word 'faith.' People get suspicious when you ask them to take you on faith. It's been overdone, Skipper."

It was a calculated risk. I was going to have to work with the guy; I couldn't have him thinking I was a sucker for inspiring, patriotic speeches, even if I had been a little slow-witted earlier. There was a moment of silence; then he threw back his head and laughed uproariously.

At last he drew a long breath and wiped his eyes. "My apologies, son," he said. "I forgot I was dealing with a pro. I've got in the habit of schmaltzing it up a bit for the impressionable civilians. No hard feelings, I hope."

He held out his hand. I shook it and retrieved my fingers, more or less intact. There was no reason to change a winning game, so I went on: "Even if you want to, you can't get rid of me, sir. I've got orders to stick around and look after you like a baby. I just got instructions from Washington, and the word is you're kind of a helpless old character who could get into serious trouble, forgetting that World War II was a long time ago. So if you need your nose wiped, sir, or your diapers changed, or the nurse doesn't bring your two a.m. feeding on schedule, just let me know right away, please."

Again, it was nip and duck. We sat there for several seconds while he fought back an attack of angry seniority. Then he grinned slowly.

"Very good, Mr. Helm. Very good indeed. Now we know where we stand, don't we?"

I wasn't so sure about that, but at least we'd redistributed the local balance of power slightly. I said, "That was the general idea."

"Well, finish your goddamned *pølse* so I can spread out the chart and show you the general layout…"

He'd obviously had a lot of practice at explaining geography to stupid subordinates. By the time he was through I knew the North Sea like my favorite fishing lake near Santa Fe, New Mexico—it had damned well better be my favorite since, in that dry country, it's just about the only water around, besides the Rio Grande, big enough to swim a trout. But here there was more water, a hell of a lot more, and we weren't concerned with fish.

He showed me the locations of the submerged oil and gas fields: the British operations over to the west—one named Indefatigable, in true British fashion—the Belgian, Dutch, German, and Danish areas to the south; and the Norwegian fields, Ekofisk, Frigg, and particularly Torbotten, the latest discovery way up north where nobody'd really expected to hit anything, he said. We also discussed a bit of strategy dealing, mainly, with the Elfenbein problem. I offered a solution he didn't think much of.

"You're not going to bluff, Ivory like you bluffed that little boy of his," he warned me.

"Who's bluffing?" I asked. "Anyway, nobody'll call me. Dr. Elfenbein's been around. He knows better than to confront a man in my line of work with a direct challenge. He knows, or thinks he knows, that we homicidal types are all unbalanced, dangerously unstable, apt to go completely berserk if crossed. He won't risk it, not if he's looked up my record, as he undoubtedly has."

"You're running hard on that record of yours, son. One day you'll rely on it and it won't work."

"Maybe," I said. "But it's what you hired me for, so let's make use of it while it is working. I wouldn't be fool enough to try it on Denison; but if I can't back down a white-haired little laboratory genius, even one with a criminal bent, I'll turn in my invisible ink. Who's he working for, anyway?"

"What?"

"Ivory," I said. "Who's his client here, who's paying his freight?"

"We haven't been able to determine that. As far as we know, Elfenbein is working on speculation, hoping he can find a customer once he gets hold of something to sell." Priest shrugged, dismissing the subject. He went on: "You have two contacts to arrange, Matt, in Trondheim and in Svolvaer. Well, the arrangements have already been made, and Diana knows them, so I won't waste time on them here; but your job is to see that the people up there get met, and their material picked up, according to plan. Just remember, a lot of these folks aren't quite as brave as they were back when their country was in the hands of the Nazis. They're helping me out, but they're not very happy. Anything out of line, and they'll crawl back into the woodwork; so be careful."

"Yes, sir," I said.

"The important delivery is the one near the end of the line," he went on. "You'll get plans for a certain piece of machinery invented by a drunken, middle-aged, oilfield bum who once was a bright, young, mechanical genius with a knack for explosives. He sank a small troopship for us and did a fine job, but he was one of the sensitive ones, you know the type, and he started seeing drowning Germans in his dreams. Do you ever see dead men in your sleep, son?"

"No, sir," I said. "I'm told I have no imagination."

"Well, this chap had too much imagination, and it more or less finished him; but once in a while he gets lucid and tosses off an invention, something so simple nobody ever thought of it before, if you know what I mean. This gadget of his is one of them. He named it after me, you know."

"So I understand."

"Don't think the gesture was flattering, Mr. Helm," Priest said, smiling thinly. "The boy—well, he's no boy now, but he was then—hates my cold-blooded, murdering guts, and told me so, in several languages, at the time. Apparently he feels this is just the kind of lousy device that ought to be named after a bastard, like Sigmund, the sadistic, heartless slob everybody else in Norway considers a hero. I'm just giving you a rough idea of his attitude, using his words as well as I can. To put it differently, it's his big joke. Everybody else will consider it a tribute to a national hero; only Johann and I know what he really means by it. And now you."

I said, "The motivations are getting a little complicated, but I think I'm still with you, sir."

"Don't fall for this Sigmund crap, is what I'm trying to tell you," Priest said. "My job was to do as much damage as I could, and I did it. Some of them hated me for it and some of them loved me, and to hell with all of them. Well, that's putting it too strongly. They were good tough men. Some of them still are. But you know how these things go. A bunch of mean, ragged bastards, scared shitless, prowling through the *fjells* like hungry wolves, becomes, in the history books, a band of clean, noble patriots led by a saint on a white horse. You sneak into a village one night and slit the throats of five poor, stupid Nazis from behind and ten years later you're reading about the goddamned battle of Blomdal complete with cavalry, band, and bugles. But just don't expect that if you say Sigmund they're all going to knock themselves out helping you. Some of them got hurt, including some who didn't expect it, and didn't think it was fair it should happen to them. Fair, hell! Who ever heard of a fair war, for God's sake?"

"What happened?" I asked.

"Well," he said, "you know the standard German method of retaliating for guerrilla attacks back in those days. What the hell made them think we'd pay any attention to their lousy hostages, son? We were getting shot; if somebody else got shot, too, we were just as sorry as we could be. It was too damned bad, and all that, but we had a war to fight and we just got the hell on with it. If those people wouldn't get out into the hills and fight with us, the least they could do was stay in town and die with us, was the way we felt at the time."

The room was very quiet after he stopped talking. Then a truck drove by outside, and he reached for his mug and finished off his beer and ran the back of his hand across his mouth.

"The old man's getting garrulous," he said dryly. "Let's get back to business. In addition to the Siphon drawings, we need some information about the area that's kind of specialized and not in the oil and gas journals. Johann's done the work on Torbotten; he'll hand it over with the plans. He's in bad shape, he needs what I'm paying him, but don't discount the possibility of a doublecross anyway. In other words, make sure there's a girl at the right place at the right time, but be careful."

"Yes, sir," I said.

He didn't go on at once. The door opened, and the waitress came in with another beer. I wondered about ESP and decided there was probably a buzzer under the rug at the head of the table where he sat.

"As for the Trondheim contact tomorrow," he said, "take care of it if you can, but don't risk anything for it. It's the stuff on Frigg and Ekofisk, but we're not too interested in Frigg at the moment. It's a gas field, and we probably won't be set up to handle gas for quite a while, if ever. Anyway, it's shared between the Norwegians and the British, being right on the boundary line between their respective areas, so it offers political complications. Ekofisk also presents problems. For one thing, there's a deep ocean trench between the wells and the Norwegian coast, so the oil is going to have to be pumped the other way, west or south, which makes it tougher to get at. Also, Ekofisk is being handled by a whole mess of companies working together: Phillips, Aloco, and a bunch of others. That makes finagling kind of difficult, if you know what I mean. So if the Trondheim drop starts looking too risky, forget it. We'd certainly like to have that southern information on file, for future reference, but at the moment it's not essential. Largely, it's a diversionary tactic. We have people picking up information around

the British operations, too, even though we see no way
of using it right now. That way, even if some rumors get
around, nobody'll know just where to look for trouble.
But the place we've really got our eye on, at least for a
start, is Torbotten."

I glanced at the big chart on the table. "It looks kind
of chilly for well-drilling, way up there," I said. "Or for
anything else."

"The Gulf Stream off shore keeps that coast from
getting too damned cold," Priest said. "Not that you
can't freeze your ass off, I did plenty of times, but you
don't have a lot of heavy ice to contend with. Actually,
Torbotten is ideal for our purposes—well, it depends
kind of on what Johann has turned up, but up to now it
looks very good. It's not too far out in deep water, it's
all Norwegian, and best of all it's being developed by
a single outfit called Petrolene, Incorporated—a name
that may sound faintly familiar to you—controlled by a
gentleman with the high moral principles of a wolverine.
Of course, the operation is being conducted under strict
government supervision and the Norwegians are being
very tough—the contracts they've been insisting on lately
are truly heartbreaking, I'm told. Oslo runs none of the
risks and gets all the money, said my informant with tears
in his eyes."

"Your informant wouldn't have the same initials as the
city of Los Angeles, by any chance?"

"Don't be naïve, Mr. Helm." Priest's voice was dry.
"Nobody deals with Lincoln Alexander Kotko face to

face. He has very efficient negotiators to talk for him, while he sits in his Swiss chalet or his French chateau admiring the view and getting a nice tan on his shaved head—I understand he has the theory that women find bald men irresistible. So far, I gather, the evidence is all in his favor. Of course, his money may have something to do with his amorous successes, but I don't suppose anybody dares suggest that to Mr. Kotko. Well, the hairless sonofabitch is going to have to come out of hiding if he wants what I've got to offer. I'm not risking men's lives for it, and women's too, just to turn it over to some errand boy like Denison." He threw back his head and finished the latest beer in a single draft like a Viking polishing off a horn of mead. "Now you'd better shove off, son. If there's anything I've left out, Diana can probably fill it in for you. I'll be keeping out of sight—north of here, somebody might recognize me who shouldn't—but I'll be in touch later, or some of my people up there will."

"How will I know them?"

He frowned. "It's been a long time since I played this secret agent game… If you speak some Swedish, you've got a pretty good notion of how Norwegian's supposed to sound. If they can pronounce *pølse* correctly, they're mine. If they say *pelsay*, or *poal-see*, shoot them. Okay? Give my regards to the girl. Here are the things I brought along for her. How are you kids getting along?"

It was part of the act. I wasn't all that young, and he wasn't all that old, but he'd always favored the elder statesman role. I told him Diana and I were getting along fine. After all, that wasn't too far from the truth. It was a hell of a lot closer, I figured, than some of the information that had been presented at the conference now being adjourned...

10

The unseen captain up on the bridge had a method for getting his ship away from the dock that was just as simple as the system he'd used for bringing her in. He merely cast off all the docklines except the same workhorse wire cable; and then he put the old bucket into gear, or whatever you do to get action on a vessel that large. Maybe, he also put the rudder over—my rudimentary seamanship said it would be a logical move—but I couldn't check that from where I stood. Anyway, the ship moved ahead slowly until the cable came taut. With the bow held, and the propeller still turning, the stern swung outwards gradually. When it was aimed at the open harbor, he gave her reverse. The cable went slack, a dockhand threw it off the cleat on the pier, a couple of deckhands hauled it aboard the ship, and we were clear.

Standing at the rail beside Diana, I watched the colorful, sunny little town recede as, moving forward once more, the vessel headed for the open fjord beyond the reefs and breakwaters.

"I didn't see the Skipper. I guess he must be serious about starting to keep out of sight," Diana said. I'd given her a condensed and censored report of the morning's events while watching her eat a hearty lunch in the ship's dining room. I mean, the Denison angle wasn't really any of her business that I could see.

I said, "Washington may have authorized this very illicit operation, in a panicky moment but if anything should go wrong they'd undoubtedly prefer not to have the gent in charge recognized as a U.S. naval officer, even a retired one. Apparently, there are quite a few folks along this coast, particularly farther north, who remember him from World War II."

"Yes, I gather he's kind of a hero to these people," Diana said. She hesitated and glanced at me a bit uncertainly. "But even so, I've been wondering... Doesn't it seem a little strange to you, Matt, that he'd be able to persuade them to help him as they seem to be doing, considering what his objective is?"

I grinned. "Sweetheart, join the club. You have just restored my faith in the intelligence of the so-called weaker sex. Strange is hardly the word for it. I think we can safely assume, on the basis of the evidence to date, that whatever Captain Priest is up to around here, it isn't what he says he's up to, no matter how often and elaborately he says it, complete with maps and statistics."

She frowned at me in a worried way. "But… but what are we going to *do*?"

I sighed sadly. "First the girl lifts me up, way up; then she casts me down, way down."

"What do you mean?"

I said, "Did you throw off all your ladylike inhibitions, all your lovely concerned morality, just to come over here and lead the Skipper into paths of righteousness and veracity? That isn't the way you were telling it a few hours back."

"But—"

"I thought you were rebelling against your dull, safe, worthy, and scrupulously honest life. I thought you were through with saving the blackfooted ferret, and similar displays of social consciousness."

She laughed quickly and stopped laughing. "You mean, we should go right on working for him even if… even if we suspect he isn't telling us the truth?"

"We know damned well he isn't telling us the truth," I said. "As a matter of fact, he came right out and said so. So what? My orders make no reference to the truth. And whatever Captain Priest is up to, it can't be a hell of a lot wickeder or more illegal than what he's going around saying he's up to—like robbing these poor Scandinavians of their offshore oil. If we're capable of accepting that, and we damn well did, the chances are we won't be too damned shocked at the truth when he finally dispenses with the security razzle-dazzle, as he calls it, and lets us in on the secret. My chief says he's an ingenious and effective operator, and my chief doesn't toss words like that around lightly. Okay, let the old pirate proceed with his ingenious and effective operation, whatever it may be, and to hell with him. Our job is to pick up his mail up north, not to pass judgment on his manners or his morals... Oh, oh. Look who we've got here, just as pretty as two pipes in a shooting gallery."

The Elfenbeins, *père et fille*, if you'll pardon my lousy French, had come out on deck to admire the passing view. They were a little late to see the coastline at its best, since the clouds were pulling together again, cutting off the sparkling sunshine of a few minutes earlier. I glanced at my companion.

"I'll see you in your cabin in just about five minutes," I said. "Stop by my place on your way. There's a first aid kit in my suitcase; take it. Five minutes. Don't be surprised if there's company with me."

Diana hesitated and glanced at the June-and-September couple by the rail. Her eyes showed quick excitement. "Can't I help here?"

"You're too damned bloodthirsty," I said. "You'd shoot them just to hear them go thump on the deck. Go on, beat it."

As far as the basic survival skills are concerned, the worst thing that can happen to a man in our general line of work—and you could say that Dr. Adolf Elfenbein was, at least, in a closely related business—is for him to gain success and authority. He forgets what it was like down in the jungle out of which he climbed. He starts to feel invulnerable; kind of sacred and untouchable. He knows that down in the lower echelons people still fight and die, but the blood can't spatter him and the bullets can't reach him any longer, up on the serene, safe eminence to which he has attained. At least he gets to thinking they can't.

Elfenbein looked up questioningly as I stopped in front of him. I said, very politely, "My name is Matthew Helm, sir. I think it's time we talked, don't you?"

His blue eyes looked a little surprised, his pink preacher face a little disconcerted, before he got his expression under control.

"You're the man who murdered Bjørn," he said coldly. "He was not a very valuable man, just local Norwegian help hired for the occasion, nevertheless I can't see that it leaves us anything constructive to say to each other."

I said, "Well, if we're adding up old scores, sir, you're the man who sent Bjørn to murder Mrs. Barth. And I'm the man who doesn't like people trying to kill people under my protection. And I'm the man who, therefore, has just informed your pretty boy Erlan Torstensen, also involved in the attempt, that he'd better run along and make himself invisible before I squash him like a cockroach."

The girl stirred. "Oh, then that's why... Erlan sent us an incoherent message we couldn't understand."

"That's why," I said, reminding myself not to forget that to the best of my knowledge there was no ship-to-shore phone service. If they'd received a message here on board, somebody must have brought it aboard; and nobody'd said a thing about his leaving, whoever he might be. Of course, the girl hadn't *said* they'd got the message on the ship—they might have attended a rendezvous on shore while I wasn't around—but it was the only safe assumption to make. I said, "My information is that handsome Erlan hopped into his sports car and drove like hell out of that little town back there. I must have made a big impression on him... And now that we've got the cheap Norwegian help out of the way, sir," I went on, addressing myself to the parent once more, "I suggest we shake hands like civilized human beings and talk this thing over before more people get killed. How about it, sir?" I held out my hand.

Although the reference to civilized human beings didn't do any harm—the crookeder they are, the more civilized they like to think themselves—I'm sure it was the sirs that really did the job. Kids nowadays won't say sir or ma'am to their elders; they consider it demeaning, or something. They don't know what a useful tool they're passing up. When a guy damn near six and a half feet tall, a guy considered dangerous in some quarters, approaches you deferentially and calls you sir, why, it makes you feel very important, particularly if you already have a tendency towards feeling very important. I could see the little white-haired gent in front of me kind of swelling slightly, proudly, pigeon-like, as he condescended to take my hand...

The girl was smarter. Her eyes narrowed abruptly and she started to cry a warning, but she was too late. Before she'd got it out, I'd yanked Dr. Elfenbein close and slammed a knee into him hard. My left hand pulled his face against my shoulder to stifle the moaning gasp he let out. He was short enough to make this practical. I held him there by the back of the neck so he wouldn't attract attention by slipping to the deck. There were still a few passengers out here, although most had gone inside after we emerged from the harbor. I took out the gun and pointed it at the girl, turning slightly so it was hidden by my body from the rest of the ship.

"Your daddy seems to have been taken suddenly ill, Miss," I said. "We'd better be careful it doesn't prove fatal, hadn't we?"

Her eyes were wide and shocked. "You... you must be mad! You can't—"

"Get away with it?" I said cheerfully. "Why, you're perfectly right, Miss Elfenbein. Of course I can't get away with it. That's strictly impossible, ma'am. I mean, where will I go, afterwards, on this little ship? They'll catch me, sure. They'll try me and electrocute me, or whatever they do in Norway. Of course, it'll take months. Meanwhile—" I put the muzzle of the borrowed automatic against the body of the man I held. "—meanwhile your father will have been long buried, thoroughly perforated with nasty little 9mm bullets. If you think it's a fair exchange, just shout for help."

Greta Elfenbein started to speak, licked her lips, and remained silent.

I went on, raising my voice slightly, "You'd better take his other arm, ma'am. I'll help you get him below.

The sudden way it hit him, I'm afraid it can't be just seasickness. Has he been having dizzy spells or trouble with his heart…?"

The ship was now far enough out to feel the seas kicked up by the brisk tail wind helping us up the coast. She responded with a long, slow roll that made my job of half-carrying Elfenbein below less easy than it might have been; but the girl made no move to take advantage of my off-balance moments. Two decks down, Diana was ready for us. When I kicked at the stateroom door, it opened. She had my revolver in her hand.

"You first, Miss Elfenbein," I said. "Sit down on that berth to the left, please, with your hands in plain sight on your knees. No, a little farther over, if you don't mind, to make room for… There you are, Doctor. Feeling better now?"

Elfenbein's face was pale and damp and his thin, white hair was disheveled, revealing that there was quite a good-sized, pink, bald patch on top, normally hidden by careful combing of what remained. He started to speak—maybe, like his daughter, he felt obliged to tell me I couldn't get away with it—but he checked himself. His eyes, however, were wicked in his mild face. I realized that he wasn't really a very nice man. Well, neither was I.

I gestured to Diana to sit down on the other berth, facing Greta. "She's your responsibility, Madeleine," I said, to remind her who she was supposed to be. "Just don't make any loud, fatal noises unless you have to."

"I understand, Matt."

I glanced her way. She had her elbows on her knees, and she was supporting the revolver with both hands the way I'd shown her. She seemed to have the situation under control. Greta Elfenbein looked pale and subdued, as if weapons and violence didn't agree with her. It could have been an act, but I remembered being told that the girl had been innocently studying music in Switzerland when her mother had died and she'd been brought home to her father.

She bothered me. I couldn't quite see where she fitted into a professional caper. The data on the female Elfenbein were contradictory. There was the fact to be kept in mind that the first time I'd met her she'd gone for a gun—but I reminded myself also that she hadn't got it. She'd been too conventionally concerned about her dignity and her nylons to make the headlong dive that would have done the job. All in all, she was a subject that could use a little more research, but this was hardly the time for it.

"What do you want, Helm?" That was Dr. Elfenbein. "What do you hope to achieve by this muscular melodrama?"

"Achieve," I said. "Nice word, achieve. I hope we're going to achieve some information and cooperation, Doctor. First, I'd like you to inform me exactly how you came to know enough to be on this ship with your daughter and your hired Norwegian henchmen, prepared to take swift and drastic action, convinced that it would be worth your while to do so. And then I want you to cooperate by getting the hell off it. Off the ship, out of the caper, out of our hair."

The little man had stroked his thin, white locks into place. "You must be joking, sir," he said. "You can't really believe that I'll tell you everything you want to know, and then obediently disembark at the next port, simply because you tell me to."

"Suit yourself," I said. "But before you make up your mind for sure, why don't you ask your daughter to tell you just once more exactly what happened to Big Bjørn, the dangerous fellow you hired to toss helpless ladies into harbors?"

Elfenbein sighed. "So much melodrama! You are really threatening us with death if we do not leave this ship?"

I said deliberately, "It was a very simple job as far as I was concerned, Dr. Elfenbein. Just a quiet boat-ride up the coast with an attractive companion, an elementary escort job, with no real danger in sight—at least I'd been advised of none. Suddenly you barged in and tried to make World War III of it. Okay, if war's what you want, I'll give you war. One of your boys is already taking a codfish census thirty fathoms down, if I've got the depth right and they have cod around here. Another's on the run; he believed that I meant what I told him. It would be too bad if you were to lose your life, and cause me a lot of trouble, simply because you refused to understand what was said to you in plain English. Would you rather hear it in Swedish, sir? Or I can take a crack at German, although my pronunciation's lousy. I even know a few Spanish words if they'll help."

The little man smiled faintly. "The linguistic display

will not be necessary. Let us say that I accept as a working hypothesis that you'll assassinate us if we don't leave this vessel. But there was some talk of information, and dead people do not communicate very well. Are we, then, to be tortured first, before we're killed?"

He was a little too calm, a little too self-assured, even for an experienced crook. After all, he was supposed to be a refugee from a scientific laboratory, not truly a graduate of the underworld jungle. Considering that he'd just been roughly manhandled and kneed where it hurt, he was holding up too well for a sheltered Ph.D.—at least for a sheltered Ph.D. without any hope of assistance.

I grinned at him wolfishly. "And what's so unthinkable about torture, Professor?" I pocketed my borrowed automatic, brought out my knife, and did the one-handed, flick-it-open trick that's mostly for show. It does impress some people. I saw his eyes widen slightly, but he did not speak. I said, "The logical approach here, of course, is through the young lady."

That got to him. "If you dare—"

I went on without paying him any attention: "It's a real pity, she's pretty, but it's not my fault if people won't listen to reason. It's altogether up to you, Doctor. If you really prefer to have your daughter spend the rest of her life as Three-Finger Greta, or One-Ear Elfenbein—"

I won't bore you with the rest of the Torquemada patter. I was marking time, waiting for the long, slow roll of the ship to reach the proper degree of tilt, whatever the nautical term may be. When I felt it approach, I lunged towards the girl. Elfenbein responded predictably, making the intercept, his right hand reaching out. I grabbed it with my left and slammed it against the wardrobe beside him and drove the knife through it, pinning him there. He gave a choked little scream. Beautiful. The man in the corridor outside couldn't stand that. He started to smash his way in, just as I yanked the door open leaving him nothing to smash...

11

If I do say so myself, it was neatly done. The timing was right on, as the cats say. The endless, lazy roll of the ship to starboard—there were times when you thought she'd keep on lazily rolling through three hundred and sixty degrees—did all the work for me, once he got himself going. Head down like a charging bull, unable to stop, he hit the far wall of the cabin, actually the side of the ship, with a jolting crash.

I'd thrown myself backwards onto the berth, knees up, to let him go by. Now all I had to do, as he came to rest on all fours, dazed, was drive a heel at the back of his head. He collapsed in the narrow space between the berths; a youngish man, at a glance, with a sharp, brownish sport coat and the kind of carefully/carelessly styled crop of medium-long hair the executive types are wearing these days. I reached across to take a small automatic pistol from his hand—a tiny .25 Colt; I hadn't seen, one of those in years. They really went in for miniature firearms up here in the Arctic. I checked it over. It was loaded, with one in the chamber, ready to go. Well, as ready as those diminutive firearms ever get. There are tales of the anemic little bullet being stopped by a sheepskin coat. You'd hardly call it professional artillery, is what I'm trying to say.

After closing the cabin door, I looked at Dr. Elfenbein. He wasn't looking very professional at the moment, either. His brain might have earned him a high place in scientific circles, but his threshold of pain was too low for this kind of work. Of course, I don't suppose the man crashing past had done his transfixed hand any good; but anyway, he had fainted.

The two girls were curled up at the ends of the two berths in almost identical positions resulting from what might be called, scientifically, the nylon-protective reflex. Long years of practice at preserving fragile and expensive stockings have given the modern woman a very fast reaction time when it comes to keeping her legs out of trouble, and it carries over to slacks. Both Greta and Diana had apparently got their, trousered limbs tucked up under them instantly, leaving the passage clear for the charging intruder.

Diana asked calmly, "How do I get this thing down without killing anybody?"

I took the revolver from her, cautiously. On my last visit to the armory in the basement far below Mac's office, I hadn't been able to obtain the old-fashioned shrouded-hammer pocket model I really prefer. These days of shortages, one uses what one can get; and this was a standard, lightweight, police-type arm, hammer exposed, and now cocked. I showed her how to let it down.

"How did you happen to cock it?" I asked, returning the weapon to her. "I told you, there's no need to cock the piece and shoot single-action except for pinpoint accuracy. A long, strong, smooth pull on the trigger does the job, cocking and firing it in one motion. That's why they call them double-action, or self-cocking, revolvers.'

"But you said no unnecessary fatal noises," Diana said. "The girl started over to help her daddy when you reached for the door. I wondered if I was supposed to shoot, and then, well, I remembered all those books where the menacing click of a cocked hammer… you know. So I hauled it back, and it did make a nice little click, and what do you know? It worked. She stopped right there." Diana looked down curiously. "Who's he?"

I said, "Probably a guy who sneaked aboard with a message, earlier. He may also be the reinforcements the Torstensen boy was sent after, although he doesn't look like very heavy muscle to me, not with this peashooter he's packing."

Diana grimaced. "Any more guests, and we'll have to move the show to the ship's ballroom, if any. Where are we going to put him?"

Her voice was nice and steady, maybe a little too steady to carry complete conviction; but for a beginner she was doing fine.

"Are you just going to sit there *talking*?" That was

Greta Elfenbein. "Are you just going to *leave* him there like that?"

Her eyes were on her parent, slumped against the big wardrobe at the end of the bed with one hand up, like a bag of old clothes suspended from a hook.

"That's right, ma'am," I said. "Just like that, I'm going to leave him. Until he comes to and talks. Information was what we were trying to achieve, remember?"

Greta licked her lips. "But you *can't...*" She hesitated. "If I... if *I* tell you what you want to know, will you...?" She stopped, as if she'd run out of breath.

I didn't like it. I mean, it's not a moral business, and you're supposed to use what leverage you can get. I hadn't felt a bit guilty about using the daughter to make an impression on Elfenbein, presumably a hardened sinner like me and playing by the same rules—anyway, the torture routine had been largely a gambit to flush out the gent outside the door. But I wasn't sure about this girl yet. She might be just an innocent music student dragged along on her papa's expedition for reasons yet to be determined. Even if she wasn't particularly innocent, using her daddy's blood to break her down didn't make me feel very proud of myself. Well, I hadn't been sent here to polish my self-esteem.

"What can you tell me?" I asked. "Who's our Sleeping Beauty on the floor, for starters? Can you tell me that?"

She licked her lips again. "That's Mr. Yale, Mr. Norman Yale. He works for the Allied Oil Company."

I frowned. "The Allied Oil Company? Aloco... Wait

a minute!" I remembered my recent conversation with Hank Priest. Things were beginning to come together. "That's one of the outfits developing Ekofisk, along with Phillips and a bunch of smaller fry, isn't it?"

"Yes, of course." She hesitated. "I... I guess the Aloco people have hopes of, well, secretly helping themselves to a slightly larger slice of the pie, if you know what I mean."

"And they heard about our little project, and figured we had some interesting machinery they could use, or the plans for the same, and hired your daddy to get it for them?" Greta Elfenbein nodded reluctantly. I recalled the Skipper saying that Ekofisk was difficult for various political and geographical reasons, but he hadn't said it was impossible. Apparently some Aloco executives didn't think it was impossible, either. I went on slowly, thinking aloud: "So when Dr. Elfenbein ran into a snag on this ship, a snag named Helm, he dispatched a messenger, Torstensen, to report the problem to his principals. And they sent him Mr. Norman Yale to provide advice and assistance, not to mention a lousy little .25 caliber popgun. You say Yale works for them. How?"

"Well—" She was going to wear out her lips, licking at them. She'd already gone through all the lipstick she'd had on, not that she'd been what you'd call a heavy lipsticker. "Do you know a man named Denison?" she asked.

"I know who he is." That wasn't the complete truth, but it was certainly no lie.

Greta said, "I think you could say, Mr. Helm, that whatever Mr. Denison is to Petrox, Mr. Yale is to Aloco.

A… a troubleshooter, I think you'd call him."

I looked down at the feeble firearm in my hand, and at the stylishly dressed and barbered young man at my feet, who was showing signs of reviving.

"Oh, dear," I said softly. "Oh, dearie me! You mean this Madison Avenue type is supposed to be a match for Paul Denison? Excuse me a moment, I've got to call my broker; I want to make sure he unloads Aloco fast. Denison eats bright young characters like this with his Chivas Regal. One peanut, one cashew, one Norman Yale. Crunch, crunch, crunch, slurp… Come on, Buster, let's see what you really look like."

Diana slid aside to cover the Elfenbeins across the way while I heaved the newcomer up and dumped him at the outboard end of the berth where she'd been sitting. With five people in the stateroom, it was a little like operating in a sardine tin. Yale's eyes were open by the time I got through.

"What… where… oh, my head!" His eyes came to a focus, not on me, but on a spot diagonally across the cabin. "Oh, my God!" he said. "Is that a *knife*, right through his *hand*? Oh, my God!"

I looked at him hard, wondering if he was for real. "And this is a gun," I said. "Your gun. Where'd you get it?"

"Well," he said, "well, of course we don't *approve* of violence, but under the circumstances they thought it might prove useful; and I did have some marksmanship training in the Army before I was assigned to public relations…

He was straightening his artistic necktie as he talked.

He was a handsome specimen, almost as pretty as Erlan Torstensen in his brown-haired way but much more adult and sophisticated, of course. At least he undoubtedly considered himself so.

"Public relations?" I said. "Is that what you're doing for Aloco?" When he frowned quickly, I said, "Oh, Miss Elfenbein performed the introductions while you were napping."

"Yes, of course," he said, with a reproachful glance at the girl on the other side of the little cabin. "Well, P.R.'s what it says on the door. Actually, I'm more or less responsible for the corporate image, regardless of what that involves, if you know what I mean. Any threat to the company's reputation..."

"I see," I said. "Any threat like that and you'll handle it. With or without a gun."

"If I can't, I know where to hire men who can," he snapped, showing his teeth suddenly, like an overbred show dog displaying the dangerously erratic temperament lurking beneath the gorgeous looks. Reconsidering, he went on smoothly: "Let me withdraw that statement, Mr. Helm. It was not intended as a threat, I assure you. Obviously, there's been a serious miscalculation. We were told we'd be dealing only with members of a hastily organized and fairly amateurish government agency with rather shaky support in Washington. It was only recently that we were informed that Captain Priest had been able to enlist real *professional* help. If we'd known that at the start, maybe... He shrugged. "Anyway, I've been authorized to offer terms; that's what I'm really here for."

"You have a funny way of establishing diplomatic relations, gun in hand."

"I... I didn't know what was happening in here. I heard a cry; I thought I'd better intervene quickly. Obviously a mistake. I apologize. What about it, Mr. Helm?"

"What about your terms?" I asked. "Let's hear them, and I'll forward them to my chief in Washington, but I'd better warn you he's not much at negotiating—"

Yale cleared his throat. "I see no good reason to bother your chief about a detail like this, do you?"

I looked at him for a moment; then I shot a meaningful glance towards Diana Lawrence. "You picked a hell of a spot to broach the subject, *amigo*," I said to Yale.

He shrugged his shoulders once more. "You can keep her quiet, I'm sure, one way or another, Mr. Helm. It would have to be done in any case, wouldn't it? Anyway, she's your problem."

"Well, okay," I said. "How much?"

"Twenty-five big ones?"

It's really funny how many of them take for granted everybody can be bought with money—or maybe not. The ones who are for sale themselves probably can't comprehend the psychology of folks who aren't. Obviously, slick young Mr. Yale would happily have sold Washington to the British, New York to the Dutch, and Aloco to Mr. Lincoln Alexander Kotko, for twenty-five thousand dollars and it simply hadn't occurred to him that somebody might refuse such a deal—except perhaps to hold out for twenty-seven five.

Actually, it was a very flattering offer. It meant that somebody at Aloco had checked on me, and considered me a real menace to the company's reputation and profits. Unfortunately, they hadn't checked quite far enough. They hadn't got to the fine print that said that while I was a real lousy citizen, capable of all kinds of dirty tricks, maybe even treason, I just didn't happen to be all that fond of money. I don't say I can't be bought. Maybe some day somebody'll offer me something I really value; then we'll see just how loyal and patriotic I am. However, unlike Norman Yale and Paul Denison, I just don't happen to set all that store on cash.

I was aware that Diana was watching me kind of uncertainly, wondering whether she ought to start getting indignant and reproachful. I was tempted to tease her by carrying the act a little farther—besides, it would have been interesting to know just how far Yale had been authorized to go. Was I considered merely a twenty-five-grand government slob, or a fifty-grand U.S. creep, or maybe even a hundred-grand All American louse? But Elfenbein was stirring uneasily in his sleep, and there wasn't time for any more comedy. Well, not much more.

"Half a million," I said, and was a little startled to see that for a moment I was taken seriously. There was a funny little silence. I went on plaintively, "Hell, that's only a fraction of what you folks are expecting to make on this deal, Yale. It's got to be, or you wouldn't be taking the risk."

His eyes had narrowed. "Half a—"

"Take it or leave it," I said.

"You've got to be kidding!"

I grinned abruptly. "Friend, you're catching on. It's nice to be smart, isn't it?" I stopped grinning. "Now, if you have any more funny jokes, why don't you save them for a better occasion? Right now, I've got some advice for you, Mr. Yale. You're going to sit right in this corner. You're not going to move a muscle. You're not going to open your mouth unless directly addressed by me. If you disobey any of these instructions, this young lady will put a great big hole through—"

Suddenly I slammed the little pistol, flat in the palm of my hand, against the side of his head, hard. He bounced sideways against the cabin wall and slumped there, staring at me with big, brown, shocked, and angry eyes.

I said, harshly, "In case you're wondering what that was for, Mr. Norman Yale, it was for looking at Mrs. Barth the way you just did and thinking that I was obviously bluffing and she wouldn't shoot, not a nice young lady like that. It was to save your life, *amigo*, because I'm not bluffing and she will shoot... Okay, Madeleine, he's all yours. I'll take care of the ones across the room."

"I've got him, Matt," Diana said quietly, sliding past to, take the middle of the berth close to her prisoner. "Matt, I—"

Whatever she'd teen about to say, she checked it. I knew what it was, anyway. She'd been going to tell me that she'd had perfect faith in me; absolute confidence that I wouldn't sell out, not even for half a million.

I grinned. "You're a lousy little liar."

"I didn't say anything," she protested, but there was a spot of color in each cheek.

"His name was Wetherill," Greta Elfenbein said abruptly.

"What?" I glanced her way.

"That's what you want to know, isn't it?" Her voice was impatient. "You want to know who betrayed you, who gave Papa the information, that brought us to this ship? That's what you asked. Well, I'm telling you. The man was one of your people. He was paid a good deal of money. His name was Robert Wetherill. Now... now will you *please* take Papa down?"

Diana stirred indignantly beside me. "That's not true! Robbie would never have—"

I glanced at her sharply. "Keep him covered, dammit! Robbie? The guy you said was dead?"

Greta Elfenbein laughed sharply. "Of course he's dead. When they learned he'd betrayed them, they murdered him—or isn't it murder when one government agent kills another? Of course they made it look like an automobile accident." She went on quickly before Diana could protest: "Please, Mr. Helm, now will you pull out that dreadful knife? Please?"

"And have you clam up just when you're speaking your piece so nicely?"

"I'll tell you everything I know if you only... if you'll just take him down. I promise!"

Diana was faming, obviously on the verge of bursting with counter-accusations; as if I gave a damn, at the moment, who'd killed a guy who'd been dead before I arrived in Norway. I gave her a sharp little sign to remind her that her business was Norman Yale, and reached around and got one of the ship's towels from the rack by the little sink in the corner. I wondered how soon we'd start getting complaints from the stewardess about all the disappearing linen—I'd already shot a hole in part of this cabin's quota. I folded the towel once and laid it across the unconscious man's lap. Then I took the strain off his arm, yanked out the blade, and placed his hand on the towel so he wouldn't bleed all over himself and the bunk.

"How about some Kleenex?" I asked Diana.

"Right there on top of my back by the foot of the berth." Her voice was cool and unfriendly. "The first aid kit you wanted is on the edge of the washbasin, in case you didn't notice."

"You can start talking again while I clean up," I said to Greta. "What did Robert Wetherill have to say?"

She glanced at her parent, whose color seemed to be returning, although he still hadn't opened his eyes.

"Very well," she said. "I'll keep my part of the bargain; but I can't tell you everything he said because he did a lot of talking to Papa when I wasn't there. There was something about a fantastic invention cooked up by a drunken oilfield mechanic—well, we'd already heard about that from the Aloco people. That's why Mr. Yale got in touch with Papa in the first place. Papa had put out feelers, the way he does, and turned up Mr. Wetherill, who was willing to talk, for a price."

I'd wiped off the knife, folded it, and put it away. "Shut up, Madeleine," I snapped when Diana started to speak quickly, obviously to protest this further slur on her dead associate's name. I reached for the first aid kit and got out some sterile gauze pads and a roll of bandage for Elfenbein's hand. "Go on," I said to Greta.

"Mr. Wetherill confirmed the existence of the invention. I wasn't in on those discussions but Papa made sure I was there when Wetherill described how you people were going to pick up all the information up the coast. The railway-station restaurant near the docks in Trondheim and the little rocky hill above the parking space behind the Svolvaer airport. The courier would be a woman. Wetherill didn't know who, but he told us the ship and cabin number so we could identify her when she came aboard. She would carry a pair of special binoculars for identification: Leitz Trinovid 6x24s. It's a very expensive little glass, and it has been discontinued. The smallest currently listed is the seven-power, Mr. Helm, and that now costs close to five hundred of your American dollars. We had a terrible time locating a dealer who still had a specimen of the smaller model in stock."

"I see. *You* were going to be the courier." Her presence suddenly made sense.

"Of course. Mr. Wetherill supplied me with all the information I'd need. In addition to the binoculars there's a kind of password. The other person offers to buy the glasses, apologetically, saying he couldn't help noticing them and he'd been looking for a pair for a long time. Then I—well, the courier—will say: 'Oh, I wouldn't part with them for all the oil in Arabia!'" The smaller girl glanced towards Diana triumphantly, but spoke to me: "Ask her! If you haven't been told all the details yet, Mr. Helm, ask her if I haven't got it right! And if I do, how could I have got it except from her precious Mr. Wetherill?"

There was a little silence then Diana said reluctantly, "Well, that's pretty close, but it doesn't mean—"

"Never mind," I said. "Miss Elfenbein, we stop at Molde, up the coast, in a few hours. For your sake, I hope we see you there. On the dock. With your luggage, your daddy, and your tame P.R. man. Persuade them, doll. Cry, scream, kick, and yell but get them to hell off this boat. Okay, let's wake up Papa…"

Then I saw that Papa was already awake, watching me steadily, unblinkingly, like a snake. There was a cold, vicious hatred in his eyes. Again, I got the impression he wasn't really a very pleasant person, but then, who is?

12

The ship's captain apparently used the same undocking technique everywhere, going ahead against the wire-cable spring line, as I think it's called, and then backing free as soon as the stern had swung out far enough to give him maneuvering room. At least he used it in Molde just as he had in Ålesund.

As we drew away stern first, I waved a friendly hand at the little group standing beside the cluster of suitcases on the dock: the dark-haired girl in the gaily checked slacks, the white-haired man with the bandaged hand, and the tousle-haired young executive type in the sharp sport coat. I didn't really expect to get a response, and, except for a glowering look from Dr. Elfenbein, I didn't. The wind turned sharper and colder as, moving forward now, the ship picked up speed out of the small harbor.

I said, "Let's go have a beer in the lounge. I guess it's still inhabitable; they don't seem to turn on the terrible telly until six."

Shortly, Diana and I were installed in a couple of the comfortable, shackled-down chairs in the first-class lounge. The TV was, happily, blank and silent and a waitress from the dining room was plying us with the best the ship could legally offer in the way of booze, pretty feeble stuff. I took a taste of the Norwegian brew and decided that it tasted no worse than any other beer. You'll gather I'm not really an *aficionado*.

I said, "Okay, now that we're out of the wind, tell me. Am I correct in deducing, from the way you kept trying to stand up for him, that you had a thing going with Mr. Robert Wetherill?"

Diana hesitated. After a moment, she shook her head and said wryly, "No, you're not correct, darling. I would very much have *liked* to have a thing going with Mr. Robert Wetherill, but that's not quite the same thing, is it?"

"Does that mean he just couldn't see you, or that he was looking elsewhere?"

She sighed. "Now who's clairvoyant? If you must know, Robbie's attention was firmly concentrated elsewhere. As a matter of fact, it was really rather funny, I guess, if you had a good sense of humor. There was I yearning after Robbie, who couldn't see me; and there he was yearning after Evelyn, who couldn't see him. And she, well, I think she kind of hoped the Skipper, once he got over the loss of his wife… No, I'm not being fair. I don't *know* that. We weren't quite close enough to compare yearnings. But it would have been like her. She was a very dignified and proper girl, you know, much too dignified and proper to get involved in a hot and messy affair with somebody her own age; but a discreet liaison with a distinguished older man… Oh, damn, I'm being catty, and I promised myself I wouldn't, particularly now she's dead."

I was a little surprised at Hank Priest, with his wartime experience. The group he'd got together—the youthful U.S. part of it, at least—sounded like just the kind of half-baked outfit I'd feared I was getting involved with, with everybody distracted by private little loves and hates and jealousies, and nobody tending to the public business, weird though it might be, that was supposed to be the organization's chief concern.

I said sourly, "It's a wonder any of you got any work done, with all this round-robin yearning going on. But I think you're right about Evelyn Benson, not that it makes much difference now."

"What makes you think so?"

"Something she said when she was dying. Tell me, what's your feeling about our commanding officer, Diana?"

She looked a bit surprised; then she thought for a moment and said carefully, "The Skipper? Why, I think he's a pretty good guy who ran into a bunch of bad luck and is keeping himself very, very busy so he won't have to think about what he's going to do with the rest of his life, and that empty house back in Florida, and the boat he used to love working and cruising and fishing on, that he can't bear to go aboard now after what happened on it."

It was a pretty fair analysis, I decided, as far as it went. I said, "Did you ever feel sorry enough for poor, bereaved

Captain Priest to try to console him, to put it discreetly, in a practical way?"

She spilled a little beer on her knee, jerking around to look at me, shocked and angry. Then she saw I'd been deliberately trying for a reaction, and grinned.

"You louse! The answer is no. What put that idea into your head?"

I offered her my handkerchief to mop with, but she rejected it in favor of a Kleenex from her purse.

I said, "Not what, who. Evelyn Benson. She thought you had, or at least wanted to. 'Doting' was the word she used to describe your attitude towards your employer."

"She must have been crazy—"

"Not crazy, just jealous. I don't know exactly how your duty roster read, but I gather that she was kind of a field girl and you stuck pretty close to headquarters, meaning Hank Priest. And apparently she was so infatuated with our retired naval gent that she took for granted that any woman exposed to him daily, like you, couldn't help but feel the same way. Which seems to confirm your hypotheses."

She looked at me, frowning a little. "What are you trying to prove, Matt?"

"I don't know," I said. "I'm just trying to get all these relationships cleared up. Most of them probably don't mean a thing. Now tell me about Wetherill, Robert, defunct."

Diana winced. "You don't have to be so callous… Ah, nuts. Life goes on, and all that jazz. Robbie was… well, he was a very nice guy in spite of being a patriot."

"The DAR wouldn't like the way you put that," I said with a grin.

"Well, you know. Love it or leave it... and you always have to love it their way, the way it happens to be at the moment. If anybody tries to change it to something a little better, they want to ship him off to Russia or Africa or anywhere. But, well, aside from being a rabid reactionary, he was swell. The Skipper's pretty reactionary too, you know, in certain areas. I guess it's all those years in the military. What America needs, America gets, and to hell with all the poor backward Scandihoovians. Considering that his ancestors came from around here, it seems a funny attitude."

"If it *is* his attitude," I said. "We're not too damned sure about that, remember. He could be kidding somebody, and it could be us."

She shrugged. "Well, he certainly acted as if Robbie was a kindred spirit, and I was just a token liberal he'd hired on to satisfy the ADA or somebody. I felt kind of outnumbered when they got to talking."

I looked at her curiously. "But you still yearned for this Robbie guy?"

She said rather stiffly, "Don't be silly. Who the hell loves a man for his *politics*, for God's sake? Personally, I thought he was a sweet guy, kind of innocent if you know what I mean; and he treated me as if I were his lousy kid sister and told me all about the great, unrequited passion of his life. Ugh!"

"And then he died in an auto accident. Where?"

"Outside Oslo, while we were getting things set up for all this. Have you seen those Norwegian roads, the high ones? A mountain goat could break his neck."

"But you suspected, as the saying goes, foul play?"

She said judiciously, "When you're playing games with people like Dr. Elfenbein and somebody dies unexpectedly, you can't help wondering, can you? We'd heard he was interested and had people snooping around. Robbie had been assigned to check the rumor—Operation Ivory—and if it turned out to be true, to find out whom Elfenbein was working for. Then he died." She shrugged. "Obviously, we had to consider the possibility that he'd got too close to something they didn't want us to know."

"Aloco?"

"What else? You saw that slick P.R. creep with the little pistol who tried to bribe you." She grimaced. "I'd bet he'd sell his grandmother for a quarter and give back twenty cents change. And you heard what he said: anything he couldn't handle, he knew where to hire people who could. Those big companies will do anything to protect their lousy corporate reputations. And Parson Elfenbein, as you call him, would do anything to protect a lucrative job. Matt?"

"Yes?"

"I don't think that little man likes you very much, judging by the way he looked at you. You'd better watch yourself as long as he's around."

"I always do," I said. "No matter who's around. But you'd better watch yourself, too."

"What do you mean?"

"I have a hunch friend Elfenbein has the modern hostage mentality: if the guy you want to hurt—or the society—is too big or tough or elusive, just grab somebody easier and take out your hate on them. In this case, you." I grimaced. "Well, to hell with it. It's been a delightful, relaxing, ocean cruise, Mrs. Barth, and tomorrow we go to work. Trondheim at the crack of dawn, the schedule says. Contact number one."

There was a brief silence. "Matt."

"Yes?"

"Am I *supposed* to be scared?"

"Drink your beer," I said. "You're the little girl who loves being scared, remember?"

13

Back down the coast in Bergen, I'd heard they were feeling very cocky nowadays, because the latest census figures indicated they'd overtaken Trondheim and were now the largest city in northern Norway. It seemed like an odd cause for pride, these crowded days. If I were a Trondheimer, I reflected, I'd concede the population title graciously, happy to know that people were settling elsewhere and leaving my home town alone.

Trondheim was still a sizable community, as far as I could make out from the ship. It looked like an old, historical, well-established place; apparently it had not been systematically wrecked by the withdrawing Germans back in '45. The guidebook said there was an old cathedral, intact and worth seeing. There were also, apparently, some massive ex-Nazi submarine pens at the end of the harbor, now used for peaceful ship repairs and associated activities. I couldn't make out either of these points of interest but it was only a little after six on a misty and drizzly Arctic morning, and the visibility was terrible.

Not terrible enough, however, I thought wryly. What I needed, if I was going to be subtle, was a fog with less than ten feet of visibility, that would allow me to get myself—and later, Diana—off the ship without being seen; but maybe that was too much to ask for.

The water looked too cold and dirty for swimming. I'd never learned to fly without an airplane—as a matter of fact I wasn't much good at flying with one. That left only one way to get ashore, and I made my way down the damp, steep, cleated gangplank to the pier, flipped a mental coin, and turned left.

The Trondheim railroad station is quite near the docks. The roof of it had been pointed out to me by the ship's purser. However, there are all kinds of tracks and railroad yards in between, and to reach the station, I'd been told, I'd have to either go left a couple of hundred yards around the end of them, or right a quarter of a mile to an underpass tunneling beneath them. My simple-minded plan was just to make the circle tour and see what Diana might have to cope with in keeping her—well, Madeleine Barth's—rendezvous in the station restaurant, time unspecified. In the meantime, she was staying in her cabin with my .38 for company, although she'd complained that by this time she and Mr. Smith and Mr. Wesson had very little left to say to each other.

It was a damp walk in the penetrating drizzle, and I hoped the gent behind me had forgotten his raincoat and was getting good and wet. I wasn't quite sure where I'd picked him up, but suddenly I was just aware of him back there. Well, he'd keep. I paid him no attention. I just hiked along the curving road and made my way through a muddy construction area—one of these days, I hope, they'll stop rebuilding the world and let us settle down to live in it. Then the station was ahead of me, a big building obviously designed by folks who'd had the old-fashioned notion that railroad stations were fairly important structures and ought to look it.

The restaurant was at the near end, a big, high-ceilinged cafeteria. I went in and got a cup of coffee and a piece of pastry, which wasn't as good as the stuff I remembered eating in Sweden some years back; but maybe I'm prejudiced because my ancestors came from there. Anyway, it beat the plastic doughnuts served up in equivalent U.S. eateries.

Sitting in a small booth, I surveyed the room, sparsely populated at this hour of the morning. The only individual at all out of the ordinary was a well-dressed, elderly gent sitting half a dozen booths down the aisle; and he was distinctive only because he had with him a pair of handsome hunting dogs—German shorthaired pointers. That's the good-sized spotty one with the stubby tail. Well, all the Continental breeds have docked tails, as far as I know. In case you haven't got them straight, the cute little ones are Brittanies, the handsome, red-brown fellow is a Vizla, and the odd, smoky-gray guy is a Weimaraner. Anyway, that's what I was told by a Labrador fancier, but he had no use for any dog that wasn't black. He wouldn't even have a yellow or chocolate Lab around the place, although the colors are perfectly legitimate, according to the breed standard I'd had to read in the line of duty—I was pretending to be a guy who knew something about dogs, at the time.

Sipping my coffee, I wondered idly if maybe the dogs might not be a secret signal of some kind. After all, there had been an old man with a dog in the restaurant in Ålesund where I'd last talked with Hank Priest. I toyed with the notion playfully. One dog, all clear. Two dogs, condition yellow. Three dogs, condition red...

It was an intriguing idea, but I decided regretfully that I probably just kept seeing dogs in restaurants because the relaxed Norwegians allowed dogs in restaurants, and more power to them. By now the gent outside—he hadn't followed me in—had had time to get nicely soaked, I hoped. I went out without looking around and hiked off through the drizzle in the direction from which I hadn't come. Pretty soon I had him behind me again. Here the road ran along a kind of canal or inlet. There were some beautiful, sturdy fishing boats tied up along the sides. You can say what you like in favor of fiberglass, and it may well be the boat material of the future if the petroleum from which it's derived holds out, but for pretty, it doesn't compare with wood, particularly varnished wood.

Then the road curved right, away from the canal, and ducked down into the underpass beneath the railroad tracks. I'd reached the end of my orbit in this direction and would shortly be heading back for reentry. It was a long tunnel, not very well lighted. I stopped when I'd come about thirty feet from the entrance.

I didn't have long to wait. I heard his footsteps coming. They never paused. He just marched around the corner, a husky familiar figure with that wide-brimmed hat, and walked up to me. I was happy to see that he was actually pretty wet, although he did have a raincoat. We faced each other for a moment.

"You make a lousy shadow, Paul," I said. "I hope you weren't really trying. I taught you better than that… What the hell are you doing?"

There was a black-and-white-striped barricade, like a sawhorse, standing at the side of the tunnel. Apparently there had been some construction or road-patching done down here, too. Denison had hung his hat on the end of it. Now he was taking off his raincoat and jacket, together. He laid these across the horse. Then he took a snub-nosed Colt revolver from a waistband holster and tucked it into the pocket of the coat. He reached down and got a flat little knife from under his pants leg somewhere, and stuffed that in with the gun, and turned to face me.

"There's been enough horsing around," he said. "You can't kill me; L.A. will put too much heat on your outfit if you do. But I can't kill you, either. If I do, Mac will say to hell with Mr. Kotko and send out the executioners, the termination squads, anyway. Agreed?"

"Okay so far," I said. "Which brings us where?"

He stood there for a moment, his handsome, tanned face wet and shiny in the dusk of the tunnel. "It's a funny damn thing," he said slowly. "Do a guy a good turn, and often he'll detest you the rest of his life for putting him in your debt. Do him a bad turn, and pretty soon you find yourself hating the self-righteous sonofabitch you double-crossed… It ought to be the other way around, don't you think?"

"Well, I'm not exactly fond of you these days, Paul," I said.

"Ah, but you don't *hate* me," he said softly. "You'll flatten me like a mosquito, given a chance—or try—but you don't live it and sleep it. I know you. Hell, after the first, you probably never thought about me once a year. I was just a bit of unfinished business you'd take care of if you ever got the word to go; meanwhile it was ancient history and to hell with it. But I've been looking over my shoulder for seven years, waiting for you, you bastard."

As he said, it was kind of a backwards situation. By any reasonable standard, I was the injured party. The whole thing was ridiculous, but he was rolling up his shirtsleeves, and what he had in mind was fairly obvious, if fairly childish. Well, hell, when it came to a personal matter, like an old betrayed friendship, I could be as childish as anybody. I removed my hat, coat, and jacket, and laid them beside his. I stuck my gun and knife into the coat pocket as he had. Then we had to stand there a moment, looking innocent, as a car made its way through the long tunnel.

I said, "Hell, I haven't done this since grammar, school. We used to go out behind the gym where the teachers couldn't see us."

"That's enough talk," he said. "Let's fight."

He put down his head and came in swinging. It was rather touching in a way. I mean, he was putting himself into my hands. It was his party, and he was indicating how he wanted it run; but there was nothing compelling me to play by his infantile rules. There are a number of adult responses to that clumsy windmill attack that leave the other party in a very bad shape. We're taught most of them and he knew it because he'd been there. If I wanted to trot out the fancy stuff, he was telling me, that was my privilege; but it could cancel all obligations between us, because this time he was playing it straight...

I met him and traded blows with him blocking, chopping, feeling him out awkwardly. It would have looked like hell in a ring or gym. The honest-to-God fact was that we weren't very good at it. The manly sport of boxing wasn't part of the repertory of dirty tricks we'd been taught, so we didn't look very professional as we circled each other, fists up, looking for openings. Then I slipped one through and caught him on the mouth, and at the same time he got me hard in the ribs. Stung, we both forgot about caution and started slugging heedlessly. Abruptly he broke away.

"Hold it!" he panted. "Car coming!"

We leaned against the tunnel wall, looking as peaceful as possible, while a small truck came through heading for the docks.

"Ding-dong bell," Denison said. "Second round. Ready?"

We went at it again. Twice more we had to stop and

act innocent while vehicles passed. It was, I suppose, a stupid damned business, two grown men pounding each other with knuckles. My own theory had always been that you leave the guy alone or you leave him dead. There are often sound arguments for removing people permanently but none, I used to feel, for beating them up.

Well, I'd been wrong. Denison had found one, or made one. Remembering a man called Mark, and a man called John, and a girl named Luisa, all dead due to his treachery, I found myself taking a good deal of satisfaction in each blow that landed solidly. I found it even more satisfying when he began to give ground and I drove him backwards savagely, looking for a way to finish him off. He slipped and went to one knee.

Old reflexes came into action; I started the lethal kick that would do the job right, and stopped with some difficulty. This crazy fight wasn't like that. Instead of killing him, I stepped back politely to let him get to his feet. I was surprised to see him try, and fail to make it.

"Soft living, Luke?" I gasped. My voice sounded harsh and rusty.

"Hell, you can hardly stand up yourself, Eric," he panted and I realized that he was perfectly right. "Give me a hand, you sonofabitch," he breathed.

The thought of a final trick passed through my mind as I stepped forward to help him up; but of course there was no trick. He leaned against the striped sawhorse, breathing deeply and raggedly, while I steadied myself against the tunnel wall trying to catch up with my own respiration.

"I guess that's enough exercise for one morning," he said at last. "If you want to say you licked me, you're welcome."

"Go to hell," I said.

"You understand, I don't regret a goddamn thing," he said without looking at me. "Not any of it. Except maybe that I couldn't put you down just now."

"Sure."

He drew a long, uneven breath. "Well, I guess we haven't settled anything except that we're the world's two lousiest boxers. They'd have booed us out of the ring... Matt."

"Yes?"

"You can send the girl in safely. I've had somebody keeping an eye on Elfenbein since you put him ashore with a mangled hand—some day you'll have to tell me about that. Whatever you did to him, it made him mad as hell, but he's a pro and he's playing it cool nevertheless. He's letting this drop go by, figuring to get the stuff from you later, before you hand it over to your naval captain up north—I guess he knows Priest has specified he's to make delivery to L.A. in person, no substitutes accepted. Maybe Elfenbein figures letting you make this first contact peacefully will throw you off guard, or something."

"You seem to know a lot about what Elfenbein figures," I said.

Denison grinned. "Hell, that fancy Aloco P.R. boy has dollar signs for eyes. Norman Yale. I've had him on the payroll for weeks and I think he's collecting elsewhere as well. A real clever lad, playing us all against each other, and crying all the way to the bank about his lost integrity.

Well, I'm in no position to criticize anybody for liking money—I'll say it for you, Matt—but the little shithead doesn't seem to realize he's messing with folks who play for keeps. However, as long as he lasts he's very useful, if slightly expensive."

"Has Dr. E. got himself any additional muscle?" I asked.

"That's another reason he's leaving this drop alone," Denison said. "He's got three plug-uglies on the way and he doesn't want to make his move until they arrive. You can figure on being hit in Svolvaer, one way or another. But here you're okay."

14

I was waiting by the ship's gangplank, entertaining myself by calling myself a naïve and incompetent jackass for trusting a man who'd already betrayed me once—how gullible could you get?—when I saw Diana returning, at last, along the rain-wet road. She had the bright scarf she'd used before tied over her head to protect her hair. She was wearing her own gray slacks and sweater, and Evelyn Benson's tan raincoat, left open despite the weather so as not to make too obvious the fact that it was slightly too small for her. The cased binoculars were slung casually over her shoulder.

Even at a distance, I could tell everything was fine. Although she'd got pretty wet hiking to the railroad station and back, wet enough that she was no longer bothering to avoid any but the largest puddles, she walked lightly and briskly, almost skipping along through the cold drizzle; obviously a girl who was happy and pleased with herself for carrying out a dangerous mission successfully.

I drew a relieved breath and made a silent apology to Paul Denison, the calculating louse. He'd managed to change our relationship drastically this morning, and I didn't think for a moment it had come about by accident. First he'd let me have the satisfaction of beating him to his knees—well, one knee—and now his report on Elfenbein had saved me a lot of unnecessary precautions; and what the hell, seven years was a long time to stay mad at a guy, whatever he'd done.

The trouble was, he was applying his psychology to the wrong man. Mac had indicated what was expected of me. He had said there was no *current* word on Paul Denison. He had said that, *until the situation changed or could be changed*, Mr. Denison was untouchable. He had said that he hoped he'd made himself clear; and he had.

The literal record made by the phone monitors said one thing, in case anybody cared to investigate later; but any agent with half a brain and a little experience could, and was expected to, read a totally different set of instructions from that record. The cold fact was that the sentence of death had once more been passed on Paul Denison.

What I'd actually been directed to do, in careful Washington doubletalk, was change the situation in such a way that Mr. Denison could at last, in the jargon of our great fellow-organization with its lovely estate down in Virginia, be safely terminated with extreme prejudice. The termination squads, as Paul himself had called them, had not been alerted—it's very seldom that Mac puts together that kind of a group these days, and never to deal with just one man—but a single terminator, if you want to call him that, had. Me.

Diana came running up the gangplank and stopped in the shelter of the deck to yank off her kerchief and shake it vigorously. Her hair, judiciously darkened by the dye Hank Priest had supplied, was further darkened around the edges now by rain. She looked damp and flushed and pretty, all breathless from hurrying and I discovered—it seemed to be a morning for awkward personal discoveries—that I was so glad to have her back that it frightened me a little. I mean, it's always advisable in the business to keep clearly in mind that everybody's expendable. It's much better not to get emotionally involved, today, with an associate, male or female, whom you may have to write off tomorrow in the line of duty.

"Don't look so grim, darling," Diana said, smiling. "Everything's wonderful. Were you worried?"

"Sure," I said. "Of course, the Skipper said this drop wasn't really essential, so I wasn't too concerned about that; but when you didn't get back I started wondering where the hell I could scrounge up another female for the important Svolvaer contact. Not to mention those special glasses."

She laughed. "I love you, too, you coldblooded creep," she said. "My God, I'm soaked to the skin! How about buying a girl a cup of coffee to warm her up?"

Inside the dining salon, I helped her off with her wet coat—well, the late Evelyn Benson's wet coat—and hung it over an empty chair. I went to the end of the room and returned to the table with two cups of coffee.

"Nothing to eat?" I asked.

"Heavens, no! I stuffed myself in that damned restaurant, waiting. He let me eat everything on my plate and go back for seconds before he deigned to wander by at last and notice the binoculars. The old jerk! Did you know that they let *dogs* into restaurants around here, Matt?"

"Oh, that guy," I said. "He was there earlier; he must have had a long wait. Didn't you see any dogs in Oslo or Bergen?"

"Well, I guess so, but I must have figured they were seeing-eye dogs or something. But this old character had those two big bird dogs with him, right there in the cafeteria with everybody eating. Crazy!"

She was all hopped up with her experience; she was talking too brightly and too fast, about anything but what was really in her mind: the long scary wait, the tense contact, and finally the triumphant knowledge that she'd actually done it. She, Diana Lawrence, the timid friend of the blackfooted ferret and the whooping crane, had actually pulled off a risky assignment without benefit of protective seat belts, ignition interlocks, crashproof bumpers, or miracle antibiotics. She'd done the civilized unthinkable. She'd deliberately gambled with her life; and she had won. She'd never be quite the same girl again.

She was smart enough not to want to spoil it by discussing it yet. And of course I wouldn't have dreamed of pointing out that it had actually been a pretty simple little errand and the risk hadn't really been very great.

After all, you couldn't judge this girl and her achievement by hardboiled undercover standards. She'd been brought up on the modern philosophy that any risk is totally unacceptable and everybody's supposed to live forever, or at least present the body, intact and unscarred, to the geriatric intensive care ward for final processing, after a long, safe, and uneventful life.

"What's crazy about it?" I asked. "I think it's great."

"Dogs in restaurants? But isn't it *unsanitary*?"

I grinned. "Where's that brave and independent female spirit who's mad because everybody keeps protecting her from germs and auto accidents against her will? As a matter of fact, I took a course in how to deal with attack and guard dogs once and we were told that dogs have very clean mouths and if we were bitten not to worry too much, assuming we survived the bites. Now, if we were bitten by a human guard, that was different, and we'd better get medical aid fast before infection set in; a human bite is almost as poisonous as that of a rattlesnake. Maybe, if we let all the dogs in and kept all the people out, we'd have a lot nicer and safer restaurants."

She laughed. "I didn't know you were a dog man, Matt."

"I'm not," I said. "Not really, but I had to travel with a mutt once—actually a very well-bred and well-trained young retriever, part of my cover for the assignment—and I got damned sick and tired of being treated like a leper accompanied by a rabid wolf. Hell, that pup was a lot better behaved than most of the humans we met along the way. And he was a damned sight better company than a lot of agents I've worked with. Present company excepted, of course."

"Thank you, sir," she said. She'd had time to wind down a bit now and she glanced at the binocular case on the table. "But, talking about agents and their work, aren't you even going to look at it?" She pushed it towards me.

"Why should I?" I asked. "When you obviously have, and are aching to tell me all about it?"

"More clairvoyance, Mr. Helm?" She grinned tomboyishly. "As a matter of fact, I did slip into the ladies' room and take a peek—"

That figured. Wanting desperately to grab the stuff and run, she'd forced herself to walk calmly down the hall and spend a little longer in the building, just to see if she could.

"Tut-tut," I said. "Not very smart, Agent Lawrence. Statistically, a public john is a very dangerous place."

"But your great good friend Paul Denison had assured you I was perfectly safe, remember? Not that I believed it. I was scared stiff the whole time; but that's what you told me."

"Sure, safe from Elfenbein," I said. "But he said nothing whatever, nor did I, about your being safe from Denison, even behind the door marked DAMER. Here, as it happened, you were, because his employer is concerned chiefly with Torbotten and doesn't give a damn about Ekofisk and Frigg, at least not at the moment. But don't ever count on Paul's being a friend of mine, or yours. Basically, he's a friend of Paul Denison and nobody else." I glanced down. "Well, what did our doggy contact slip into that slightly-too-large case when he took the money out?" I'd noticed earlier that the leather container, although it had all the right markings, didn't fit the glasses inside quite as well as it might have, for obvious reasons.

Diana said, "Well, it's an envelope full of onionskin paper, with a lot of numbers and funny symbols and a lot of words in Norwegian that I couldn't understand. It looked like the kind of super-technical stuff I probably wouldn't understand if somebody translated it into English."

I said, "At least they're keeping it simple. No microdots or microfilms or any of that jazz. Or tapes. After all that political mess in Washington, I couldn't look a tape in the face."

"Well, you'd better take charge of it," she said. "You can have the responsibility of protecting it. I've done my part; I got it here at the risk of Denison and double pneumonia. Do you really think we have to watch out for Denison? After all, he's kind of on our side, isn't he? He wants Mr. Kotko to get this material and the Svolvaer material, doesn't he? Just as we do?"

"Not necessarily just as we do," I said. "We don't deliver direct to Kotko, do we? We deliver to the Skipper who delivers to Kotko, isn't that right? At least that's what I gathered, indirectly, from something he said in Ålesund, and Denison kind of confirmed it this morning. Of course, nobody tells me anything directly. It's more fun to watch me work blindfolded."

"Poor Matt," she said. "But you might try asking, some time. The answer is, yes, the Skipper will make contact with us on the ferry that goes from the Lofoten Islands to Narvik on the mainland. It's an overnight boat-ride, starting from Svolvaer at nine in the evening. The Skipper will take over everything as soon as he thinks it's safe; he'll take it from there, and get it to Kotko."

"Sounds great," I said. "Of course, we've got to get it first…"

15

They had some peculiar machinery on that ship. It ran all the time. In a way it was very restful. There was never that sudden, shocking, dead hush in the middle of the night when they pull into a port and everything shuts down and you lie in the eerie silence listening to the distant thumps and bumps on deck and waiting for all the shafts and gears and pistons, or whatever it is that runs the bucket, to go into soothing, rhythmic action once more so you can go back to sleep...

That last night on board, I awoke anyway, some time after midnight. Something told me we weren't moving. I rose and glanced out the porthole and saw the lights of a little harbor reflected in the still water.

"Where are we?" Diana's voice asked from behind me, thick with sleep.

I said, "If I remember the schedule right, tonight it's either Brønnøysund, Sandnessjøen, or Nesna. Take your choice. Of course, this late in the season, they seem to be passing up some of the minor stops, so it may be that one or two of those candidates aren't in the running. In the morning we hit Ørnes, followed by Bodø and Stamsund. Then comes the moment of truth, Svolvaer, at twenty-one hundred hours, nine pee em to you. Since the ferry to the mainland leaves at nine, you said, we probably couldn't make the connection if we wanted to. Anyway, we've got a bit of business to transact, so we'll have to stay over in the Lofotens at least one full day."

"We?" she said, invisible in the darkness. "Oooh, listen to the lousy male chauvinist! Anybody'd think he was the one who'd hiked endless miles in the freezing rain to keep the gas tanks of America from going dry, dry, dry. Anybody'd think he's the one who'll be standing all alone, like a target in a shooting gallery, on a windy hill beside an airstrip hewed from solid Arctic granite, or whatever kind of geology they have around here... Matt."

"What?"

"About Robbie. I've been thinking. Robbie might have betrayed us. I don't think he did, but I suppose it's possible. But he'd never have betrayed Evelyn. He'd never have done anything to put her into a position where she might get hurt."

"And he didn't," I said. "At least he did his best not to. Whether it was Wetherill or somebody else, he was very careful not to give the Elfenbein forces the name of the courier, remember?"

"What does that prove?"

"Well, whoever talked out of class had all the other

information. He knew about the specific drops, the binoculars, and the whole password routine. Little Greta rattled it all off word-perfect, if you recall. Is it likely that her informant really didn't know who the Skipper was sending north to pick up the stuff? But he held it back, that's the significant point. He fixed it so they couldn't grab Evelyn on her way to join me, and dispose of her before she got to Bergen; they didn't know her. They had to wait until she stepped aboard the ship and asked for a certain cabin. In other words, he'd arranged it so she'd be safe until she'd arrived where she'd be under the protection of that infallible super-bodyguard, M. Helm."

"Do you like kicking yourself because it feels so good when you stop?" Diana murmured. "Well, never mind. Do you want to know something? I'm still scared. When I think of what happened to Evelyn, and Robbie, I get all jellylike inside, particularly when you mention nasty words like Svolvaer and Elfenbein."

I grinned in the dark. "You love it," I said. "You told me so yourself. It makes you feel alive. It makes you feel real."

"It makes me feel real, all right," she said. "Come here and I'll show you how real I feel." I went, and she showed. It was a very convincing demonstration for a girl who had, at our first meeting, impressed me as being rather pale and dull. A long time later, she said, "Matt."

"Uhuh."

"Is it considered very improper to talk about love? Among secret agents, I mean?"

I lay in the warm, crowded little berth and listened to

the steady beat of the ship's machinery. "Very improper," I said.

"Well, I'm a very improper person, darling. At least I seem to be getting that way fast after long years of strict propriety—well, more or less strict. And I'm falling very much in love with you, I think." After a while, when I didn't speak, she said, "Did you hear me?"

"I heard you."

"Well?"

"Physical relations, even intimate physical relations, are permissible between operatives," I said formally. "Emotional attachments, on the other hand, are frowned upon, ma'am."

"Then it's just as well that I'm not really an operative, I'm just a girl," she said. "May I ask, sir, if you feel no emotional attachment whatever?"

I said, "You're an inquisitive bitch. I'll take the Fifth on that one, Judge. Go to sleep."

She laughed softly, and fell asleep in my arms. The following morning I slipped ashore at one stop and made a call to Oslo. In the evening, after an otherwise uneventful day of steaming through spectacular scenery frosted with snow at the higher elevations—we were now north of the Arctic Circle—we landed in Svolvaer in the dark.

There seemed to be nobody waiting, hostile or friendly, to greet us on the lighted dock. There seemed to be no sinister figures lurking in the shadows. Presently some taxis materialized. I commandeered one. It transported us and our luggage to a hotel not far from the waterfront;

a blocky, red, frame building several stories high, with one of those tiny elevators beloved by Europeans. After the formalities at the desk had been concluded, the diminutive cage carried us up to our room—all pretense of chastity had been discarded, and we were now, for the record, Mr. and Mrs. Helm—where we were greeted by the usual tiny Norwegian beds, two of them, side by side in the middle of the floor.

They displayed another Norsk sleeping trick, which is to pass up the normal bedding arrangements in favor of a single bottom sheet. A bolster or comforter protected by a kind of linen bag serves as a unified substitute for top sheet and blankets. This all-in-one contraption is carefully sized so it's too small to tuck in all around. On a cold night, you keep nice and warm chasing the slippery, elusive thing as it tries to escape to the floor.

Some time after we'd settled down sedately in our separate toy beds like the blasé married folks we were now supposed to be, I heard the whistle from the direction of the docks signaling the ship's departure. It made me feel deserted and lonely. I'd become kind of dependent on that floating home, I guess, and on the competent captain I'd never seen. It was like being expelled from a warm, safe womb into a cold, hard, friendless world.

"Matt."

"Yes," I said.

"Maybe I should have gone to the airport right away," Diana said worriedly. "What if you're wrong. What if our contact expected…"

"He'll wait till morning," I said. "He's supposed to be a timid type, and he didn't pick an exposed hilltop for the drop for nothing. He wants to see who's sneaking up on him. He can't do that in the dark. And I'm not going to have you scrambling around strange Arctic rocks in the middle of the night. You might fall and break a leg, and I'd have to shoot you; and I'm short of cartridges for the only gun I have that's worth a damn—just Bjørn's one clip, with one shot gone already."

"You're all heart," she said. "I'm so glad you care. Good night, darling."

I didn't sleep, of course. Not tonight. I was all caught up on my sleep. I'd had plenty of sleep on the ship, despite distractions and there were things to be figured out—but I couldn't figure them out.

Actually, I'd worked all the combinations in my head already, several times. Now I made a last effort to see if there wasn't something I'd missed, some other way it could be done. If there was, I couldn't find it. It would have to be a sacrifice play. All I could do, besides keep the losses as low as possible, was make as certain as possible that the gambit would pay off. That, I reflected grimly, would make it all worthwhile as far as the big boys were concerned—the big Washington boys, one in particular. They never concern themselves much with minor losses as long as you can present them with major payoffs.

At eleven o'clock, still wide awake, I got up and started dressing in the dark. I heard Diana stir.

"No," I said. "No lights, doll."

"What are you going to do?"

"Sneak out of here, making like the invisible man, I hope. When you keep your airport appointment, I'll be somewhere around. It's several kilometers out of town, according to the guy at the desk. I'd better do it on foot and keep out of sight while I'm doing it, and I want to be there ahead of anybody else with the same idea, so I'm giving myself plenty of lead time."

There was a long silence while she thought it over. When she spoke, her voice was quite steady: "All right, if you think it will work. I certainly won't mind a bit of moral support out there; but if you won't be here to hold my hand when I leave for the rendezvous, you'd better brief me now. For instance, when should I start?"

"Wait for daylight," I said. "At this latitude, this time of year, the sun won't actually be up until well after eight, but there's a long morning twilight. It'll probably start getting light, after a fashion, some time around five. Wait until you can really see. As I said, I don't think our contact will risk approaching you until it's good and light out there, and anyway, I need reasonable illumination to cover you properly."

"Should I... should I kind of talk to myself in here when I get up, to make it sound as if you're still here?"

"Swell," I said. "We'll make a lady superspy of you yet."

"What about transportation? Should I figure on walking, too?"

"That's not necessary," I said. "To put it bluntly, you're just as vulnerable on foot as you are in a cab. We're gambling that they'll play it cool, like in Trondheim, until we actually have the information they want. That's the logical thing for them to do, wait until it's all in one place before they grab it."

"What makes you so certain they're even around, Matt? Maybe you really put the fear of God into them, isn't it possible, in spite of what Denison said? There hasn't been a sign of anybody since we left them on the dock back in Molde."

I said, "Dr. Elfenbein has been masterminding his specialized brand of larceny too long to be scared off by a little hole in the hand. It'll only make him more determined to beat us. This is just his *modus operandi*, as we sleuths call it. He used it on me in Bergen, remember, leaving me strictly alone, no signs of surveillance, until the time came to hit and hit hard."

"You're such a cheerful man to work with," she said. "Always looking on the bright side."

Finished dressing, I sat down on the edge of her little bed. "Of course, I may have it figured wrong," I said. "The crystal ball is a little cloudy. It could happen earlier than I think. That could leave me hiding behind a rock way outside town twiddling my thumbs while you're impersonating Custer's Last Stand somewhere along the route, or even in here."

"Like I said, cheerful," she murmured. "Any advice to cover that happy eventuality?"

"Here are some extra cartridges for the gun I lent you," I said. "Keep them handy. I showed you how to reload. And remember, a firearm is not a magic wand, and you're not anybody's fairy godmother. I think I mentioned that before."

"Mention it again," she said. "Let me see if I remember."

"You've got to *shoot* the thing to accomplish anything significant," I said. "Just waving it around chanting ancient incantations like 'Put your hands up,' or 'Drop that gun,' or 'Don't come any closer or I'll pull the trigger,' won't buy you a thing. Yank it out and fire it or leave it alone. And if you shoot it, do a good job. Use both hands like I showed you, hold steady, keep firing, and really perforate that target. Never mind the Cossacks attacking from the left flank and the Apaches galloping in from the right, whooping and hollering. Get that guy in front of you and get him good. You'll be surprised how discouraging one thoroughly dead gent can be to a lot of people." I hesitated. "Oh, and don't let anybody talk you into giving up that pistol, no matter how prettily he pleads."

"What do you mean?" she demanded indignantly. "I'm not likely to—"

"You've never been there, sweetheart," I said gently. "You don't really know what you're likely to do until you do it. Just don't fall for that line about how we're all reasonable people here and just hand over that gun, you know you're not *really* going to shoot it, my dear, so please pass it across and let's talk things over in a civilized manner... Don't give it to *anybody*, and if somebody tries to take it, figure that's all the proof you need of his hostile intentions, and blast him to hell right then."

She gave a short little laugh. "It sounds as if I'll be wading knee deep in blood, come morning.".

"Probably not," I said. "If you're ready to use that revolver on the slightest provocation, if you're absolutely certain in your mind that nobody but nobody is going to take it from you until it's empty and you're dead, you'll probably make it without firing a shot. People don't like to go up against a hairtrigger lady just licking her lips in happy anticipation of a gory massacre. If you march straight at them, letting them know you're prepared to make your fight right there, live or die, they'll probably let you through. But if you start trying to figure out some easy, safe, noiseless, bloodless way of doing it, if you start worrying about laws and morals, and how much racket you'll make and what the folks back home will think, if you attempt one of those idiot stick-them-up-or-I'll-shoot routines you've seen in the movies, well, it's been nice knowing you, kid. I'll put some posies on your grave, if I can find it…"

I didn't know where the back door of the hotel was located, and it didn't matter anyway. If there was one, and if they were working at surveillance, they'd have it covered. I was betting, however, that Dr. Elfenbein would be a victim of his own *modus operandi*. Once they find something that works pretty well, they tend to get hung up on it, particularly if they have a tendency towards believing they're smarter than other folks. I was gambling that, enamoured of his own cleverness, Elfenbein would keep his people well back so as not to alert us, until the time came for action. After all, he undoubtedly knew where we were, and he certainly knew where we'd be going in the morning, or Diana would. He didn't have to keep watch on us.

Whether I had him figured right or wrong, nobody followed me away from the hotel. After making sure of this, I hiked back towards the center of Svolvaer and past it, and found the taxi waiting near the dock at the point the driver had indicated, never mind how, while taking us to the hotel, earlier. I got into the rear, and he drove away.

"Sorry to keep you waiting," I said, and we went through a little secret-agent business.

"You are Eric," he said, when the formal identification procedure had been concluded. "I am Rolf."

"Happy to know you, Rolf," I said. "What are your instructions concerning me?"

"The man in Washington signals, by way of Oslo, that you are to be helped in every way possible, short of homicide. That is not my specialty. I understand yours. What do you need, friend Eric?"

I told him.

16

"Sigmund!" said the old lady. "That wicked, bloodthirsty man with a heart of stone!"

She was a rather striking old lady, with white hair done up in a bun at the nape of her neck; and a seamed, peasant face as rugged as the rocky island on which she lived. From the lined old face poked a pair of young, bright-blue eyes. Her English was considerably better than average for her generation—I doubt they taught it in the schools back when she was that age, although they do now—but otherwise she was the kind of old lady you'd expect to find, in a long, old-fashioned dress, rocking peacefully by the fire of a picturesque old Scandinavian farmhouse as she knitted warm winter clothes for her grandchildren's children.

Actually I'd found her, in slacks and a sweater, sitting on an unfortunate couch, the Nordic equivalent of Grand Rapids modern, in a fairly new little house that, with certain concessions to local tastes and weather conditions, could have been lifted bodily from any U.S. housing development catering to lower-middle income groups. The slick little living room had no more character than a motel unit. It differed from its American counterpart only in that there was no television set. Instead, there was a goodsized and fairly expensive radio, to which the old lady had been listening when Rolf showed me in. She'd turned it off, politely, to entertain me, while Rolf disappeared to make certain arrangements.

I said, "You should make allowances, Mrs. Sigurdsen. All men have hearts of stone when there's a war to be fought."

"All men do not let hostages die, *min herre*. All men do not send brave volunteer fighters to their deaths in order to create a mere—what do you call it, diversion, distraction? All men do not sink ships and wait on shore to cut the throats of those who escape the icy waters. Even Germans, even Nazis, are human beings, *min herre* although I will admit I had some doubts at the time. But not to be slaughtered when they are helpless and lined up on the beach in stiff rows, like dead fish. Six hundred Germans died that night and half a dozen of our men, including one of my sons, were sacrificed in cold blood so that the killing could take place. Sigmund! And now he comes again; and again the men follow him, like so many sheeps—"

She stopped as Rolf came back into the room. "Grandmother!" he protested. "Whatever you think of Sigmund, he is this gentleman's good friend."

"Then this gentleman should know what kind of a good friend he has; a man who will let him die without a moment's hesitation, just so he can kill, kill, kill."

"Grandmother, please!"

It was a new slant on Hank Priest, who'd always seemed to me a fairly conventional gent for a military man. Of course, you don't make a career of the armed forces if homicide bothers you terribly; but I hadn't realized the Skipper had made quite such a hobby of it in his younger days. *Ingenious*, *effective*, and *ruthless*, Mac had said. Well, I was hardly in a position to pass judgment, considering my own profession.

I followed Rolf out of the house and got into the taxi beside him. "How did it go?" I asked.

"Communications were satisfactory," he said. "The aircraft will be there at o-seven-thirty as you requested. It will land at the usual signal. The formalities are being arranged, so there will be no official interference. You must not mind Grandmother. My uncle, the one who died, was her favorite son, I think."

"Sure," I said. "Tell me about it... Oh, take me somewhere near the airport road, where I can get out without being seen. I'll walk from there."

"Very well." He turned a corner, and said, "The way it started, I was told, was a guerrilla raid on Blomdal, a little village down the coast. Five German soldiers were killed. The Nazi colonel was very angry. He took hostages, ten for each dead man. If the guilty did not give themselves up, he proclaimed, the hostages would die. Nobody surrendered. The fifty hostages were shot. Sigmund disappeared. He was not heard from for months.

It was thought that remorse had affected him, perhaps, or that his superiors in England had disapproved of his behavior and withdrawn him permanently. The Germans relaxed. Then one night there was a strong attack—at least it looked like a strong attack; actually it was carried out by only a handful of men—on a munitions depot at Varsjøen, back in the hills. But a big attack had been expected. A quisling had given information. The Germans were ready. They had a great trap prepared, utilizing every soldier who could be spared; they were going to catch Sigmund at last—"

"Did the men know they were being sent into a trap?"

"It is said they did not. It is also said that the informer had actually been fed his information by one of Sigmund's agents. All this has been said, but it has not been proved. The facts are that, with most of the Nazi soldiers engaged back in the mountains, Sigmund was free to make his arrangements on the coast by Rosviken, through which a troop transport was scheduled to pass that night."

"Rosviken," I said. "The Bay of Roses. Nice."

"Yes, there were red roses blooming there that night," said Rolf, apparently a poet at heart. "Everything went as planned. The explosion occurred at the proper time and place. The ship sank. The German troops that were not killed outright, and did not die of exposure or drowning, were dispatched by Sigmund's guerrillas as they struggled ashore. In the morning, on the door of the Nazi headquarters, was a neat sign in German. I'll try to translate: TEN FOR ONE IS THE GAME,

HERR OBERST. YOUR MOVE."

I whistled softly. "Our naval friend plays rough."

"I was only a boy at the time," Rolf said, "but I remember that there was much talk against Sigmund by those who thought it was too terrible a thing even for war—you heard my grandmother. But others, well, it was a bad time for Norway, and there were many who took new heart, hearing that the brutal Nazis had for once been given a taste of—how do you say it?—their own medicine, by someone as strong and brutal as themselves. Because the joke was on the Nazi Oberst, the colonel. He could not, even if he wanted to, even if he had the authority, execute five or six thousand Norwegians in reply. Not up here in the north where there are not so many people. There would have been no one left to do the work. He was removed shortly afterwards in disgrace... Here you are, Eric. Good luck."

"Sure," I said, getting out. "Thanks."

"Just walk straight down the road to the left."

It was a long hike in the dark, but it was easy walking along a reasonably good, gravel road, and at this time of night there was no traffic. For a while I had the sea, or an arm of it, gleaming on my right; then the bay ended, and the road swung out onto a peninsula of sorts, and there was the airstrip behind a chain-link fence. The road branched, the main thoroughfare such as it was leading left to what seemed to be an unfenced boarding area, while a smaller track swung off to the right. I took this, and found a little dirt parking lot behind a knob of rock, the top of which could be reached by climbing a fairly steep footpath, visible even in the dark. Obviously, this was where the local folks came to watch the flying machines land and take off. Obviously, it was also the hill specified for the rendezvous.

I climbed up there and looked around, first glancing at my watch: two o'clock. It seemed unlikely that there'd be enough light for our timid contact man to make his appearance much before six, not with the sky overcast and a fine rain falling. And if I'd calculated correctly, Elfenbein could hardly have got his people out here yet.

Again, I was betting on human nature. There are advantages to hiring mercenaries on a temporary basis— you don't have to pay them when they're not working for you—but you don't have the control over them that you do over men, or women, who depend on you for their regular paycheck. I doubted that some stray thugs picked up in an Oslo alley, or wherever they'd been recruited from, would accept an order that involved waiting in ambush half the night in an Arctic drizzle. Even if they did say *ja*, I was betting that, being sensible men, they'd stop their car somewhere along the way and kill a couple of hours, at least, with the heater running, before they exposed themselves to the cold and wet.

I studied the situation carefully, therefore, in the misty darkness, as if I had all the time in the world. After all, if anybody was ahead of me, he'd already seen me, and I'd worry about him when he made his move. There was another dim, rocky rise back along the road, from which

I could watch the approaches as well as the rendezvous; but that was too obvious. I decided on a slight elevation even farther back, and made my way there, and settled down to wait.

Four hours is a long time to sit on a wet hunk of granite in the dark without moving. Fortunately, it was a windless night; I probably couldn't have survived the wind-chill factor, as they call it nowadays, if an icy breeze had been blowing. I was pretty well protected from the rain by an overhanging rock behind me, but that didn't help as much as it might have, since I'd already got pretty damp, walking. What I needed was a pair of insulated duck boots, a goose-down hunting jacket with a waterproof parka over it, warm mittens, and a heavy hood or cap. What I had was city shoes, a lined raincoat designed to keep me warm and dry while making the safari between the house and the car, a pair of thin, leather gloves, and a soggy felt hat. It wasn't the most comfortable morning of my life.

I'd told myself four hours, so as not to get my hopes up, but I'd actually expected action before then. Elfenbein was bound to plant some men out here before daylight. It was the obvious move, of course, but it was also, I thought, the only move. He had no alternative, unless he was a lot brighter than I was and had been able to think up something I couldn't. Apparently, geological genius or no, he wasn't quite that smart, which was just as well for me.

They came without lights, just a car's black shape

moving along the shore. It stopped where the road made
its turn around the head of the bay. Two figures got out,
indistinct blobs in the darkness. Okay. Denison had said
three, and there they all were, if you counted the driver. I
hadn't expected Elfenbein himself to appear at the battle-
front. It wasn't his style or what I figured to be his style,
and he had a crippled hand. The car drove away. The two
left behind came along the road. They stopped to hold
a consultation; then one headed for the rocky elevation
I'd rejected as too obvious, while the other disappeared
towards the parking area.

The stalk was easy. I don't know where Elfenbein got
them, but an Oslo alley was actually a pretty good guess.
Certainly they weren't outdoorsmen. I found the first one,
the nearest one, smoking a cigarette; you could smell him
a quarter of a mile away. I just followed the scent in, and
heard him fidgeting uncomfortably among the rocks up
there. He'd be facing the parking lot, the scene of future
action, I figured. He was. I came in behind him silently,
dropped my looped belt over his head, drew it up tight,
and held it for a moment against his frantic struggles;
then I released it briefly.

He made a harsh sound, halfway between a choked
gasp for breath and a terrified scream for help, very
horrible and effective in the still night. I bore down again
until he was unconscious, and slipped into his neck the
needle of the little drug kit we carry, using the injection
that lasts four hours. There are some that last forever,
and I had those, too; but it didn't seem necessary or

diplomatic to clutter up the Norwegian scenery with a lot of awkward dead men.

The other came in to the scream like a hummingbird to a feeder full of bright, sweet syrup. He hesitated for a moment at the foot of the little hill.

"Karlsen," he hissed, but Karlsen didn't answer. "What's the matter, Karlsen? Is something wrong?" Well, it translated to that, approximately.

Then he started climbing the rocks. He jumped a crevice gracefully—that is, the jump started out gracefully. I spoiled it by reaching up and grabbing a foot, slamming him face-down on the rocks. I hauled him down, half-stunned, and gave him a sleepy-shot, too. I stuffed him into the crack in which I'd been hidden, and went back up to Number One, who'd actually picked himself a pretty good observation post. Sitting there beside him, I reminded myself not to be too proud. There were people around who didn't smoke on duty or march naïvely in to investigate desperate screams. It wouldn't do to forget it.

The exercise had warmed me, so the rest of the wait was almost tolerable. Gradually, very gradually, things got lighter. Details began to show here and there. A little traffic began to move on the shore road, but the parking area remained empty. The rain had stopped; but it wasn't a climate in which you dried off very rapidly, so my comfort quotient remained at about the same level, low but not unbearable. Five thirty came and went. Now, in the hotel room, Diana would be dressing, I figured, making suitable remarks to a nonexistent male companion. *Is it considered improper to talk about love, Mr. Helm?* What did she think we were, anyway, a couple of happy kids on a Vermont ski-tour? *Love,* for God's sake!

After another long half hour, I heard the car coming, bouncing along the gravel, turning onto the dirt track to the parking area, splashing through the puddles left by the rain. It nosed up against the rocks and stopped. A small girl got out from behind the wheel. It wasn't Diana, of course. She'd have come in a taxi, not a private car.

I don't suppose I'd even hoped she'd make it. You can give them instructions until you're purple from lack of breath but they simply will not believe what they're told in perfect English, or any other language. Not if they're amateurs, they won't. *I'm not an operative, I'm just a girl,* she'd said; and obviously she'd been as right as could be. Well, I'd taken it into account. I'd made allowances for it, if you want to call them allowances.

I watched Greta Elfenbein climb the path to the lookout, take her little binoculars from the case slung over her shoulder, and pretend to admire the craggy, snow-capped Lofoten scenery around her.

17

I had to hand it to our contact. He'd been there all the time, back among the glaciated rocks of the little airport peninsula. He must have arrived very early, even earlier than I, or I'd have seen him come; and he'd stayed silent and unmoving while I scouted the area and found myself a hiding place. He'd remained motionless watching the other two delivered by car. He'd witnessed, more or less, as well as his angle of view and the darkness permitted, the three-man Battle of Svolvaer. He'd waited in his secret spot, betraying nothing, until the girl drove up, parked her car, climbed the hill, and waved her identifying binoculars conspicuously for his benefit.

Now he appeared at last. I was suddenly aware of him among the rocks and brush far off to my right, looking like a gray teddy-bear, in a heavy, hooded, insulated Arctic coverall inside which, I reflected sourly as I shivered in my damp city clothes, he'd probably spent a very comfortable night—a little too warm, if anything.

He moved closer and disappeared behind a boulder for several minutes. When I saw him again, he was a changed man: a smallish, middle-aged gent in a dark suit and a sporty leather cap. On his back was a pack, stuffed, presumably, with his survival gear. It didn't make him any more conspicuous in that *ryggsekk* country—rucksack to you—than a lady carrying a purse is conspicuous on a New York street.

He passed below me, and I got a good look at him: the Skipper's drunken, bitter, genius. He had an ordinary, sharp-featured, small-man's face. He didn't look like a genius, but they often don't. He didn't look particularly bitter, but that's hard to tell at fifty yards. The big trouble was, he didn't look much like a lush, either; and they mostly do. Well, as I'd already sensed, a lot of things about this operation weren't exactly what they seemed.

He stopped and shrugged the pack off his back and dropped it behind a scraggly bush. Moving quite openly now, he walked up to the small car that had brought the girl—actually a diminutive station wagon. He looked inside and seemed satisfied. I gave him silent thanks for doing that job for me. Wherever Elfenbein's third hired hand was hiding, it apparently wasn't in Miss Elfenbein's back seat. The man in the dark suit started climbing the path up to where Greta awaited him.

It was my turn to move, and I slithered out of my den and wiggled through the rocks and brush, heading in the general direction of the parked car by a fairly well-protected route I'd picked out, waiting. I found a handy hole nearby and crawled in. It was great ambush country. I wondered how many other armed gents with dubious motives had stashed themselves away among the rocks over the centuries, in that convenient Nordic scenery.

By the time I was established, they'd made themselves acquainted up on the lookout hill. They were admiring the girl's unique and priceless little binoculars. The man was permitted to look through them. He approved what he saw. He made the offer. The girl said she wouldn't dream of selling for all the oil in Arabia—well, she said something obviously negative. The man gave a resigned shrug, wound the strap around the glasses, lifted the case hanging from Greta's shoulder, and put the instrument away for her, tenderly. He raised his cap in polite farewell, came down the hill, retrieved his *ryggsekk*, and hiked away in the direction of Svolvaer. If he'd been hitting the bottle all night, as the Skipper's description would have led me to expect, he certainly carried it well.

Now the girl was coming down the path, still in the red-checked slacks she'd worn on shipboard. She was really kind of a cute little thing, protected by a jaunty yellow raincoat and sou'wester hat—well, that's what they were called years ago when they were made of heavy oilskin and considered high-fashion headgear by the rugged fishermen on the Grand Banks schooners. There's probably some cutiepie name for them now.

I waited for her to reach the car. That missing third man made me nervous. I waited until the last possible moment, hoping he'd reveal himself if he was around.

Then I rose with the Llama pistol in my hand.

"Please hold it right there, Miss Elfenbein."

With the car door half open, she froze; but I saw her move desperately, sweeping her bleak surroundings, looking for the help she'd obviously been promised would be there if she needed it. I moved forward.

"They're sleeping soundly, ma'am," I said. "Let's not disturb the poor fellows. After traveling so far to give your dad a hand, I'm sure they can use the rest."

She licked her lips. "Did you kill them like you did Bjørn?"

"No, I just put them gently to sleep, as I said. Where's Madeleine Barth?"

Her head came up. I could see hope and courage return, at the reminder that she wasn't really in such a bad spot, after all.

"My father has her! She is his prisoner. And if anything happens to me—"

"Aren't you being just a wee bit stupid, Greta? It cuts both ways."

"What do you mean?"

"I've got you," I said. "And I can be just as nasty as Papa—"

I stopped, listening. The sound of a plane motor was in the air, faint but growing stronger. I glanced at my watch: six-forty. The boys were early. According to the arrangements proposed by me, and made by Rolf, they weren't supposed to arrive until seven-thirty. I'd given myself that much time to get the job done. Well, early was better than late. The job was done. I'd be happy to get out of here sooner than anticipated, although I'd have preferred to be leaving with other company.

I took the cased binoculars. Greta made no protest. The case wasn't properly closed; it couldn't be, with all that paper stuffed inside. Apparently Dr. Elfenbein, unlike our team, hadn't taken the trouble to construct a specially oversized case for the job. There were two envelopes. One contained a lot of scientific-looking stuff in Norwegian, very much like the stuff in the envelope already in my pocket. The other went in more for mechanical drawing. There wasn't time to examine it closely. I put the two envelopes where they could keep company with the third. I was a success. I'd obtained the secret formula upon which depended the fate of great nations, or something. Now all I had to do was deliver it.

"Okay, get into the car," I said, and when she was behind the wheel and I was sitting beside her, I went on: "Now start up and drive us around to the boarding area. Leave the car pointing straight out to sea."

There was nobody around. Maybe there was never anybody around unless a plane was due; or maybe Mac had pulled some strings somewhere. Rolf had said the formalities were being arranged. The sea was a few hundred yards beyond the airstrip. There were spectacular rocky islands out there, rising abruptly from the water to heights entitling them to mantles of snow, but I wasn't really interested in scenery. I was thinking of a pale, slim girl with funny greenish eyes; but she wasn't significant, either, any more than the view, not any longer. All agents are expendable, I reminded myself firmly. Nobody lives forever, particularly if they get themselves mixed up with ingenious, effective, and ruthless individuals like a certain Henry Priest—and a certain Matthew Helm. Anyway, with the daughter for leverage, maybe I could pry her loose later, when I had the time and if she lasted that long.

I looked towards the approaching plane, frowning, because it wasn't sounding quite right. Then I saw it take shape in the misty distance, and it wasn't a plane at all, but a helicopter. Well, come to think of it, Rolf hadn't said anything about airplanes. He'd used the word aircraft, covering everything from gliders to Zeppelins. But I'd kind of been figuring on the pilot making a swing over the runway to look things over, before he went around and came on in. With a chopper, he could take his time and see everything he needed to see, hovering if necessary, as he made his landing on the first pass.

I said, "Turn the car a bit, facing that way."

Greta obeyed. I reached across to get the headlight switch and gave the signal; three and two. She made no attempt to take advantage of my awkward position; but when I straightened out, she said rather accusingly: "You're just going to fly away and leave your assistant behind?"

"That's right," I said. "What was your daddy's plan, anyway?"

She hesitated, and shrugged, realizing that it was a little too late to be concerned about security.

"The same as it has always been, right from the start,

Mr. Helm," she said. "To remove your Mrs. Barth and substitute me. Those two men were supposed to protect me if you tried to interfere. We hoped they'd be able to trap you, of course: but even if they didn't, if they just drove you off, well, I'd get the material on the Sigmund Siphon and the Torbotten oil field—as I just did. You'd still have the Ekofisk and Frigg data, but we'd have your Mrs. Barth. An exchange would have been arranged—"

She stopped, because I was laughing. "Oh, dear," I said. "Oh, dearie me. And I'd docilely turn over the papers, any papers, rather than see my precious Girl Friday get hurt? Oh, my goodness gracious me, Miss Elfenbein, what a pretty dream world you folks live in, to be sure!"

"You mean you wouldn't have—"

"We don't play the hostage game, ma'am. We can't afford to. We let it be known that it's no damned use anybody holding any of us for ransom, because it won't be paid. Your daddy should have checked a little more thoroughly."

"You'd let her die—"

"If necessary," I said. "At the moment, it isn't necessary. I've got you, and your papa's smart enough to know that one pretty girl is just as vulnerable as another, I hope. But please don't figure it's ironclad insurance. If you make enough trouble that it's simpler just to shoot you and roll you into a handy ditch, well, to hell with Mrs. Barth. She didn't make it. We don't have much patience with people who don't make it. She had her instructions. She had her gun and plenty of ammunition... How many shots did she get off before your goons managed to disarm her, just as a matter of curiosity?"

"None, Mr. Helm. Because she had no gun when they broke into the room." I started to speak and checked myself. After a moment, Greta went on: "By the greatest good luck for us, she'd lent her gun to your Captain Priest and he'd stepped out for a moment. We were watching, we saw him tucking it away as he came out of the room, and heard him thank her for the loan. Naturally, we grabbed the opportunity while he was gone—"

I drew a long, long breath. "Thanks, that's what I wanted to know. Just one more question. There were three men, one driving the car. Where'd the driver get to, since he doesn't seem to be around?"

She hesitated cautiously once more; then she laughed. "It doesn't matter now, I suppose. Papa has a good deal of respect for you, Mr. Helm; and while Aloco's Mr. Yale is still with him, I'm afraid he doesn't think much of Norman as a bodyguard. The third man had strict orders to come straight back, just in case you managed to escape the ambush here and went looking for Papa."

I grinned. "Nothing like a dangerous reputation, I always say. Well, let's go take a ride in a whirly-bird…"

It was a relatively big machine to pull itself up by its own bootstraps—or lower itself down, as it was doing now. The only bigger ones I'd seen close up had had U.S. marked clearly on the fuselages. A private chopper this size, capable of carrying four people, would be worth somewhere around a million bucks; it would also be worth a lot of status in executive circles. But of course it wasn't a private chopper, at least not at the moment. Regardless of its civilian markings, it was operating on official U.S. government business. I couldn't help wondering just how our people had managed to promote such fancy airborne transportation in this chilly corner of the world, but that's the kind of question you never ask.

We waited clear of the spray and small stones driven out from under the machine as it settled to the rain-wet runway. Then the rotor slowed, just ticking over idly, and the door opened. I shoved the girl ahead, and hurried forward with her, ducking low although there was actually plenty of clearance under the big, slow-turning blades, even for a man of my height. Greta clambered through the doorway or hatch. When she was inside, I pulled myself up, and stopped, looking at a revolver aimed at my face.

"Welcome aboard, Eric," said Paul Denison.

18

It was one of those moments. You know you've goofed, and goofed badly; and what the hell are you going to do about it—if anything?

I had my options, of course. I could hurl myself backwards onto the runway and, if I didn't knock my brains out, roll aside, make that lightning draw that had earned me worldwide renown—actually, we're supposed to be smart enough to have a weapon in hand when it's needed, and to hell with that fast-draw jazz—and shoot it out heroically. The trouble was, I happened to know that Denison was an excellent marksman with very fast reflexes. If I did anything melodramatic, I'd hit the pavement dead if he wanted me dead. And even if he missed, and I actually got a gun out, I wasn't quite certain that I wanted him dead, at least not yet. The crystal ball was still cloudy; and I wasn't sure it was that kind of a last-ditch situation, worth cluttering up the neighborhood with a lot of bloody stiffs, mine perhaps included.

There was, of course, the verbal option: I could tell him he couldn't get away with this, and what the hell did he think he was doing, and I'd get him for it if it was the last thing I did, and if I didn't Mac would see that he was properly terminated, immediately. However, I wasn't a Hollywood hero and there were no cameras or mikes aimed my way—just the lone Colt .38—so I didn't waste time being brave with my mouth.

I said, "The gun's under my belt. The knife's in my right-hand pants pocket. Do you get them, or do I?"

He grinned. "Good old matter-of-fact Eric." He reached out. "I'll take the gun. You get the knife. Division of labor. Okay?"

A moment later, minus both weapons, I was occupying the seat beside the pilot, a sandy-haired, moustached gent, who, like a lot of those fly-boys, didn't seem to figure guns and knives were any of his business. He just drove the airborne buggy and kept his mouth shut.

Behind me, Denison said, "Okay, Jerry, take this thing upstairs. Swing either north or south and get out of sight fast. There'll be a plane coming in from the coast shortly, and we'd rather they didn't see us, don't you know, old chap?"

I waited until the roar and clatter of takeoff had subsided and the air strip was receding into the mists behind us. Then I asked, "What's with this old-chap business, *amigo*?"

Denison chuckled. "Ah, hell, us glamorous mercenaries are all supposed to be dead-eye, stiff-upper-lip British types who used to shoot elephants for a living. Anyway, Gerald here *is* an old-chap type, and one kind of tends to mimic it, don't you know?"

"Up yours," said Jerry/Gerald without turning his head.

"Well, he's picked up a little Yankee slang along the way." Out of the corner of my eye, I saw Denison glancing at the diminutive occupant of the seat to his left. Greta Elfenbein was sitting very still and keeping very quiet; she didn't give the impression of being happy with the situation. Denison said, "You seem to've switched girls since I last had you under surveillance, Eric."

"That's right."

"Left your partner to Elfenbein and took the daughter in trade, eh? Very neat. I figured you might pull something tricky like that. Happy to see you haven't lost your touch."

"I'm happy you're happy," I said. "Who talked?"

I was thinking of Rolf, reluctantly and of the grandmother who hated Sigmund. But Granny wouldn't have known enough about my arrangements to betray them to Denison unless Rolf had told her, deliberately or carelessly; so it came back to the friendly taxi driver, our man in Svolvaer.

"Nobody talked," Denison said. "Or, let's say, you did." I glanced around quickly, maybe indignantly. He gestured with the revolver. I turned my head forward again. He laughed.

"Seven, eight, nine years ago, you talked," he said. "Don't you remember? You talked quite a bit, about getting into the mind of the other man and looking at the situation through his eyes. Sitting at the Master's feet, I drank in his golden words, if that's what you do with golden words. Maybe you eat them."

"Go to hell," I said.

"In due time; don't rush me," Denison said cheerfully. "Another thing you said, another nugget of wisdom I've treasured through the years, is that if there's only one logical thing for a man to do, and he's a logical man, you can probably gamble safely on his doing it. Consider this morning, Eric. You're certainly a logical fellow; and there you'd be, I figured, with all that valuable data... Oh, let's have it, if you don't mind. The valuable data."

"Be my guest," I said. I took the three envelopes from my inside pocket, held them back over my shoulder, and felt them taken away. "Do you read scientific Norwegian?" I asked.

"I read neither scientific nor Norwegian," Denison said. "But L.A. does. He sat down and learned it when he got involved with Torbotten. He's not really stupid, you know, just because he's heard that bald men are supposed to be virile, and because he shuns public appearances, and has all that money. Anyway, my job is to deliver, not decipher. I'll let him figure it out."

There was a little pause while the helicopter cruised high over a maze of islands and rocky reefs against which the gray Arctic sea broke sullenly. We'd swung north, and I wondered if we'd come, as far as Altafjord where the *Tirpitz* was sunk. The minisubs sneaked in and crippled her, and the planes finally finished her off, but it wasn't easy. But we probably weren't that far up the coast.

I'd have been just as happy to sit watching the watery scenery roll away below us in silence—well, silence except for the steady racket of the machinery. I didn't feel much like talking. You don't after you're made a bad booboo. Denison, however, was obviously in a euphoric, chatty mood, and there were things I didn't know that I wanted to know, and guesses I'd made that I wanted confirmed. I couldn't afford to pass up the opportunity.

"You were telling me how smart you were," I said, to start him going again.

"Well, as I was saying," he responded readily, "there you were with all that valuable data, on the edge of an island airport with hostiles all around you. Would you be stupid enough, under constant threat of attack, to hold to the original schedule and wait over twelve hours for the ferry to the mainland—oh, yes, your plans are common knowledge, thanks to a few bucks and Mr. Norman Yale who got them, I gather, by virtue of a few bucks and a traitor in your ranks named Wetherill. Well, standing by an airstrip, would you call for a taxi, a boat, a horse, or a snowmobile? No, I decided after careful consideration, a logical chap like you would do none of those things. You'd send for an airplane. Clever, huh?"

"Brilliant," I said.

"And when would you schedule it?" Denison asked rhetorically. "Well, the drop was set, I gathered—both drops were set—rather loosely for the first convenient time after the ship was seen to dock. It was up to the contact to keep track of its arrival. That took care of possible delays due to fog or breakdowns. In Svolvaer, I didn't figure the evening when you arrived would be considered convenient. Your boy wasn't the kind of hero, I'd been told, who'd like playing tag in the dark. The morning, then, as soon as it was light enough for him to feel safe. Okay so far?"

"Right on, man," I said.

"So I checked some celestial tables and found that first daylight was some time after five, but with the usual lousy weather around here it probably wouldn't really be light until six or six-thirty. Okay. You'd want to give yourself some leeway. If your man was late arriving with the merchandise, you wouldn't want to have that bird circling overhead impatiently, maybe scaring him away. Say you'd give yourself a full hour or a little more; that meant you'd have your plane arriving at seven-thirty or eight. But there was a strong possibility, actually, that your contact would want to get the damned drop over with as quickly as possible after visibility allowed. I took a chance, and came in forty-five minutes ahead of the earliest time I figured your plane would be due, gambling that you'd already have your business transacted, and that you'd be anxious enough to get away that you wouldn't be suspicious of a little discrepancy in timing..."

That was the trouble, of course. I'd had plenty of warning. It had been the wrong kind of aircraft at the wrong time; and my subconscious had been nagging me to wake up, but I'd chosen to ignore it. I'd been too busy patting myself on the back for the great job I'd done, and kicking myself in the pants for the girl I'd sacrificed to do it, to pay attention as I should have.

"Very clever," I said sourly, "but after all, what's the point, Paul? I mean, so you've got the stuff, but you'd have had it tomorrow or the next day, or Mr. Lincoln Alexander Kotko would, as soon as my current chief got around to taking it from me and handing it over. Why make with the guns and helicopters, except to make me look bad?"

"Well, there's that, of course; I don't deny it," Denison said frankly. "Show up the Master at his own game, and all that sort of thing. But that's just a little private bonus. The fact is, this tame naval hero of yours makes me nervous. He's got some odd contacts along this coast, and when I try to check up on him and what he's doing, I meet the goddamndest case of community lockjaw you ever saw. And then, of course, he's made a real point of his delivering the goods to Mr. Kotko, in person. My job is protection, chiefly, and when somebody's all that eager to get into the Presence, I start worrying. Okay, L.A. likes the oil deal, crooked as it is—after all, it isn't every day you're offered a piece of government-guaranteed and government-sponsored larceny—and he was even willing to come to Norway and sacrifice his sacred privacy briefly to put it over. But after he got here, I got a hell of a bad feeling about the whole thing, Eric. Damn it, it *smells* wrong; and I decided that Captain Henry Priest wasn't really a nice enough fellow to be allowed to associate with my saintly employer, if it could possibly be avoided. After all, look what he just did to you, or tried to do."

"What's that?" I asked. It was one of the things I'd guessed, from the way things had happened, but it wouldn't hurt to hear it said.

"Well, I got this from that same young P.R. man with the FOR SALE sign hung so conspicuously on his nose. I wasn't the first purchaser, you understand. Captain Priest had been there with the greenbacks before me. The deal that had been made between them was, Elfenbein would get the stuff, using his daughter as planned; he'd deliver to Norman Yale and get his money—Aloco's money— as promised; but Yale, instead of handing it over to his bosses at Aloco, would slip the stuff to Priest for a substantial consideration. Oh, they were going to muss him up judiciously, and he'd claim to have been set on by a bunch of desperadoes, probably including you, who overpowered him and took the papers after he'd put up a valiant but losing fight—that gray-haired old routine."

"I wondered what happened to good old-fashioned loyalty," I said sadly.

Denison chuckled behind me. "Your girl—your other girl, the one who got left—is probably asking that question right now, *amigo*."

"Forget I brought it up," I said. "So Priest was going to get the stuff from Yale, who'd get it from Elfenbein, who'd get it from Greta here. And what were Mrs. Barth and I supposed to be doing all this time?"

"Getting thoroughly double-crossed," Denison said.

"At least your girl had to be, obviously. They couldn't have two pretty young ladies with binoculars turning up at the rendezvous. Furthermore, Yale explained, they needed Mrs. Barth as a hostage, since they might have to trade for the data you were carrying if they couldn't catch you with it." I heard him chuckle again. "I didn't laugh out loud at that, but I wanted to. The amateur mind is delightfully naïve, isn't it, Eric? But you'd think a pro like Elfenbein would know better."

"They all watch too many sentimental movies," I said.

He went on: "Anyway, Yale told me that he'd pointed out to Priest that Mrs. Barth had been armed and briefed by you, and seemed to be a tough young lady. Disarming her would get a bit hairy, not to say noisy. Priest said not to worry, he'd take care of it. Apparently he did."

"He did," I said.

"You don't seem very shocked or surprised by his perfidy, Eric."

I said, a bit grimly, "He's a practical man, our Skipper. With Yale on the payroll, he could take his choice, but he had to make up his mind. Should he sabotage Elfenbein with Yale's help, and let me get through to the contact as originally planned? Or should he sabotage me, and get the stuff from the Elfenbeins via Yale? That was the unexpected way to do it, and I guess he hoped it would throw you off if you had any tricks pending—of course, he didn't know you'd bought Yale out from under him. And then there's the fact that I don't think Hank Priest really trusts me. He knows I don't really work for him, but for a guy in Washington. He preferred to deal through somebody he could bribe." I shook my head. "No, Priest doesn't surprise me; but you do, *amigo*."

"How so?"

"Why did you bet on me?" I asked. "You had Yale right there. Obviously, after spilling all this to you, he was ripe for the big deal. If you'd just paid him a little more, he'd have double-crossed Hank Priest completely, and brought the stuff to you instead. All you had to do was sit tight and wait for him to drop it into your lap."

"And if I'd done that, I'd still be sitting tight and waiting, wouldn't I?" Denison said. "Hell, man, I'm not a dumb sailor like Priest. I'm your old friend Luke, remember? And in the great Siphon sweepstakes, I was going to put my money—L.A.'s money—on the winning nag; and I knew damned well it wouldn't be Elfenbein or Yale or any other half-assed crook. So I bet on you, my reliable old pal Eric, and you came through for me just as I'd figured you would."

I said, "That's very flattering. I appreciate the testimonial, even if it makes me out a horse." It was time to get the conversation away from the Skipper and his odd tricks, so I said, "Incidentally, I just remembered I met another guy named Denison once, a long time ago. He was an F.B.I. man and a real stuffed shirt."

"No relation," Denison said. "No badges or stuffed shirts run in this family... Matt."

"Yes?"

"What's the current word?"

"What do you mean?" I asked evasively, although I knew perfectly well what he meant. He didn't say anything. I said, after a moment, "Well, if you must know, the word is I'm supposed to take care of you as soon as I can arrange it so there'll be no political backlash."

He sighed behind me. "Goddamn it, that gray bastard in Washington never forgets, does he? So what's to prevent me from getting you out of my hair right now?"

"Not a damned thing," I said cheerfully. "In fact, it's a hell of a fine spot. I recommend it. Just pull the trigger and open the door. No problems, just a nice big splash a couple of thousand feet down. Of course, he'll send somebody else, sooner or later."

"And of course, actually you'll play hell trying to arrange it so L.A. won't light a fire under you. Even if you make it look like an accident, he won't believe it; and he's got more political clout than a lot of Prime Ministers. No, I don't really think you'd better try it, Matt. L.A. looks after his people; and I'm the best he's got, if I do say so myself. I've saved his life at least three times since he put me on the payroll, not to mention straightening out a number of cockeyed deals that might have cost him a lot of money... Well, no sense being hasty. Let's see how it breaks, *amigo*."

I didn't give a large sigh of relief but that's not saying I didn't want to. The morning's intermittent rain turned to gentle snow as we came over the mainland. The moustached pilot took us away from the coast a bit, wiggled and twisted through some nasty little white mountain passes, and then brought us into a pretty, Alpine-looking valley with a gravel road down the middle, on which the snow wasn't sticking yet. The chopper settled down beside it, among some wet, unhappy-looking cows that scattered to give it room. From there, a driveway led up to an expensive-looking house built onto, or into, the side of the mountain above us, all glass and angles and flying bridges.

A tall man in a long fur coat had been standing on one of the out-jutting porches, watching us land. On his head was one of the high fur hats I associate with Cossacks in winter. He didn't wave any greetings. He just waited until we were down, and then turned and walked into the house, unbuttoning his coat as he went, and pulling off his hat. His head was as brown and shiny and hairless as a hazelnut.

19

We didn't get to meet the Invisible Millionaire immediately, but there were a couple of hard-looking characters to greet us at the door beneath the flying-bridge porch. They had the sharply tailored, south-European look the syndicate boys favor but I didn't take it too seriously—any more than I took Denison's wide-brimmed hat seriously, now that I realized it was supposed to put you in mind of safari headgear, not Buffalo Bill's chapeau. We all play these little imitative games when we want to appear kind of tough and special.

"Any problems?" Denison asked.

"Everything's been quiet, Mr. Denison," said the taller and darker of the pair.

"Take these two back into the store-room and lock them up with the skis," Denison said. "Watch out for the man, he's tricky. He'll skewer you with a ski-pole if you give him half a chance. I'll be back down as soon as I've seen L.A."

It was almost worthwhile being taken prisoner, the amount of flattery I was getting. Denison headed for a nearby flight of stairs. The shorter and blonder of the hard boys said he'd better stay on the door; Mr. Kotko wouldn't like it left unguarded. The taller one had already pulled out a big Browning automatic, the first honest-to-God firearm I'd seen on this job aside from my own revolver and Denison's. This was the 9mm Hi-Power, as they call it, using the long, he-man nine, not the short ladies' job chambered by my confiscated Llama. It would shoot thirteen times before running dry, fourteen if you stuffed an extra round up the spout before ramming home the magazine. Very handy if you've got thirteen or fourteen stupid men coming at you single file...

The store-room was cut into solid rock, being at the rear of the house where it backed against the hillside. As Denison had indicated, it was used primarily for ski equipment, presumably belonging to the folks from whom the place had been rented. At least I figured it was rented. Desolate northern Norway didn't seem like the kind of place Mr. Kotko would pick for one of his permanent love-nests—he liked to maintain his well-publicized privacy in fairly public places, as I recalled. And if he'd just come here temporarily with an illicit oil deal in mind, it seemed unlikely that he'd have prepared himself for winter sports, the season for which was still a month or so away.

I wondered if the skis were employed locally or if they were put on the train by their owners and hauled up to Abisko in Sweden, on the craggy backbone of the Scandinavian peninsula, some thirty miles east of us, assuming we'd been deposited somewhere near Narvik on the coast. The fact that there'd been hardly any snow in the cow-pasture in which we'd landed, indicating a fairly low altitude, made this a reasonable assumption. As for the skis, that was just idle curiosity. Skis weren't likely to figure prominently in the forthcoming activities. At this time of year we could hardly expect to glide away swiftly into the sheltering blizzard—anyway, for all I knew, my diminutive companion was strictly useless on skis, for all she'd gone to school in Switzerland.

I had plenty of time for cogitation. Taking Denison's warning literally, our escort established us against the rear wall of the room, facing the rock, with our hands flat against it. Then he proceeded to remove every last ski-pole in the place, quite a job since he used only one hand and never turned away from us, keeping us always covered with the Browning. When he had all the sharp, spear-like metal poles stacked against the wall in the hall outside, he went out, slammed the door shut, and turned the key in the lock.

I lowered my arms, looked at my, hands, and rubbed them together to get rid of the traces of the chalky, calciminelike white paint, if that's the right word, with which the whole storeroom was finished.

"How are you on skis, Miss Elfenbein?" I asked.

"As a matter of fact, I'm rather good on skis, Mr. Helm," she said. "But that is not much use to us here, is it? Even if we could get free, the snow was melting almost as fast as it fell, when we came in."

"I know, I was just talking," I said. I looked at her curiously. "You haven't been saying very much."

She shrugged a little defiantly. "What was there to say? 'Release me, sir, or I will scream for help'?"

I grinned. "Good girl."

"Thank you. But if I were a good girl, I would be back in the conservatory in Switzerland, making little marks on music paper. If I were even merely an intelligent girl, that is where I would be." Her slight accent seemed to become stronger under stress. She shook her head ruefully. "And it is not as if I were passionately fond of my parent, Mr. Helm. How can you love a man you disapprove of, who never paid you any attention until he needed a housekeeper and an accomplice in crime."

"But you came when he called," I said.

"He is my father. My mother was dead; there were only the two of us," she said softly. "And he did need me. I suppose that is the point. After all these years he looked at me, at last, as if I were a human being and not just an obnoxious pet my mother insisted on maintaining. He asked me to help. And of course I had always wondered about... about the glamorous and exciting things he did... Exciting!" Suddenly she was crying. The tears ran down her cheeks unchecked as she said, "I most certainly c-came to the right p-place for excitement, d-didn't I, Mr. Helm? This should be exciting enough for anyb-b-body, d-don't you think?"

Well, that made two of them. Diana had been looking for risk and excitement, too. Maybe a whole generation was, after all the years of concentrated safety and ecology. Maybe there was a worldwide backlash against the protection-and-purification zealots. I wondered what Diana was thinking about it now, and I decided that what Diana was thinking wasn't anything I really wanted to wonder about. I held out my handkerchief.

"Blow and wipe," I said. "Let me help you off with that raincoat, you won't need it in here."

"But what are we going to *do*!" she wailed. "How are we going to get *out* of here?" Then she drew a long, ragged breath. "I'm sorry. I did not mean to be a baby… What is the matter, Mr. Helm?"

I'd started laughing; I couldn't help myself. She'd asked how we were going to get out and I had suddenly realized that the last thing I wanted was out. I was exactly where I wanted to be, or at least I was within one flight of stairs of where I wanted to be. Everything was working out great, thanks to the kind of cooperation of my old comrade-in-arms, Paul Denison. I was amazed at my own stupidity in considering, even for a moment, making a fight of it at the Svolvaer airport.

"Mr. Helm—"

'I controlled my unseemly hilarity, with an effort. "It's all right, I'm not hysterical, Greta," I said. "You don't mind if I call you Greta, do you, Miss Elfenbein? It's all right. I just… I've been so busy being mad at myself for getting caught that it never occurred to me… Hell, I couldn't have worked it better if I'd planned it."

"What do you mean?"

"Well, look," I said, "there I was standing on the bleak, lonely Lofoten Islands with the documents everybody wanted, and what could I do with them? Knowing, because you'd told me—well, I'd done a little guessing, too—that he'd deliberately pulled the rug out from under me, I could hardly turn them over to the guy I was supposed to be working for, Captain Henry Priest. Sure, I'd arranged for a plane to get me out of there, over to the mainland, but what could I do there? Except try to find my way to Mr. L.A. Kotko, the man to whom the stuff was consigned? That might have taken some doing, since I had no idea where he was staying; I didn't even know if he'd actually arrived in the area. But along came my good friend Paul Denison and hauled me straight here by helicopter express—"

I stopped, hearing quick footsteps in the hall. There was a sudden, loud, clattering sound.

"What the goddamned lousy hell?" That was Denison's voice. It sounded angry.

"I'm sorry, Mr. Denison. You said not to let him near any ski-poles, so I took them all out and stacked them—"

"Oh, for Christ's sake!"

There was more clattering as Paul kicked poles out of his way. The lock rattled. The door burst open. My good friend Denison marched inside, looked for me, found me, glared at me, and strode up to me and knocked me down.

"You bastard!" he panted, standing over me. "You

bloody bastard! I should have known when you let yourself be taken so easily… Where are they?"

"What?"

He kicked me in the hip. "Don't *what* me, you sonofabitch! Where are the real data: Ekofisk, Frigg, Torbotten? Where are the real plans of the Sigmund Siphon? What sneaky place did you find to hide them…"

And there it was, the whole damned jigsaw puzzle with the last piece in place. I should have guessed, of course, but I hadn't. It wasn't the brightest operation of my life, not by a long shot. I reminded myself that it could still be the last operation of my life, if I didn't pull myself together and start applying a few brains to the problem, if I could find some to apply. Denison was still frothing at the mouth and roaring like an enraged grizzly.

"Denison!"

The voice sounded weak and distant, but it silenced him abruptly. He drew a long breath.

"Yes, Mr. Kotko," he called.

"What the devil are you doing? I ordered you to bring them up here fast!"

"Yes, Mr. Kotko." He kicked me again, in the same place. "You heard the man. Move! You, too, girl!"

I got up and, with Greta following, limped through the door, over the fallen ski-poles, and up the stairs to meet Lincoln Alexander Kotko, a privilege reserved for only a few.

20

It was a big, paneled room, self-consciously and expensively rustic—knotty-pine luxury, Scandinavian style. One wall was glass, looking out onto the elevated veranda and the valley; but the stormy day outside didn't yield quite enough light despite the large opening, so some lights were on. Kotko was waiting for us behind the big pine table that, littered with papers, was apparently serving him as a desk.

He wasn't a bad-looking fellow, for a gent in his fifties. He was quite tall, within a couple of inches of my own height and he had no middle-aged protuberance amidships. Obviously, he was proud of his lean, hard figure, making a point of displaying it in snug, wine-colored stretch pants and wine-colored turtleneck, very sporty. His deeply tanned face was handsome in a hawklike way, with a blade of a nose and kind of hooded brown eyes—an impressive gent, until he opened his mouth. I'd thought his voice had sounded weak because of the distance. I'd been wrong. It was weak and pitched a little too high; a boy's voice in a man's body.

"Have you searched them thoroughly?" he demanded in that thin voice.

Denison said, "Not yet, Mr. Kotko. I—"

"Well, get at it! Do I have to tell everybody their business around here? Search them now!"

"Yes, Mr. Kotko." I noticed Denison wasn't using the great man's initials. He spoke to the tall guard who'd accompanied us upstairs: "See if the girl's got it on her, Wesley. You're looking for papers, any kind of papers. I'll handle this one."

He did a thorough job, working his way downwards, until he came to my socks and stopped. I saw him throw a quick glance up at me. His face had paled slightly.

"What is it? Did you find something, Denison?" Kotko was watching us.

"No, sir. I'm just trying to untie this damned double knot in his shoelace… Okay, you, step out of them." He checked the shoes and placed them on the rug in front of me. He glanced up once more. His eyes were oddly pleading. "That's all. You can put them on again, but don't try anything, Helm, or you'll regret it."

He stepped back a little. I put my feet into the shoes and bent over to knot the laces. Still bending, I smoothed my left sock—one of the snug, nylon-reinforced, elastic knits—over the tiny .25 Colt pistol I'd taken off Norman Yale. Denison should have found it earlier, of course; but his success in reading my mind and anticipating my escape plans had made him overconfident and careless. He'd been so sure he knew what weapons I was carrying—the two I'd shown him before our slugfest under the railroad tracks—that he'd even overlooked the trick belt I was wearing, although it was a fairly standard gimmick even seven years ago.

I saw him remember it now, and dismiss it from consideration. Chiefly an escape tool, it was not a factor here. The little automatic was a very different matter, but the trouble was, he simply could not afford to disarm me under Kotko's watchful eye. Denison's privileged position was already in danger. The papers he'd brought were unsatisfactory. The Sultan was displeased. If Paul should discover the popgun on me now, and confess that he, the royal bodyguard, had permitted me to come armed into the Presence, as he'd called it, it would be the end of everything he'd worked for. It was safer just to leave me the weapon and hope that I'd find no occasion to use it; or that he could shoot me down fast if I did, and palm the toy gun before anybody else caught a glimpse of it.

"Nothing? On either of them?" Kotko's voice was harsh. "Well, bring them here, Denison. You get back downstairs, Wesley. They had coats when they came in, didn't they? Check those, and any place in this house where they could have hidden it or thrown it. Tell Gerald to report as soon as he finishes searching the helicopter… Bring them closer, I said, Denison!"

The tall guard disappeared into the corner stairwell, that was protected by a handsome pine railing. Denison

ushered us forward. Greta, with a pink spot of humiliation
in each cheek, was pulling up her slacks and smoothing
down her sweater. Denison fined us up neatly, facing his
employer, like two naughty sailors brought to the ship's
captain for punishment.

"You're Elfenbein's daughter?" Kotko snapped at
Greta, after looking us over deliberately. "Well, that means
nothing here; we are not intimidated by minor crooks.
Your father has chosen to interfere in our business. If you
have to suffer the consequences, that's your misfortune.
You are the one who received the documents this morning
from the Norwegian contact, isn't that right? You had
them first, before this man got hold of them?"

Greta licked her lips and nodded.

"Yes, that was the plan that was reported to us," Kotko
said. I blinked slightly. I hadn't heard wrong. The man
was actually employing the royal, or editorial, *we* to
refer to himself. He went on: "You received them, Miss
Elfenbein, and then, presumably, this man took you
prisoner and confiscated them. On or near that hill beside
the Svolvaer airport?"

Greta nodded again. The touch of color had faded and
she looked quite pale. "Yes," she whispered. "Yes, that is
correct, Mr. Kotko."

"They were the right papers?"

"I… I don't know. I didn't look. I wanted to quickly
get away from there, first." She licked her lips again.
"Even if I had looked, I would not have known whether
they were right or wrong. I do not know anything about

oil, Mr. Kotko, and I do not read Norwegian."

His eyes narrowed. "If you didn't look at them, how do you know they were in Norwegian? According to our information, this man had the material that was picked up in Trondheim, earlier. You never saw that, either. You never saw any of it."

Greta said carefully, "The information was supposed to have been collected by Norwegians. A Norwegian had drawn up the plans. At least that was what we were told, Papa and I. We… we naturally assumed those people would be writing in their own language."

"Well, you were right!" Abruptly, Kotko slammed the flat of his hand down on the papers before him. "At least these documents are Norwegian—Norwegian gibberish! Obviously dummies, made to be substituted for the genuine material. Where do you think the substitution occurred, Miss Elfenbein?"

"I didn't—"

"No, of course you didn't. All these documents are fakes, not just those you picked up this morning. That means the substitution must have been accomplished by someone who had all of them in his possession. Tell me, Miss Elfenbein, was this man out of your sight at any time after he took—"

Well, you can cut the dialogue to fit: the standard, stupid, interrogation procedure, getting nowhere because there was nowhere to go in that direction, no matter how much infallible logic and deductive genius was displayed by everyone concerned. The answer was right on the desk, but it was an answer Mr. Lincoln Alexander Kotko wasn't ready to face. Sooner or later I'd have to persuade him of the truth, but he had a lot of blustering to get out of his system first, and I left him to it. I was studying a phenomenon I'd discovered back in the shadows by the big, lighted fireplace.

I'd thought, after the guard was sent downstairs, that there were only the four of us left in the room: Greta and I, Denison and Kotko. Gradually, I'd come to realize that there was a fifth person present. Under normal conditions, she wouldn't have gone neglected so long. I'm usually fairly quick at spotting slender but well-proportioned blondes, but the corner was dark and my attention had been elsewhere. Her presence didn't really surprise me, of course. Kotko might not have brought skis to Norway, but if his reputation was to be relied upon, he wouldn't have made the journey alone.'

Her hair was long and silvery, almost white. She seemed to be average height or slightly above, but it's hard to judge the vertical dimensions of a girl sitting down, or a man for that matter. Her horizontal dimensions were adequate and interesting. She seemed to have a good complexion but her eyes were painted in an exaggerated way. The elaborate makeup went oddly with the fact that her nose was definitely snubbed, or *retroussé* as we say in French.

She was wearing a costume that seemed more suited to the Riviera in summer than Norway in the fall: a shirred, blue, elastic halter that left her midsection bare—some day somebody's going to have to explain to this innocent lad what's so fascinating about navels—and thin white pants riding so low on her nicely rounded hips that it seemed unlikely they'd stay on if she stood up. The pants, snug enough above, flared into yards of material below. One of the things that intrigues me about Women's Lib is how the ladies complain so bitterly about the impractical sheer stockings and unsafe high heels forced upon them by masculine tastes, and how, allowed free choice, they immediately insert themselves into impractical white trousers that will show every smudge, dangerously wide enough to trip them headlong down the first flight of stairs they come to.

The silverhaired girl was sipping beer from a slim, tall, pilsner glass. It was her movement to reach the bottle for a refill that had caught my eye. Otherwise she sat perfectly silent, perfectly still, just watching and listening.

Kotko had now proved to his own satisfaction, and logically demonstrated to everyone in the room, that the substitution must have been performed by me between the time I took the second batch of papers from Greta and put them with the first, and the time I handed the three substitute envelopes to Denison. That meant, he proclaimed, that since I hadn't been out of Greta's sight, she must have seen me cache the real, valuable documents somewhere, unless...

His timing was good. Right on cue, Gerald, the moustached pilot, appeared at the head of the stairs. He paused as he reached room level, then came forward at Kotko's signal.

"Well, Jerry?"

"There is nothing in the aircraft, Mr. Kotko. And Wesley says they hid nothing in the entrance, the hall, or the store-room. Here are their coats. Also nothing."

Denison asked, "You're sure?" His voice was sharp.

Jerry turned his head a bit. "Fuck you," he said, quite pleasantly.

Kotko said, "If Gerald says there is nothing, if Wesley says there is nothing, there is nothing. All right, Jerry. Keep yourself available."

"Righto, Mr. Kotko."

When he'd gone, Kotko looked at the small girl before him, rather sadly. "You heard, Miss Elfenbein? He did not hide them in the helicopter, or in this house." He sighed, and came around the table to stand over her. "Where did he hide them, Miss Elfenbein? By your own story, you must have seen—"

"I didn't!" she gasped. "I didn't see anything. Why don't you ask him, instead of b-bullying me?"

"Miss Elfenbein," he said deliberately, "we are not asking Mr. Helm, because Mr. Helm is a trained government professional who will not speak unless he chooses to speak, not unless we employ drugs that we do not, unfortunately, have. Mr. Helm has been subjected to interrogation before, we are informed. He has had a great deal of practice at keeping his mouth closed under duress, and is reported to be quite good at it. How much practice have you had, Miss Elfenbein? How good are you?" He gave her a sudden, violent shove that sent her sprawling. "Never mind ogling the young lady, Denison," he said, moving forward. "Watch the man."

"I'm watching him, Mr. Kotko."

It was out of character. I mean, the great man should have seated himself calmly behind the table, lighting a casual cigarette perhaps, keeping up a flow of clever conversation to show how little it all meant to him, while the menials did the dirty, rough-'em-up work for him. Instead, he moved in and performed the operation with his own hands. It took him about ten minutes, working methodically and without haste, to reduce a rather nice-looking young lady to something resembling a mauled and bedraggled and bloodied kitten that kept trying to crawl away on all fours whimpering that it didn't know, didn't know, didn't know...

I drew a long breath and reminded myself that I didn't owe a damned thing to any Elfenbeins, quite the contrary. When the tall figure with the shaved head paused for breath, I spoke harshly: "If you've had your fun, Kotko, let's talk some sense for a change."

He turned to look at me with a funny, glazed look in his eyes. "*Mister* Kotko," he said.

I shrugged. "How long is it going to take you to wake up, *Mister* Kotko? How long is it going to take you to realize you're looking for something that doesn't exist? There are no real documents; there never were. There is no Sigmund Siphon. There never was."

21

Greta Elfenbein crouched against the wall, sobbing helplessly, with her hair straggling damply down her blood-smeared face. The blood had made a mess of her white sweater and spotted her gay pants, and it hadn't done the room's rug any good, either; but it was nosebleed blood, a dime a pint, no indication of any serious damage. It had been a reasonably careful mussing-up job; just enough to persuade a sheltered young lady to talk, if she had anything to talk about.

Kotko studied her for a moment, coldly, decided she wasn't worth any more exertion, and walked up to me wiping his hands on a handkerchief, which he dropped into a nearby wastebasket.

"What are you trying to say?" he demanded.

"I'm not trying to say it. I've said it."

"Don't get flip with me, government boy!" I noticed he had discarded the royal plural. He turned sharply. "What do *you* think you're doing?"

The girl with the long blond hair had crossed the room to kneel beside Greta. When she looked around, I understood the reason for the elaborate eye makeup. Her right eye sported a rather spectacular shiner, visible now in the light from the big windows.

"I'm just sticking her back together little, Linc," she said calmly. She had a nice, throaty, sexy voice—well, she would have. She went on: "You can take her apart again later, if you feel like it. More fun that way, huh?" She spoke to the weeping girl: "Come on, darling, cooperate. Misty can't pick you up all by herself. Here, hold this against it so you don't get it all over... That's the girl!"

Kotko watched the two of them make their unsteady way into the corner by the fire. The silvery blonde who'd called herself Misty seated her patient in one of the big armchairs. Kotko shrugged and turned back to me.

"That's a very funny story you just told, Helm. I don't like funny stories, or people who tell them."

I said, "We've been conned, Mr. Kotko. We've been tricked into playing charades to entertain each other, particularly you. Or maybe it would be more accurate to say that you've been the audience, and we've been the dolls putting on a thrilling little puppet melodrama entitled *The Great Norwegian Oil Robbery*. The U.S. government, Elfenbein, and that model of youthful integrity, the handsome, hungry P.R. boy from Aloco, not to mention yours truly, we've all been dancing on invisible strings to persuade you there was a great plot afoot that could be turned to your benefit. Benefit, hell! You had the Torbotten concession, or whatever you oilmen call it, quite legally; but you didn't like the terms of the contract so you tried to improve on it a bit, right? But how long do you think you'll be drilling and pumping out there after the Norskies discover that you tried to help yourself to a larger serving than you were signed up for? We've all been suckered, Mr. Kotko, but guess who's the biggest sucker of the lot!"

He had a good poker face. He said without expression: "I don't think our Norwegian friends like being called Norskies."

I said, "Hell, I'm Svensk by blood; I can call them anything I damned well please. We've feuded for generations, in a neighborly fashion. They even went to a lot of trouble to louse up their language so it wouldn't look like Swedish the way it used to. Does the subject interest you, Mr. Kotko? Do you want to hear a lecture on Norsk-Svensk relations? Norway used to be ruled by Sweden, you see, so—"

He slapped me hard across the face. "I told you. I don't like funny stories. Or funny men."

I said, "That wasn't very smart, Mr. Kotko. Why go around making new enemies when you've got enough old ones to go around, some you don't even know about." He didn't rise to that bait, so I went on smoothly, "Are you ready for a bit of sensible action for a change, like taking a look at what's actually on that table? Or do you have to beat up somebody else first? Go on, take another swing. Be my guest."

He stared at me bleakly for a moment. "There's nothing on the table. Nothing but valueless paper. The *real* information, the *real* plans—"

I glanced at Denison. "Is he always like this? Doesn't he ever listen?" I swung back to Kotko. "Goddamn it, I just told you! There is no real information. There are no real plans. All there is, all there ever was, is what's on that fancy-pine table. Now, can we go look at it and see if it'll tell us something; or do you want me to kill some more time chattering brightly while you make up your cotton-picking mind? I can tell you a yarn I heard in a bar once—I don't vouch for the accuracy; the guy was drunk and so was I—about what happened when the Nazis invaded Norway. There was this old fort, see, in Oslomfjord—"

Kotko was staring at me hard, as if debating whether or not to slap me once more. He turned sharply, walked around the table, and leaned over the papers there.

I went on talking, "—this old fort in Oslofjord, Oskarsborg; with two elderly cannon dating from the days when artillerymen actually made up affectionate pet names for their pieces. These big old coastal guns were called Moses and Aaron, as I recall, don't ask me why. Something Biblical like that, anyway. They were really ancient, this fellow told me, so old I guess Nazi intelligence had kind of discounted them. Anyway, on that day in April, 1940, without any warning or declaration of war, there came the Nazi invasion fleet up the fjord led by the heavy cruiser *Blücher*, a fine modern warship in the van

of a great modern armada, invincible, irresistible. Taking
Oslo was going to be a Sunday picnic. But suddenly, the
guy said, there was a sound like a freight train rolling
through the sky. The shores of Oslofjord started shaking.
The Oskarsborg fortress had opened up. Big old Moses
and Aaron were speaking at last, after all the long years of
silence. Two military antiques against the whole German
Navy, they were doing the job they'd been put there for,
they were defending the capital of Norway. When they
ceased firing, the *Blücher* was sinking in flames, and the
great Nazi armada was fleeing for its life. Oh, it landed
elsewhere later, but most of the invasion command had
gone down with the flagship; and what with the delay and
confusion, the Norwegian king and government, whom
the Nazis had hoped to capture in Oslo, had escaped—"

"Shut up."

"Yes, Mr. Kotko."

"Come here."

"Yes, Mr. Kotko."

"What do you expect this gibberish to tell us?"

Moving deliberately so as not to startle Denison into
doing something hasty, nervous as he undoubtedly was
about that pistol in my sock, I walked around the table to
stand beside Kotko. I pointed to a column of figures.

"What does that say?"

"Nothing," he said.

"There are words beside the numbers," I said. "It's got
to say something."

"All right, take this line," he said, putting his finger

on the paper. "It translates to something like 'Barrier Density .0918 percent.'"

"And?"

"I've been dealing with petroleum and oil fields for a number of years," Kotko said. "I've never heard of a barrier density. I don't think there is any such thing. And if there were, a density should be expressed not in percents, but in units of mass and volume, like grams per cubic centimeter, shouldn't it? And it's all like that, damn it, like that poem by Lewis Carroll, *Jabberwocky*. It's all scientific jabberwocky, Helm."

Baffled and bewildered, the guy sounded almost human. I had to glance towards where the blond girl was trying to make Greta Elfenbein look slightly less like a battlefield casualty, to remind myself that he wasn't a guy of whom I really approved.

"In other words," I said, "somebody went to a lot of trouble to make it up. Jabberwocky doesn't come easy. It takes, you might say, imagination. Why not just copy a couple of pages out of a Norwegian technical magazine if all you wanted was some scientific-looking material to fool somebody? What about this drawing? Can you make anything of it?"

He shrugged. "It's no machinery I've ever had any dealings with. That's a detail sketch. This one gives the overall picture of the system, whatever the hell it is… Do you recognize it, Helm?"

I'd pulled the mechanical drawing in front of me. I studied it for a while, frowning. There was something faintly familiar... I swung it around so I could see it upside down. It was no time to laugh, I told myself firmly, but I couldn't help a choked-off snort, anyway.

Kotko said sharply, "What do you find so amusing?"

"It's a long story," I said.

"I'm a little weary of your long stories," he said. "Do you recognize this drawing."

"Yes, sir," I said. You can stick the needle much deeper, with reasonable safety, if you remember to call them sir and mister. "That is, I know where it came from. There were three drawings when I saw them. They've been combined in a very interesting way by a skilled and ingenious draftsman—"

"Where did you see them?" he snapped.

"In Florida, a couple of years ago," I said. "Let me give you the background, Mr. Kotko. Living overseas, you may not be aware of it, but in America we nowadays have a fine organization known as the Environmental Protection Agency, or EPA, dedicated to keeping our air and water pure, a very worthy purpose. Only sometimes, like all ecological bureaucrats, these folks get carried away by their own virtue—particularly when they find some nice, easy, obvious subjects for purification that aren't big enough or rich enough to fight back very hard. Well, in the U.S., we also have a relatively small number of private boats sizable enough to be lived on for longer or shorter periods, a few hundred thousand I'm told, certainly less than half a million. They produce only a fraction of a percent of the total water pollution in even the most crowded areas; but for some reason the EPA considers this little bit of contamination peculiarly offensive—"

"Get to the point, Helm!"

"I'm getting there," I said. "The EPA in its wisdom has decided that the human waste from a few hundred thousand private vessels is a clear and present danger to life upon this earth and must on no account be deposited in the ocean. Cities of millions discharge their effluents into the world's waters; great industries dump deadly poisons practically where they please; giant whales, porpoises, and fishes large and small use the seas for their bathrooms in a totally disgusting manner; but the yacht owner... This isn't my diatribe, Mr. Kotko. I'm just repeating what I was told two years back, as well as I remember it."

"And?"

"The EPA is—or was at that time—busy considering elaborate, not to say impossible, standards for marine plumbing on small private vessels," I said. "What you've got here, Mr. Kotko, is an imaginative and artistic version of a nonpolluting head built to slightly—but only slightly—exaggerated EPA specifications." I kept my voice expressionless. "In other words, Mr. Kotko, there's your Sigmund Siphon. A seagoing crapper."

There was an odd silence in the room. I guess everybody expected the man to explode. Even the girls were motionless, blond Misty freezing with a stained Kleenex in her hand. But I guess you don't get to be, and stay, a millionaire just by shaving your head and beating up little girls. Kotko was perfectly still for a moment, looking down at the drawing. When he spoke, his voice was steady and very soft.

"You say you saw the plans from which this was derived? In Florida?"

"Yes, sir. There were, you see, three systems being considered for a thirty-foot fishing vessel belonging to a gent of my acquaintance. He was kind of upset about having to tear up his beloved boat to install a lot of Mickey Mouse plumbing, and he held forth to anybody who happened to be handy; and I was handy for a week or so. He described the three possibilities in very colorful terms. One involved chemical treatment, the second used a combustion process, and the third employed a holding tank, meaning that you had to live with your stinking waste products until you could find an official pump-out station on shore—that was the system being pushed by the EPA. Just what you were supposed to do on a cruise in an area where there were no official facilities, or if you merely stayed off shore for more than a few days, had never been clearly explained, said my informant."

"Who?" Kotko's voice was still low, but kind of strangled.

"It's a very nice job," I said. "He got a clever draftsman to combine all three systems into one, you see. The EPA should be very pleased: first you treat it chemically, then you burn it, then you flush the ashes into the holding tank for respectful burial ashore. Foolproof; not one little pollutant can escape. Here's the seat, see, kind of an odd perspective, but when you turn it this way you can recognize—"

"Damn you, *who*?"

"You know the answer," I said. "Unfortunately, I spoiled his great moment, Mr. Kotko. He went to a lot of trouble to deliver it to you himself and watch your face as he explained it to you."

He yanked me away from the table, and swung me around to face him. It was just as well. I don't like people who maul me and, having certain plans for him, I wanted to keep right on not liking him. He was making it easy.

"You mean your lousy little retired Navy captain played this crazy joke—"

"Wake up, Mr. Kotko," I said. "He isn't so lousy and he isn't so little. If your boy here had done his homework you'd know that." I said it without looking at Denison and I went on before he could speak: "And you played a joke on Hank Priest once, Mr. Kotko. He's just paying you back in kind."

"*I* played...?" He snorted. "I've never met the man!"

"Not in person," I said. "But some years ago you gave him, by proxy so to speak, a pretty little plastic card saying PETROX on it. You told him that if he presented that card at any of your installations, he could get all kinds of nice petroleum products for it. Well, the joke was on him. A very funny thing happened a little while back, Mr. Kotko. Hank Priest took your little card to his local marine Petrox station, or dock, and haha, what do you know? It was as worthless as that nautical pisspot he's just presented to you, which won't produce any oil, either."

Kotko looked genuinely shocked. "You mean, this

lunatic is holding *me* responsible—"

"You're dealing with a Navy man, Mr. Kotko," I said. "In the Navy, the man on top gets all the credit when things go right. And all the blame when things go wrong. You're the man on top. Things went wrong. The way he looks at it, it's your baby."

"The Arabs—"

I shrugged. "Don't argue with *me*, Mr. Kotko. I'm not the guy who's mad at you." That was not, of course, strictly true; but it wasn't a moment for slavish adherence to the truth.

He was still shocked and baffled. "But he had the U.S. government behind him!"

"The U.S. government is a hell of a big place," I said. "Hank Priest knows his way around Washington. He undoubtedly knew where to find the right, unprincipled officials who'd give him a little cautious backing for an illegal project if he showed them how they could make a profit out of the deal. There are a few unscrupulous people around that town, or hadn't you heard? Of course, he just wanted their support to make the deal look attractive to you, figuring, I suppose, that you wouldn't examine the details quite so closely if it was all stamped U.S. Approved."

"All this—" Kotko cleared his throat. "All this elaborate trickery and intrigue just to play a bad joke? I don't believe it!"

"Oh, not just to play a bad joke," I said. "That was only an added frill I guess he couldn't resist. He had to sell you *something*, it was necessary to his plan, and why not make it funny? But that's incidental."

"Then what—"

"You see, Mr. Kotko," I said, deliberately, "a lady named Frances Priest drowned when her husband couldn't go after her in his boat because one of your stations had capriciously refused to sell him enough fuel." I glanced at my watch. "I expect he'll be here pretty soon, depending on what kind of transportation he's managed from Svolvaer. What all this elaborate trickery is about, Mr. Kotko, is to decoy you here to Norway where you don't usually come, prepared to receive visitors although you usually don't. Well, a visitor. Now he's going to kill you."

I'd thought, with all the chatter, I'd built it up pretty well. I'd thought it would be a real blockbuster, and it did silence the room for a moment. Then Denison laughed. He turned and walked quickly to the stairs.

"Wes, Bill," he shouted. "Everything okay down there?"

"Everything's quiet, Mr. Denison," came the reply, in the voice of the taller man, Wesley.

"Well, keep your eyes open." Denison marched back. "They're good boys, Mr. Kotko. Nobody'll get past them."

It was my turn to laugh. "Luke, friend, like I just told your boss here, you haven't done your homework. Do you know who's out there? He didn't want to do it this way, I figure, he wanted to trick his way in neatly and do the job without a lot of shooting, but if he's got to blast his way in here, he'll blast, and he's got the force to do it." I went on before Denison could speak: "You told me you checked on Captain Henry Priest. What did you find out?"

His eyes wavered. "Well, just the usual things. He seems to be pretty respectable, a solid citizen."

"No trouble? Everybody chatty, willing to spill everything they know about Captain Priest?" He'd already told me the answer, but I wanted Kotko to hear it.

"Well, as a matter of fact, here in Norway they kind of clammed up, but—"

"Sigmund," I said. "The Sigmund Siphon. Did it occur to you to trace the name?"

"Sure, but—" He stopped.

Kotko said harshly, "But what, Denison?"

"Same thing, Mr. Kotko. Nobody'd talk to me about that name."

Kotko looked at me. "What are you driving at, Helm?"

"I figure they must have had you spotted since you moved in," I said. "They're local people, and a stranger like you renting a house like this isn't going to be a secret, locally. They're just waiting for the word. And when they come for you, your boy Denison and a couple of bodyguards aren't going to stop them, Mr. Kotko. Hell, at one time they took on the whole German Army; they'll eat up your protection like chocolate candy."

Denison said impatiently, "There's nobody out there, or the boys would have seen them. Who's this mysterious *they* we're supposed to be so afraid, of, anyway?"

I ignored him and spoke to Kotko. "I've got one last story for you, Mr. Kotko," I said. "Another World War II story. About a certain lieutenant in the U.S. Navy, of

Norwegian extraction, who was sent over here, code name Sigmund, to help out the Norwegian resistance. He did a pretty good job, according to some people. Other folks thought he was just a little too tricky, just a little too ruthless, just a little too bloodthirsty... You ought to pass the word down the line, Mr. Kotko. Next time your employees get snotty, I suggest they pick on someone who hasn't got quite so many violent friends in distant places, quite so many dead men to his credit. When you meet a guy like that, and you hurt him, he kills. Now, if we can't come up with a bright idea fast, you're going to die for five gallons of Diesel #2."

Kotko stared at me for a moment; then he turned on his heel. "Gerald!"

"Yes, Mr. Kotko." The voice came up the stairs.

"Get the helicopter warmed up, Jerry. We're getting out of here."

Denison said desperately, "He's bluffing, Mr. Kotko. He's trying to scare us—"

"Shut up. Or think of a good explanation for landing me in the middle of an Arctic hornet's nest. It had better be damned good, or you're through!"

I interrupted. "Mr. Kotko."

"What is it?"

"I'd stop that man, if I were you. He seems like a nice, competent sort, even if his vocabulary is kind of limited. And that's an expensive aircraft."

Kotko's eyes were narrow. "What do you mean—"

He stopped. Gerald, the pilot, must have slipped

but without slamming the door. Now we heard the
helicopter's powerplant sputter into life outside. Instantly,
as if answering the sound of the exhaust, an automatic
weapon opened up down the valley. Another, closer,
joined it. There was a moment of silence after they had
stopped, followed by the solid, jolting clap of a heavier
explosion: a grenade. We could see the flickering red light
of the burning machine growing strong at the window as
the fire took hold, even though the wreckage itself was
out of our field of view.

Sigmund had arrived.

22

It took us a little while to work it out between us, Denison and I, while the tall flames gradually subsided, and nothing moved in the piney woods flanking the valley in which the cows still stood around in the mist and falling snow looking wet and unhappy.

Then Denison went off to make the arrangements. Presently the two girls came through the room, heading for the garage stairs at the far end of the house. Greta Elfenbein stopped to look at me. Her jaunty raincoat and sou'wester concealed most of the damage but she was still kind of pink around the eyes and nose. Her expression reminded me of her father's, after I'd put my knife through his hand. There had been a moment when we'd almost been friends, Greta and I, and she'd used my hanky, but now she hated me. I hadn't behaved like a gentleman. I'd let the nasty man muss her up and bloody her nose without uttering a sound of protest. I hadn't hurled myself heroically to her rescue and got myself shot or clubbed, and she'd never forgive me. The girl called Misty urged her forward, and she turned away without speaking.

Denison returned, a little breathless. "Well, keep your fingers crossed," he said. "They're warming up the Mercedes. Here are the hat and coat you wanted. L.A. doesn't like leaving them with you. He thinks they make him look rugged and virile, like a Cossack or something."

"He's got a choice," I said. "He can leave his life here instead, if he prefers. Remember, now, don't go too far before you dump the blonde, if she still insists on playing the female lead in our little drama. Thirty yards should do it. Then take off straight down the road and don't look left or right, understand? If there's anything there, you don't want to see it. And once you get to Narvik—what did you say, ten kilometers?—get him out of this country. Sweden, Iceland, Scotland, England. Any damned place but Norway. Okay?" I paused, and spoke carefully, "Oh, and don't forget to try to get hold of Elfenbein and make that trade, will you? I'd keep the daughter here and deal with him myself, but there's a bigger chance of something going wrong at this end."

"I'll do what I can for your lady colleague," Denison said. He hesitated and grimaced. "Well, you did it, you bastard. You pulled out the rug. The way L.A. feels about me right now for letting him get into this mess, you could shoot me dead and he wouldn't lift a finger to avenge me."

I grinned. "And I might just do it, too, if I didn't need you to get that girl out of Elfenbein's hands, if she's still alive. And to keep those stumblebums of yours in line.

For God's sake don't let them shoot anybody, Paul. Just drive; never mind the heroics. The only one he really wants is Kotko, but one little shot and you'll probably be cut to pieces by the undisciplined, trigger-happy troops. I'm betting those woods are full of rusty firepower stuffed with ammunition so ancient it's turned green, but some of it still shoots pretty good. If you don't believe me, look at that chopper... Paul."

"Yes?"

I hesitated, and drew a long breath, and said it. "Look, *amigo*, as far as I'm concerned, you can invoke the statute of limitations. I can't keep my mind on a vendetta after seven years. Okay?"

"Sure," he said. He grinned abruptly. "Sorry, maybe that's inadequate, Matt, but I can't help remembering there's a gent in Washington who's got a longer memory than you have."

I regarded him for a moment. "Are you still willing to take advice from the Old Master, Mr. Denison?"

"Any time," he said cheerfully.

"Then listen," I said. "You're through with Kotko, however it breaks. He's not going to forgive you, even if you make amends by saving his life. I presume you've had sense enough to cash in on your seven soft years. I figure you've made arrangements for a new life somewhere for when this one wore out, as it was bound to do. You've got only one thing to worry about, that somebody'll come looking for you who knows how to look, right?"

"Right on," Denison said. His voice was expressionless.

I said, "Well, use your brains, Mr. Denison. Think real hard. Once you're a long way from here, maybe you can figure out how you can throw a bone to that guy in Washington, something that'll make him drop, your trail and forget you. *Quid pro quo*, I think is the Latin phrase, Mr. Denison."

There was a little silence. At last Denison said slowly, "I think I see what you mean. I'll give it some consideration, depending on how things work out. But you really are a cold-blooded bastard, aren't you, friend Eric?"

"I hope so," I said. "It's got a lot of survival value. Now I'd like that Llama pistol back, and the knife. And I want that big, impressive Browning Hi-Power and the shoulder holster your man Wesley is wearing, if only to keep him from getting brave at the wrong moment."

Denison studied me for a moment. Obviously he wanted to ask questions, like how I was going to handle it—certainly I wasn't going to hold off a bunch of tough old resistance fighters with a couple of little handguns, or big ones either—but it was my business and he didn't pry.

He said merely, "I'll get them to you."

"Before you go, tell me something," I said.

"What?"

"In Trondheim. Under that bridge, under the railroad tracks, remember? Did you maybe take a dive deliberately just to make me feel so good I'd leave you alone?"

He grinned. "You'll never know, will you, Matt?" he said. "So long now."

"So long, Denny."

I hadn't meant to call him that. It was a nickname
I hadn't used, or thought of, for a hell of a long time.
Holding Kotko's hat and coat, I watched him go. It
was too bad. I'd had a lot of fun hating him for seven
years—everybody's got to hate somebody—but the old
enthusiasm was gone. I'd have to find somebody else
to maintain my adrenalin level. Presently Wesley came
hurrying up from the garage side of the house and handed
me the armaments I'd asked for, with obvious resentment
at having to give up his own pet cannon.

"He says five minutes. Even with the ventilation
system, we can't stay in that garage much longer with the
motor going."

"Five minutes, check," I said, glancing at my watch.

Wesley disappeared. I stuck the Spanish .380 under my
belt, dropped the knife back into my pocket, and climbed
into the shoulder holster supporting the Belgian 9mm.
With my jacket back on once more, I donned Kotko's
long, sweeping, dramatic, fur coat, and put the Cossack
cap on my head. I looked into the mirror on the nearby
wall, and found my appearance satisfactory. I'd got a nice
tan in Florida and at a distance one tall, tanned gent with a
big fur hat on looks pretty much like another, particularly
on a foggy, snowy Arctic day. It might work—unless
Sigmund remembered that I'd pulled more or less the
same stunt once before on this trip, on a ship's gangplank,
with slightly different personnel.

I picked up the attaché case that had been parked
beside the table. It had the initials L.A.K. on it in gold. I

descended the piney, rustic staircase to the door by which we'd entered this house. It seemed a long time ago.

Standing there, I opened the attaché case and disarranged the neat business papers it contained so they stuck out a bit here and there. I closed it, but it wouldn't latch now; it wasn't supposed to. The sweep hand of my watch counted off the three hundredth second, but I waited until I saw the garage door under the other wing of the house slide up, and the shiny Mercedes inside begin to move. Then, holding the unfastened attaché case to my breast, making a big deal of trying to close it as I ran, I hurled myself through the door and after the car that was already turning away from me.

"Denison, what the hell—" I yelled in a high voice. "Denison, wait, come back here! Denison, you treacherous bastard—"

I faked a slip and went to my knees, dropping the case. Papers flew everywhere. I tried to gather them up, and stuff them into place, frantically; then I glanced at the receding car, and left the case, and ran, pounding through the thin, slushy snow down the tracks of the Michelin tires.

"Denison, you damned Judas—"

In the middle of the rear seat, through the rear window, I could see my own hat and the collar of my own raincoat, worn by Kotko. A struggle was going on up forward. Suddenly the car slid to a halt, the right front door opened, and the girl called Misty was shoved out to sprawl in the snow. A pale blue airplane-luggage suitcase followed her. It burst open upon impact. The tires spun, gained traction, and carried the big Mercedes away. When I came up, the girl was trying to reclaim her scattered belongings. I yanked her up by the shoulder of the blue ski-parka she'd put on over her thin Riviera costume.

"You bitch!" I shouted shrilly. "You were supposed to make them wait for me!"

"I tried, Linc, I tried. Why do you think they shoved me out of the car—"

I swung the flat of my hand against her cheek, not really hard enough to knock her down, but she lost her footing in the slippery snow and fell, maybe deliberately. It was too bad vaudeville was dead; we'd have made a great team. I turned and fled back to the house, stumbling in my frantic haste to reach shelter. Inside, I waited, panting. In a little while the girl came through the door, hugging her suitcase, from which trailed odds and ends of damp, snowy feminine garments. She was pretty damp and snowy herself. She leaned against the wall and drew a long, ragged breath.

"Wow! Did we have to be so damned realistic? Half my clothes are ruined. And if that's what you call pulling a punch, what happens when you really hit a girl, her head flying through the air like a volleyball? Do you really think they bought that corny act?"

I listened for a moment. "Well, nobody's shooting out there," I said. "The car must be pretty well clear by now… What are you doing?"

"Look at me, I'm soaked from the waist down after flopping around in that mushy snow in these damned silk pajamas! Any law against a girl's putting on some jeans?"

I put my hand on her arm, restraining her from groping through the stuff in the suitcase. "We're frightened silly," I said. "We're panicky, cornered rats, waiting for the cat to come through the door, remember? Do we worry about a little damp snow, for God's sake, when we're already wetting our pants in abject, incontinent terror? The play's the thing. What's a little pneumonia between friends, Miss... I stopped, and grinned. "What's your name, anyway?"

"Moreau," she said. "Misty Moreau. Mademoiselle Meestee Moreau if you want to be formal." I didn't say anything. I just stood there grinning at her. She made a face at me, and said, "All right, damn you, would you believe Janet Morrow?"

"Hi, Jan," I said. "I'm Matt. Let's go upstairs. Is there any more of that beer you were drinking...? Damn it, I don't suppose drinking beer goes with our cowardly characters, either. Well, at least we can sit down and be comfortable while we await our dooms with fear and trembling."

Upstairs, the fire was still burning brightly, throwing out a lot of pleasant warmth; but the big, windowed room seemed very empty with just the two of us in it. Misty, or Jan, tossed off her ski jacket and went to the fireplace, spreading her wide, bedraggled pantslegs to the heat. Without removing the fur hat and coat, I sat down in Kotko's place behind the table that was still littered with meaning less scientific documents and imaginative mechanical drawings.

"The armed forces have a saying: only suckers volunteer," I said at last. "I didn't ask you to stay. Frankly, it didn't occur to me."

"You couldn't have put on such a good act without me, could you?" she said without turning her head.

"That's right. You made it a lot more convincing. I'm not complaining, just wondering. Do you love the guy?"

"Kotko?" She laughed without malice. "Who loves Kotko? Except Kotko."

"Then why—"

"The trouble with this lousy world is, there's too damned much taking and not enough giving. What the hell? I've taken enough off the guy, and I don't mean just an occasional poke in the eye. I mean, I've got it made, salted away, I'll never be hungry again, thanks to Lincoln Alexander Kotko. So it was time to give a little, understand? It was time for me to earn my lousy loot, so I could be happy with it... Anyway, the poor bastard's got troubles enough without being shot."

"Troubles?" I said. "Like what?"

"Why do you think he hides out the way he does?" she asked, still speaking to the fire. "About ten years ago, when he went into seclusion, as they call it. Troubles like cancer, Mr. Helm. Cancer of the prostate. Under certain circumstances, they have to extract the whole works, if you know what I mean. Can't you hear all the beautiful people laughing if they knew? That's why he hid out, and shaved his head to look tough and sexy, and hired girls like me to make it look as if he still... well, you know.

And maybe that's why… well, if you can't do anything else to a member of the opposite sex, maybe there's some satisfaction in roughing her up a bit occasionally. Okay. I'm durable. At that price, I can play a happy masochist as well as the next girl."

I said, "It's a funny damn world full of funny damn people."

"Talking about funny people, what's your Sigmund doing now, and why didn't he shoot you when you were outside there, right in his sights?"

I said, "Don't be silly. And have me—well, Kotko—die without knowing why? An essential part of the nemesis routine is having a nice little speech to declaim before you pull the trigger."

"And what's he up to now? Why doesn't he come?"

"He's waiting for Lincoln Alexander to lose his nerve and make a run for it. Sigmund is a good general. He'll sacrifice soldiers for a plan, but not for nothing. He's not going to rush a man behind four walls, a man who may be armed, as long as there's a chance of catching him in the open. That's why I didn't want to get so far from the house they could cut us off from it."

She turned to toast her backside. "But why are they with him, all those men? It's none of their business, is it? They're not fighting for home and country now. And where did they get their guns? Those were machine guns we heard, weren't they? They don't give those away for cereal boxtops, do they?"

I said, "It's a hard thing to explain to a young lady

brought up on the popular theory that war is always evil, fighting is always bad, violence is always dreadful, and everybody hates it. The fact is, there are some people around, mostly men, who kind of like it."

"Well, sure. The same kind who go around in peacetime trying to find charging lions to shoot at, and fast sports cars to wreck."

"You've got the idea," I said. "Only there are more of them than you might think, and they're not all rich enough for African safaris. Take some aging citizens who've been leading worthy, conventional lives, most of them—gents who sometimes wake up in the night and remember how it was when they were young, hungry, cold, and scared, running through the mountains with the enemy at their heels. But alive and fighting back, remember that. Every so often, thanks to a certain man who knew how to lead, they'd get to turn on those bastards. They'd have the chance to strike; strike hard. They'd see those hated uniforms go down before the chattering guns… What can you strike at today in this dullsville world? What can you fight? How can you prove that you're alive?"

"Sounds like you know a lot about it," the girl said shrewdly.

"We're not talking about me," I said. "We're talking about a bunch of guys who remember a war and the individual who led them. And then they hear the name again, Sigmund. What do they care what he wants? It's a gleam of light out of the brave, bright past. So it's a private matter. He tells them so; I'm sure he told them so.

He said, this is my fight, old comrades; it's not yours—
unless you want it. And the sensible ones went back to
their wives and kids, to their stores and farms and fishing
boats. But a few stayed; enough stayed."

"The ones who are out there now," she said. "Well, my
mother did tell me all men were crazy."

"You should have heard what my daddy told me about
women," I said. "Well, the ones who decided to stay, they
went down into the cellars, back into the barns, up into
the attics; and they found the oilskin-wrapped packages
they'd hidden away all those years ago when the stupid
government told the resistance people to turn in their
arms like good little boys and girls—hell, they'd fought
the invaders with hoes and pitchforks once; they'd
learned their lesson the hard way. Government or no
government, they weren't going to be caught unarmed
again, not ever. So they unwrapped the protective oilskin
or plastic, and they wiped off the preservative grease, and
they loaded up the magazines and rammed them home,
click. Then they took a hike up the road and said, here
we are, Sigmund, where's your cottonpicking trouble?
However that reads in Norwegian... Now, come over
here beside me, Jan Morrow."

She'd heard it, too; the faint scratching sound
downstairs. Her face was a little pale, but she came and
said, steadily enough: "Sure. Here I am. What do I do?"

"I'll have my head down on my arms, on the table,
a picture of hopeless despair," I said. "You'll be leaning
over me, comforting me. You'll scream at them not to

touch me, to leave me alone. But that's all you'll do. You'll let them push you aside and hold you there, and you won't make them mad by fighting back. It's not your baby, Jan Morrow. Understand?"

"I understand."

They were still working at the lock down there. I spoke softly enough that they'd hear the steady murmur of undisturbed conversation without recognizing my voice, if they knew it.

"Sigmund," I said. "Isn't that a real name, now; a name with which to call the old gods out of the hills? Wagner went ape about Siegfried, but he was just Sigmund's pup, born posthumously, according to the old sagas. Sigmund died in a roaring battle on a bloody beach—anyway, that was the way I always pictured it as a kid. He was marked for death. Odin said: that man, that man, and that one there. They go today; see to it. But the Valkyrie, Brynhild, kind of liked our friend Sigmund, a fine figure of a Viking. She shielded him with her cloak through the hours of fighting. Odin spotted her doing it and was annoyed at this infraction of Valkyrie discipline. Sigmund saw a tall old gent with a staff and a ragged cloak approaching through the smoke of battle. The staff thrust out, and the great sword, the sword of the Nibelungs, broke into three pieces. Defenseless, Sigmund died. Brynhild, for her disobedience, was penned up inside the famous circle of fire. For further details see your friendly neighborhood opera house... Okay, it's about time, Misty Moreau. I'm terrified, a broken man. Comfort me."

I lowered my face onto the furry sleeves of Kotko's coat. The girl put her arm across my shoulders. Her long hair tickled my neck and cheek as she leaned over me. I felt her start as, losing patience, somebody below hosed down the recalcitrant lock with a machine pistol, making a fearful racket. Somebody else kicked in the riddled door with a crash.

"Linc, darling," the girl said loudly. They were coming up the stairs now "It's all right, Linc... Damn you, leave him alone! Who are you? What are you doing here? What do you want with him? You have no right—"

"Please be quiet, Miss." The voice was familiar, "Kotko? I've come for you, Kotko."

I raised my head, and shrugged off the girl's arm. Hank Priest was standing a couple of yards away, beyond the table, holding a revolver that looked very familiar. That was stupid of him, I reflected, stupid and overconfident, waving my own gun under my nose, reminding me of where and how and from whom he'd got it. Of course, he hadn't known he'd been aiming it at me, but in my mind, the legendary resistance hero with the Wagnerian name faded away, leaving only a treacherous and double-crossing old sonofabitch who owed me something.

"Wrong man, Skipper," I said. "But then, it always was the wrong man, wasn't it?"

23

For a minute or two, I didn't know which way it would go. It was very confused, very close, with a remarkable number of interesting old automatic weapons being aimed my way, and a number of hard-bitten, middle-aged Scandinavian gents, once they understood what had happened, vying for the privilege of pumping me full of World War II lead. There was also a faction that wanted to give chase to the Mercedes, until it was pointed out to them that the car was probably well into the suburbs by now and that it was hardly feasible to mount an armed attack on the city of Narvik.

The discussion took place, of course, in Norwegian but you'd be surprised at the linguistic understanding that comes to you when your survival is the subject of the discussion.

"You shouldn't have done it, son," Hank Priest said gently at last, facing me across the table.

I shrugged. "You shouldn't have done it, Hank." It

was too late for the sirs and other titles. "Nobody cares about Kotko. You can have all the Kotkos you want. Be our guest. But deal with him privately, for Christ's sake! When you drag the United States of America into your fancy act... What the hell's the matter with you, Captain Priest? It's not a bad country, as countries go; and you served it for what? Thirty years? Forty? And now you go manufacturing a lot of international trouble for it just to serve your private grudge! Not to mention abusing the friendship of a gent who hasn't got a lot of friends. Me, I don't care much. I've had tricks played on me before in the line of duty and you're no friend of mine. And maybe you've got no obligations to the kids you set up for tin ducks in your private shooting gallery; Wetherill, Benson, Lawrence. But you went to him for help and he gave it to you, trusting you, stretching the rules to lend you one of his people for a project you assured him was in the country's best interests, maybe a little crooked, but advantageous..."

"Search him, Lars. Be careful."

Priest turned away towards the girl, who was being held off to one side. Besides him, there were actually only four men in the room, although it had seemed at first like the best part of a regiment. I could hear more downstairs and there were probably still more outside. One of the four in the room had moved forward at Priest's command. I recognized him. He was the tough little seaman-looking gent who'd once led me to a rendezvous in the town called Ålesund. I remembered Priest telling me that this man had fought beside him and saved his life. He seemed to be functioning as second in command.

Lars laid aside his weapon, an old U.S. carbine, caliber .30, M-l. I never can understand what anybody sees in that bastard weapon—neither a good rifle nor a good submachine gun—but it's got a lot of friends in strange places. With another man covering me, he had me stand up and remove the big coat. He looked it over carefully and laid it aside. Then he searched me thoroughly from hair to shoes, finding the big, obvious Browning first, of course. Further exploration of my anatomy yielded up the Llama. Finally he discovered the folding knife in my pants pocket; but he was thorough, he carried his investigation clear down to the floor.

"You are well armed, Herr Helm," he said, straightening up and stepping back. "You could have given us a good fight." There was a hint of regret in his voice.

"Against that?" I gestured towards the ancient Sten gun covering me. "Anyway, I've got nothing against any Norwegians except the lousy way they garble the Swedish language. Was the pilot killed?"

"No. He jumped and ran at the first burst. We put it well aft, hoping that would happen. We have him prisoner."

"Even so, there has been much killing for a little bit of revenge," I said.

"I know nothing about that," Lars said. "Sigmund— Captain Priest—wants a man, for reasons of his own. I do not ask. We do not ask." He stuffed my weapons into various pockets of the peajacket he was wearing, and picked up his carbine, and patted it fondly. "It is enough to be in the woods once more with Sigmund and this old friend, Herr Helm. It is not so interesting a life we live today; it is good to remember the old way just once more. Now sit down, be so good, please."

Priest was questioning Jan Morrow. I heard her saying, "I don't know, I tell you. Linc didn't say anything to me about his future plans, if he had any."

I said, "Stop heckling the girl, Hank. I told Denison to send your target out of this country ASAP, to some place that had no legendary underground supermen roaming around. If you want another crack at the invisible millionaire, you'll have to do it alone in an unfriendly land."

He turned and regarded me bleakly. After a moment, he said, "Lars, take the girl downstairs. The men, too. I want to talk with Mr. Helm." When they were gone, he drew a long breath and asked, "What the hell am I going to do with you, son?"

"That's what the cowboy asked after he lassoed the bear," I said. "But you'll think of something to do. Like, for instance, what you did to that young guy named Wetherill, another sap who had a lot of faith in you, Skipper, if my information is correct. Satisfy my curiosity. Tell me why he had to fall off a mountain in his car. What was his crime?"

"So you guessed that." His voice was flat.

"There were only three choices. A real accident; and I don't have much faith in coincidences like that. Elfenbein; and why should he kill the goose that was laying the golden information. You."

Priest came to the table and faced me across the phony drawings of the Sigmund Siphon. He still looked like the same sturdy, weathered old seadog, with his pale blue eyes and cropped gray hair. He was still wearing the raincoat, tweeds, and cap of his British incarnation. There was a change, however, a kind of weariness. Well, maybe I looked a bit tired, too. We'd come to the end of the line and it had been a tough trip.

"I was sorry about Robbie," he said quietly. "You probably know I'd had him feeding information to Elfenbein, who'd been hired by the Aloco people after I'd tipped them off, never mind how, to what was going on up north."

"Except that it wasn't really going on," I said. "It was just something you dreamed up to keep them—us—all busy chasing each other. Just like that phony attack you set up at Varsjøen during the last big war, so you could hit the transport in Rosviken without interference."

He smiled thinly. "I can see you've been doing your homework, Mr. Helm. Well, Elfenbein was a real break for me. You see, Kotko was suspicious, or at least dubious. It was a far-out proposition I'd offered him, through intermediaries, and he wasn't really interested in gambling on it. After all, he already, had a sure thing in Torbotten, why risk it for a little additional profit based on somebody's pipe dream, even if the pipe dream did have U.S. support? That's why I leaked information to Aloco, hoping that the hint of competition for the Siphon would change Kotko's mind. And they did the best thing they could have done, from my point of view: they hired Dr. Elfenbein, who had a reputation Kotko respected."

"Complicated," I said.

"Not too complicated, son. Remember, all I really wanted was to get Kotko to Norway. The more confusion I could stir up, the more it would look as if something really important was going on, something worthy of the great man's attention, the hairless bastard. Well, I wanted to encourage Dr. Elfenbein, of course, make him think that he was being very clever, so I told Robbie to let himself be bribed. I told him what to say. I told him we were laying a false trail; that we were actually going to pick up all the material by a different route from the one he was supposedly 'betraying.' Unfortunately, what I didn't realize was that he was madly in love with the sanctimonious young lady, Benson, I was using as a courier. He became afraid, and rightly so of course, that the information he was passing would make trouble for her. He insisted that she be given protection, so I got you on the job. But even that wasn't enough for Robbie. He didn't think it right we should leave the girl in the dark; he insisted she should be warned she was being used as a decoy. I could see that he was becoming suspicious of the whole operation, and that if he and the girl got together… Well, I was sorry to do it, but you can see that it was necessary, can't you, son?"

It was kind of touching, I suppose. He really wanted me to understand, as between one pro and another; and I understood, all right—but it was still my gun he was aiming at me, and I still remembered how he'd got it.

"Sure," I said. "Necessary."

"It worked out very well in the end," Priest went on in that calm and reasonable voice. "You helped a lot, Mr. Helm. With a real U.S. agent on the job, one well known to his man Denison, Kotkc had living proof that our claims of government backing were genuine—I won't deny I had that in mind when I got hold of you. And with Elfenbein involved, with his impressive reputation, Kotko decided that it had to be a lot more profitable deal than he'd thought originally. I had him where I wanted him at last, hungry and eager; eager enough to come to Norway and close the deal in person." Priest grinned boyishly. "I tell you, son, it was more fun than a barrel of monkeys. All those damned thieves, government and otherwise, fighting over a glorified crapper."

"Yeah," I said. "But Wetherill died. Evelyn Benson died. I killed a guy on that ship, thinking we were doing something important enough to warrant it—"

"You killed that man because he'd put your nose out of joint, making you look like an incompetent bodyguard."

"Maybe, a little," I conceded. "Okay, I'll concede Bjørn, with reservations. But what about Diana Lawrence?"

"You left her there deliberately, Mr. Helm. A coldblooded sacrifice play if I ever saw one."

"Not that cold-blooded," I said. "I'd have been very happy if she'd made it; I simply made provisions for if she didn't. And I left her with a gun. You took it away from her. You're the only man in the world who could have done it. She had clear instructions, and she might have got through—but she made the mistake of trusting you. Like a lot of other people during the past few weeks. You had a lot of credit, Skipper, and you've deliberately used every bit of it, haven't you?"

He moved his shoulders. "When did you catch on?" he asked after a moment.

I said, "Well, the two contacts weren't exactly the cowards you'd led us to expect, one sitting in that restaurant calmly feeding scraps of pancake to his dogs, the other waiting steadily by the airport half the night, disregarding all the games being played under his nose. But of course you had to make us think they were cowards. If they weren't, there was no point to all this elaborate, cautious business with passwords and secret meeting places, all cooked up, we were supposed to think, to protect them." I shook my head ruefully. "But I didn't really like it from the start," I went on. "I mean, Skipper, a guy like you, or a guy like me, when somebody we love gets hurt, we don't go around doing patriotic good for their memory's sake—if you want to call grand larceny good. We find somebody to kill, and we kill them. The whole thing was just a little out of character, particularly when I learned how you'd spent that war."

He said, "The stupid bastards." His voice wasn't gentle anymore. "There was that sonofabitch who'd murdered Frances, I mean murdered her just as if he'd used a gun. A few gallons more and we'd have been through that pass and she'd still be alive. So I went over and showed him the error of his ways. Very well, I put him into the hospital, what the hell did he expect? If he wants to play games like that, he can damn well reserve a permanent bed in the ward! But the backlash I got, you wouldn't believe it! You'd have thought I'd knocked out a couple of teeth belonging to Jesus Christ Almighty. I'd have gone to jail, if I hadn't played the poor bereaved husband momentarily deranged by grief. I paid damages, I smoothed down the oil company lawyers, I even apologized to the sonofabitch himself and said I was sorry, I'd been beside myself, I hadn't known what I was doing... Well, I hadn't known what I was doing. I started realizing that. What the hell was I making myself all this trouble for over a lousy little pump jockey, when the man really responsible was sitting on the Riviera pinching the bottom of a blonde?"

"So you decided to go after Kotko, just like that."

He said, "That's right." He hesitated, and gave me that quick, boyish grin once more. "It was great, son, really great. I knew I had to get him to Norway where I had friends. I hadn't had a problem like that to solve since the end of the big shooting. No commanding officers, no Navy Regulations, no Uniform Code of Military Justice, just the great old feeling of being on your own with just one thing in mind: how are you going to put it over on the sonsabitches, *really* put it over on them, get them running one way while you go the other and strike where nobody's expecting you. The old razzle-dazzle, Mr. Helm. And it worked, by God. Crazy as it was, it worked!"

I said, "I can. see a bunch of dumb Washington

bureaucrats falling for it, several thousand miles away, if you made it look attractive enough. But how the hell did Kotko and Elfenbein get fooled? They're supposed to know something about oil."

Priest snorted. "Not Kotko. Not really. Basically, he's a money-man, not an oil-man. He *thinks* he knows something about oil, that's all. And he runs the kind of one-man show where everybody just tells the boss what he wants to hear. He's very proud of his reputation for spotting profitable situations ahead of the crowd. I figured, with all the smoke and dust I was stirring up, he'd be intrigued enough to want to see my pretty pictures before he made up his mind. He knew enough to know they were phony when he saw them, but by that time it was too late—or would have been, if you hadn't interfered. Why the hell couldn't you mind your own damned business, son?"

"It was my business," I said. "You made it my business. And Elfenbein?"

"Well, I'll tell you," he said. "I was worried about Doctor Ivory, I really was, at first, when I heard Aloco'd hired him. I thought he'd blow the whistle on me for sure, but he didn't, so actually he turned out to be the best card in my hand. If Elfenbein was after it, Kotko was sure to want it."

The old sea-dog was really slinging the metaphors— smoke, dust, whistles, and cards—but his rhetorical style was the least of my worries. I said, "But Elfenbein's supposed to be a genius in the field. He must have known he was being sent to hunt for an impossible gadget. How do you figure that?"

"Well, there are two possibilities. After all, the man's the biggest crook out of jail. Maybe he decided to take Aloco's money and give them the papers they wanted without bothering to tell them the stuff was worthless. If they balked at the payoff, he could threaten them with making the whole illicit deal public; they couldn't afford that. Our doctor isn't above a bit of polite blackmail. But then again—" Priest hesitated. "What if the gadget wasn't impossible? Oh, this glorified three-way sewage system is a phony, sure; but maybe it could be done, what we were just pretending to do. Maybe friend Ivory knew it could be done, and wanted to see if we'd hit on a good way of doing it. Interesting thought, eh?" He sighed. "It makes me fear for humanity, son. You never saw such a bunch of larcenous bastards in your life... Of course, I had to play some dirty tricks, too, but you've always got to play some dirty tricks. Somebody always gets hurt. That's the price you pay."

I didn't say anything. After a moment, he said, a little defensively, "The guy deserved it, son. You can't say he didn't deserve it."

I said, "I told you. You can have Kotko. Any time. We hold no brief for Kotko."

"Responsibility," said Priest. "Nobody's willing to accept responsibility these days. The Army blames its atrocities on its junior officers, and the colonels and generals stay safe behind their desks. In Washington, the little fish get hooked and the big fish get away. And the businessmen whose business is to supply us with this and that say it's all the fault of somebody else, so walk, swabbie—or drown. We've got to bring the responsibility home to them, son. They've got to learn that when they shaft somebody, they'd better lock the doors and windows, because somebody'll be coming for them sooner or later."

I looked at him, seeing a tough old gent who'd casually caused the deaths of several people in his elaborate effort to kill a man he'd never seen. Well, I've caused a few deaths myself, from time to time, and a hundred years from now an impartial jury might have trouble deciding they'd all occurred for valid and important reasons. The moral judgment wasn't mine to make.

Practically speaking, however, the fact was that Captain Henry Priest, USN, Ret., had put his country and its local representative, me, in an impossible situation. His wild homicidal joke wouldn't look very funny in the public press, with a retired U.S. naval officer getting jailed or executed for murder and international conspiracy and various U.S. government officials getting dragged into the mess, including perhaps a certain mysterious U.S. agent and his mysterious chief. And then, of course, there was the personal factor...

Mac could handle his friendships without help from me; but it was still my gun the old seadog was aiming at me, and I was just a little tired of the highfalutin rhetoric. It was time to bring the conversation down to earth.

I drew a long breath and said harshly, "You're a hell of a one to talk about responsibility, Hank, when you can't even admit that you drowned your own wife."

There was a lengthy silence. When he spoke, his voice sounded a little thin, a little distant, almost like the emasculated voice of L.A. Kotko.

"What do you mean, son? It was an accident."

"Accident, hell," I said. "Civilian landlubbers have boating accidents. U.S. naval officers don't have boating accidents. Would you have the nerve to get up in front of a court-martial and call that demonstration of nautical incompetence an accident, Captain Priest?"

It was unfair, of course. By normal standards, Frances Priest had died quite accidentally, with no serious blame attached to anybody under the circumstances; but I knew I was dealing with a man who did not operate according to normal standards. I'd spent a little time around the Naval Academy once, and I'd had enough contact with the finished product in the line of business to know how they were trained. Regardless of what anybody else would think about the incident—just plain bad luck, the average boatman would say—I knew an Annapolis man would not accept that excuse, or any excuse. There is no luck in the Navy. There's only good seamanship and bad seamanship.

"Who're you trying to kid, Hank?" I said. "You know damned well who was responsible. It was your ship, all thirty feet of it. You were in command. You made the decision to gamble on running the inlet with insufficient fuel, instead of waiting for the Coast Guard outside…" Something in his face gave me the clue, and I went on: "Or did you let your wife talk you into it? Was that the way it was? She insisted that you had to get that injured boy to the hospital *pronto* and you got mad at her for interfering with your running of the ship and stalked up forward, letting her climb into the tower and take the boat through. When the engines died, as you knew they would, you flung the anchor over angrily without checking… And what the hell kind of a naval officer is it who blames a fouled-up, short-tempered operation like that on a dumb gas pump attendant and a stray millionaire, Captain Priest?"

It was the thing that had brought him here; the thing he couldn't face. He wasn't about to face it now. I saw his expression change; now there was something ugly and mad and broken in the pale blue eyes. His hand tightened on the Smith and Wesson and he leaned over the table to fire, forgetting the basic principle that guns were invented to kill at a distance; close up, you might as well use a club.

My left hand got the revolver, deflecting his first and only shot. My right hand slipped the little Colt .25 out of Kotko's fur cap lying on the table. I got all six into him before he fell, taking his own gun—well, my gun, Diana's gun—with him. He was welcome to it now.

The tiny automatic closed after the last shot, instead of locking open as most of them do to facilitate reloading. Since I didn't want to be caught with anything that even looked like a loaded gun, I tossed it out into the middle of the rug, where they'd see it as they came boiling up the stairs. I waited with my empty hands in plain sight…

24

I woke up in a Narvik hospital. Although it was as anonymous as any hospital room, I knew it was in Narvik. Hell, I'd ridden ten kilometers over a damned rough, snowy road to get here, in some kind of a bastard jeep-type vehicle without any springs to speak of, with my shoulder on fire from three old slugs out of a practically prehistoric weapon—fortunately the ancient Sten gun had jammed after three. I even remembered stumbling up the steps to the office of a doctor who, we'd been told, remembered Sigmund and would probably make discreet arrangements if we used the right words on him. We?

I tried to remember. I wanted to remember all by myself, but the assignment had been complicated by a number of girls… Girls? I remembered, and opened my eyes, and there was the blonde, sitting on a straight-backed hospital chair, knitting. I didn't know people actually knitted any more.

"Hi, Misty," I said. "Or do you prefer Jan?" I was just

showing off my phenomenal memory.

"Oh, you're awake." She put the knitting aside neatly, sticking in the needles the way they do. She rose and came to the bed. "How do you feel?"

"Like somebody'd dug a bushel of slugs out of my shoulder. Did you get a message out like I asked you?"

"I called the Oslo number and explained the situation. There have been no police, but there's a man here to see you. American, middle-aged. Gray hair, black eyebrows. Shall I get him?"

"Just a minute." I frowned at her for a moment. She was a nice-looking kid, in her snub-nosed way and I remembered that she'd displayed considerable guts and something that might be called integrity, a rare commodity these days. "Just what the hell do you think you're doing here?" I asked. "Isn't it about time you learned not to volunteer?"

She grinned. "I didn't volunteer. For you, I was drafted, remember? They threw us both out of the car together and told me I'd better see that you were taken care of quietly, or else."

I said, "How long ago was that? And you're still here? What are you trying to prove, Jan Morrow?"

Her eyes had narrowed a little, hurt. "Do you mind?"

"As a matter of fact," I said, "I do mind. Because I think you're letting your romantic imagination run away with you. I think you've kidded yourself into some funny ideas about this business; and maybe even about me as a knight in shining armor or something, fighting dragons on behalf of poor defenseless millionaires. Well, let me tell you something about Sir Matthew Helm, doll. I didn't risk my life for Lincoln Alexander Kotko. I just risked my life to get him the hell out of there for political reasons and because I had to stop the man who was after him before that man loused things up for everybody."

"But you did save Linc's life," she pointed out.

"For the moment," I said. "But he's probably dead by this time; and if not, he soon will be."

She started to speak quickly, and checked herself. She was silent for several seconds. "Why?" she asked at last.

"It's an old story, an old betrayal," I said. "There was a man who was bought, and a man who bought. Two men died as a result, and a girl, but she wasn't one of us so she doesn't really concern us. But a little retribution is necessary; and the man who was bought prefers to live, so I think he'll take care of his buyer for us, settling the score."

"Denison is going to kill Linc? Why?"

"I told you; because Denison prefers to live. And because I asked him to."

"That's… pretty cold-blooded, isn't it?"

I said, "I knew you'd catch on, if you really concentrated, Misty Moreau."

Her face was pale. "I… I guess I was being a little romantic. Thanks for setting me straight."

"*De nada*, as we say in our fluent Spanish. Send in that guy with the eyebrows as you go out, will you?"

I watched her leave, a nicely built girl in jeans, with that long, silvery hair. I told myself I really didn't think much of girls in jeans who bleached their hair and if she just kept going and put a lot of distance between us, maybe she wouldn't be in the line of fire if somebody decided to open up on me with a real, modern machine gun that wouldn't jam, or heave a knife or a bomb or a bucket of acid. Noble. The fact is, I'm kind of a one-girl man—one girl at a time, at least. I hadn't quite got over the previous incumbent. Although this was quite a good specimen, I wasn't in the market for any silvery blondes today.

Mac came in, wearing his usual gray suit and his usual expressionless face. He closed the door carefully behind him, pulled the chair Misty had used closer to the bed, and sat down. He didn't ask about my health. He'd have checked with the doctors about that; why waste time soliciting amateur opinions when you can get the straight word from the pros?

"Priest?" he said.

"Taken care of," I said. There was a little pause. I went on, "That's the phrase you used. Take care of him, you said. I told him you'd said for me to look after him, but those were not the actual words you'd employed, and they don't mean quite the same thing in this context." He still said nothing. I asked, "How did you know, sir?"

"He lied to me." Mac looked up. Maybe there was a hint of pain in the cold gray eyes. He went on softly: "After thirty years, Eric, he walked into my office and lied to me, and thought I wouldn't know. It wasn't even a very convincing lie. Of course, I had to investigate."

"And while you were investigating," I said, "you sent him what he'd asked for: me. But with reservations. You carefully didn't tell me we were doing this one for good old Hank Priest because he was such a grand fellow and we owed him so much. No, you pulled the need-to-know gag and sent me to Norway cold, expecting to make contact with a perfect stranger. Eventually, I got smart and asked myself why you'd wanted me to look on good old Hank as a stranger. And I found out." I grimaced. "I'd like to point out, respectfully, that there's a good deal to be said for using the English language, sir. One of these days the ESP connections are going to break down. I'm going to misread the brainwaves or misinterpret the double-talk. Maybe I already have?" I made it a question.

He shook his head. "No. It had to be done. Too much was involved; too many people. He'd spread it too wide, made it too complicated, too dangerous. I think... I think he was really trying to commit suicide, Eric."

"He sure went the long way around the barn to do it," I said. "But you could be right."

"Where is he now?"

"They took him. His old Norwegian comrades in arms. Maybe they'll put him in a Viking ship and set it on fire and let it sail into the sunset... There was a man named Lars. He stopped the others from finishing me off, after the gun of the first guy up the stairs jammed up tight. Lars said that Sigmund must not be known to have died, at least not like that. He said they would handle that problem, if we'd do our best to hush up the rest. I said we'd try."

"The diplomatic circuits have been very busy," Mac said. "Judicious pressure has been applied here and there.

His total disappearance will help. But why did they follow him on such a wild and pointless adventure, those old friends of his?"

I shrugged. "I can only quote old Lars. He said, *It is not so interesting a life we lead, today.*"

"How did he die?"

We were no longer talking about Lars. I looked at the man beside the bed, and said, "The details don't really matter, do they, sir?"

"Tell me." It was an order.

I said, "I let them find two guns and a knife on me. They figured that was enough weapons for any one man, and didn't look further. I used a lousy little hideout .25, one full clip and the cartridge in the chamber. You never know what kind of a job a pipsqueak gun like that is going to do."

"Very well." He drew a long breath and changed the subject. "You may be interested to hear that Kotko is dead. The *Paris Herald* has it, in case you want to read about it in English. Here. Financier shot to death in argument with bodyguard, who has disappeared. Would you know anything about that, Eric?"

"Yes, sir," I said. "I thought you'd be willing to settle for Kotko, since he was the man actually responsible for our trouble seven years ago, and since you don't much like political pressure or the gents who exert it. I needed Denison's help and I figured it earned him a break. And I won't go after him again, sir. You can't kill everybody."

There was a little silence. "Very well. We will consider

the whole matter closed, Eric." It was a big concession. We don't usually try to tell him what we will or won't do, or get away with it if we do try. "As for killing everybody, somebody seems to be making an effort in that direction. A young man named Yale, Norman Yale, was found floating in the Vestfjord off the Lofoten Islands. Any ideas?"

"Probably Elfenbein," I said. "He may have learned that Yale was selling him out to anybody who'd buy. Or he may just have been covering his tracks after an unsuccessful job." I hesitated. "Has anybody heard anything about a girl calling herself Madeleine Barth, or Diana Lawrence?"

"No," Mac said, "there have been no reports of a woman being found, dead or alive, under circumstances occasioning comment. It's just as well. We've had enough troublesome comments already. But I think it's all under control now." He rose. "The doctors inform me that you will probably make a fast recovery, Eric, I am happy to say."

I said deliberately, "I'm happy you're happy, sir."

He looked at me for a long moment. He said quietly, "I know. I gave the instructions, and you interpreted them correctly. I have no complaints. It had to be done."

I watched him leave the room. We'd never been exactly friends, but we'd been closer at other times than we were at the moment. Well, as he'd often told me, friendship has no place in our line of work. I slid down into the bed and went to sleep. When I awoke, she was standing there, with a clean white bandage on her hand.

She was a little paler than I remembered her and she was wearing a neat, wool dress and moderately high heels. I'd never before seen her in anything but slacks. Her legs were slim and lovely and her eyes were green and angry as she looked at me, moving closer.

"You're a treacherous louse!" she said.

"Did I ever say I wasn't?"

"You left me there for them to take!"

"With instructions and a gun," I said. "Don't give it to *anybody*, I warned you. If *anybody* tries to take it from you, I told you, consider him hostile and shoot him dead. So you handed it to the first gent who asked. What do you want, sympathy?"

Diana's smile was slow but wonderful. "That's my Matthew," she murmured. "Thank you, darling. I was so afraid you'd disillusion me. I was terrified that you'd try to explain or apologize or justify yourself or something. I hope your shoulder hurts like hell, like my hand hurts."

"The pain is adequate, thanks," I said. "What happened?"

"That nasty little man tied me to a heavy kitchen chair in an old deserted farmhouse and pinned my hand to the table with a big knife and left me there to die. I sat there all night, slowly freezing to death, among other problems, until your friend Denison came and turned me loose. He'd got hold of Elfenbein somehow, and made a deal, sending back the daughter in return for the address. He said to tell you goodbye. Mr. Paul Denison was making one more public appearance—he said you'd understand—and then he was vanishing from the face of the earth, and never mind who was taking his place, or where. Oh, and he said to tell you he hadn't taken a dive under the railroad tracks, whatever that might mean." I didn't say anything. She said, "Matt."

"Yes?"

"I spent that whole night hating you."

"It probably saved your life. If you'd had nothing to think about but the blackfooted ferret and the fur seal and the whooping crane, you wouldn't have made it past midnight. Nothing like a good hate for survival."

"I know," she said. "That's what I told myself when they first brought me here to fix my hand and I heard you were here. Just keep right on hating him, I told myself, if you know what's good for you. So what am I doing back here?"

"I don't know," I said. "But I'll make a serious effort to find out, as soon as I get a little strength back."

I did.

ABOUT THE AUTHOR

Donald Hamilton was the creator of secret agent Matt Helm, star of 27 novels that have sold more than 20 million copies worldwide.

Born in Sweden, he emigrated to the United States and studied at the University of Chicago. During the Second World War he served in the United States Naval Reserve, and in 1941 he married Kathleen Stick, with whom he had four children.

The first Matt Helm book, *Death of a Citizen*, was published in 1960 to great acclaim, and four of the subsequent novels were made into motion pictures. Hamilton was also the author of several outstanding stand-alone thrillers and westerns, including two novels adapted for the big screen as *The Big Country* and *The Violent Men*.

Donald Hamilton died in 2006.

ALSO AVAILABLE FROM TITAN BOOKS

PRAISE FOR DONALD HAMILTON

"Donald Hamilton has brought to the spy novel
the authentic hard realism of Dashiell Hammett;
and his stories are as compelling, and probably
as close to the sordid truth of espionage,
as any now being told."
Anthony Boucher, *The New York Times*

"This series by Donald Hamilton is the top-ranking
American secret agent fare, with its intelligent
protagonist and an author who consistently writes
in high style. Good writing, slick plotting and
stimulating characters, all tartly flavored with wit."
Book Week

"Matt Helm is as credible a man of violence as has
ever figured in the fiction of intrigue."
The New York Sunday Times

"Fast, tightly written, brutal, and very good…"
Milwaukee Journal

TITANBOOKS.COM

ALSO AVAILABLE FROM TITAN BOOKS

Lady, Go Die!
BY MICKEY SPILLANE & MAX ALLAN COLLINS

THE LOST MIKE HAMMER NOVEL

Hammer and Velda go on vacation to a small
beach town on Long Island after wrapping up the
Williams case (*I, the Jury*). Walking romantically
along the boardwalk, they witness a brutal beating
at the hands of some vicious local cops—Hammer
wades in to defend the victim.

When a woman turns up naked—and dead—
astride the statue of a horse in the small-town
city park, how she wound up this unlikely Lady
Godiva is just one of the mysteries Hammer feels
compelled to solve…

TITANBOOKS.COM